THE GIRL AND THE BOMB

THE GIRL AND THE BOMB

JARI JÄRVELÄ

Translated by Kristian London

amazoncrossing ◖

Text copyright © 2014 Jari Järvelä

Translation copyright © 2015 Kristian London

Previously published as *Tyttö ja pommi* by Crime Time in Finland in 2014. Translated from Finnish by Kristian London. First published in English by AmazonCrossing in 2015.

Published by AmazonCrossing, Seattle

www.apub.com

Amazon, the Amazon logo, and AmazonCrossing are trademarks of Amazon.com, Inc., or its affiliates.

ISBN-13: 9781503946354
ISBN-10: 1503946355

Cover design by Christopher Salyers

Printed in the United States of America

METRO

At two thirty, I knew something was wack. It was like a flashing red light had been set off in the night sky, screaming at us to get out of there.

"Run, girl, run!" a siren voice wailed.

But instead of a red light, nothing but tattered clouds drifted lazily overhead, occasionally revealing the twinkle of a star.

I shut my eyes and listened, positive I had heard a faint clank. And not from the other side of the train, where Rust was working.

The harbor rail yard was dead to the world. Yet somehow the silence was more ominous than the crunch of footsteps running across gravel would have been. It was like someone in the darkness was holding back a sneeze so I wouldn't hear it. Or was primed to bolt out of the starting blocks and run me down.

If only overhead lines could talk.

I was sure that a Rat was lurking out there in the shadows. Not a rat, a Rat—a guy from a private security service. The word *service* means beating with a telescoping nightstick, spraying pepper spray in people's eyes, kicking, all in the name of the common good. Then the

Rat takes you to court, where you're handed down six-figure damages for a couple of paint blotches. The Rat gets a medal for the arms he breaks and the skulls he fractures.

Behind me old hoists and harbor cranes stood over the sluggish, metallic September sea; a tall rock face loomed ahead. In the daytime, this cliff was so red it bled. Now downtown's neon lights glowed above the dark wall of granite.

I waited for five minutes without moving a muscle. Two thirty-five. No more clanks. I watched the time pass on the church clock gleaming through the trees beyond the cliff. My heart was hammering a hole in my shirt. I stood absolutely still and forced myself to breathe slowly. I was holding a can of spray paint there at the railcar, standing on a homemade aluminum ladder that folded up into my backpack. Without the ladder, I wouldn't have been able to reach high enough to get up. I had already painted two interlocking wildstyle letters on the side of the train: *RY*.

It was the start of RYEBREAD, which you could only read if you knew how to interpret the blazing, overlapping letters that radiated yellow and red. They were over six feet tall. This wasn't your basic throwup; it was a real work of art.

The Finnish State Railways freight cars are metal walls forty feet long and ten feet high, begging to be painted. A single car offered an artist four hundred square feet of free space; eight hundred if you counted the other side. When a dozen cars were lined up, ten thousand square feet of empty canvas stretched out, waiting to be filled. The square footage of fifty studio apartments. That meant millions of euros if you thought about it like a real estate agent.

But it didn't cost us a dime. So long as we didn't get caught.

As the cars crossed the country, through cities and countryside, they became mobile galleries, way more practical than billboards. Advertisers didn't have the brains to use trains. We did.

JERE

I was playing Legos with my son. He had built an ancient temple I was supposed to explore. My Lego Man was wearing a Panama hat and carrying a magnifying glass. My son's temple was full of booby traps, secret trapdoors, collapsing roofs, walls, bridges, poison spears, crocodiles, snakes, rolling boulders.

The important thing was for Lego Man to fall into every single trap.

Thanks to my son, Lego Man and I shared the same name: Jere.

The first time we played together, I made a big mistake: I avoided the pits and kicked the Lego crocodiles' butts. Ville smashed up everything and ran to his room, bawling. Reminding him that he had asked me to be *really, really, really sneaky* didn't change anything.

"Don't get caught in the traps," he'd told me this time. Now I knew he meant the opposite. Lego Jere was supposed to be unbelievably, superhumanly sneaky and still fall for every trap like an idiot.

I moved the little yellow plastic figure. Lego Jere fell headfirst into a pit; he was crushed by a pile of bricks. I wondered if my son wanted the same thing to happen to me, because he kept enthusiastically squealing, "Uh-oh, Jere's in trouble now." Lego Jere's head popped off when a hidden axe swung out of a wall. When a cobra bit him he writhed on the ground until he died. His Panama hat had fallen off; there was a hole in his head where the hat clicked on. I peered in.

"He doesn't have any brains," I said. "Kaput."

"Keep going, Jere," Ville said. "Keep going, keep going, keep going. You're alive."

Lego Jere came back to life in my fingers, gathered up his scattered arms and legs, and rushed headlong into the next trap. He crept cautiously along the wall, the very wall from which a clutch of spears would soon pierce through his ribs. Completely unexpectedly.

"Keep going, keep going," Ville ordered.

"Time for bed," Mirjami announced from the doorway.

"Nooo."

"Yes," I said. "Daddy has to go to work."

"Nooo you don't."

We left the temple on the floor. I promised to continue my explorations tomorrow. My son bragged how I had at least a thousand traps to look forward to, all of which Lego Jere had to sneak past. Really, really sneak past.

"So I can't fall into the traps?"

"No! You have to get past them," Ville cried. "Promise me you'll get past them? Promise? Trying for real, Daddy?"

Ville grabbed my hand and stared at me with his doe eyes. I wondered at what age a kid learns how to be manipulative. Probably the instant he pops out of the womb. First he wraps Mom around his tiny finger, then Dad.

We were sitting at the kitchen table, and I was watching Ville gulp down his cup of hot chocolate. His cheeks were red, as if he had been the one running through the booby-trapped temple. When Mirjami had come in I brought in an armchair from the living room so she could be comfortable. She liked to sit in the kitchen and look out at the bird feeder and the world passing in the lane beyond.

"Guess how many Legos there are in the world per person," I said.

"Three," Mirjami ventured.

"No."

"A million," Ville said.

"The population of the earth is over seven billion. If everyone on earth had a million Legos, that would be an insane amount!"

"How insane?" Ville asked, rattling a spoon around his cup.

"An incredibly insane amount. The whole world would be knee-deep in Legos. There wouldn't be room for people," I said. "You're both totally wrong. I'm going to give you another guess."

"What was the question?" Mirjami said.

It was annoying how little attention she paid to what I was saying sometimes, even though she was pretending to listen.

"How many Legos are there in the world per person?"

"Four," Mirjami said.

"A million billion," Ville blurted out. "A million zillion billion."

"Wrong," I said. "Wrong. A hundred. There are a hundred Legos for every person on earth."

"Wow," said Mirjami.

She couldn't have cared less.

"I have more than that," Ville said.

"You're in a privileged position," I said, "compared to the average person on earth."

I stroked Mirjami's rounding belly. The baby was due right after Christmas. She thought Christmas was a horrible time for a kid to be born; no one ever remembered a Christmas baby's birthday. Her Grandma had been born on the twenty-third, and no one ever came to see her on her birthday, even when she turned eighty. People had dropped by a week earlier, jettisoned their presents on the table, tossed back a cup of coffee, and rushed out before it could be refilled, complaining about the bustle of the season. There had been more conversation about Santa Claus than Grandma's eight decades of existence.

"You should try to hold off until early January," I said to Mirjami.

"And how am I going to do that?"

"If the baby's born in early January, it'll be the oldest one in its age group for sports. If a baby's born in December, it's always almost a year younger than the January babies. Always trying to catch up, from the very start of its life."

"So you want me to keep my legs crossed for a week if the baby wants to be born on Christmas Eve?"

Night had fallen by the time I stepped out the door. My neighbor, Mr. Sorsasalo, had put up a small greenhouse at our fence line a couple of summers back. He had started growing grapes, hybrid vines that would survive the Finnish winter. I had been inside the greenhouse a few times; the space was so tiny that you had to hunch over and twist your shoulders sideways. The summer before, Sorsasalo had invited me through the flourishing vines to the back corner, where he had two stools and a little table. "Welcome to my wine-tasting nook," he had said. We sampled whiskey that day. Not a single grape had ripened yet.

Now from the door of his greenhouse Sorsasalo was insisting that he would harvest enough grapes this fall for at least ten bottles.

I drove to the portable trailer that served as company headquarters, changed into my uniform, and attached two different batons, tear gas, and handcuffs to my belt. Raittila invited us into his office. There were over a dozen of us and there weren't enough chairs for everyone.

Raittila said that he had set up a special deal with the State Railways for tonight. There were three times the normal number of guards on duty, and everyone would get an extra bonus if we nailed the smudger-scum. For the past three days, train cars had been waiting at the harbor as bait. According to a reliable tip, the Bacteria would converge tonight.

We were the Antibiotics.

METRO

RYE

I finished up the *E* with a sharp horizontal split-tip that looked like a viper's forked tongue.

I was in the process of writing RYEBREAD. It wasn't some advertisement commissioned by the local bakery; it was homage to the guy from Philadelphia who invented graffiti, Cornbread. In the late 1960s, Darryl Alexander McCray was in reform school and missed his grandmother's cornbread. He started writing it all over the school and when he was released in '67, he wrote his new moniker all over North Philadelphia. Later, he fell in love with a girl and started writing love letters along her path to school. Dogs leave marks by pissing on lampposts. Cornbread marked walls that the girl would notice: CORNBREAD LOVES CYNTHIA.

Cynthia had no idea who Cornbread was and wondered why the sappy phrase was suddenly popping up all over the asphalt jungle, in the weirdest places: on the sidewalk corner she passed every morning on her way to school; on drain spouts, AC ducts, building foundations. Sometimes it was just CORNBREAD. In the end, the signature spread beyond the neighborhood. High up on lampposts: CORNBREAD. So far up brick walls it seemed only birds could reach: CORNBREAD.

Darryl was shy and at school he didn't go by his nickname. An invisible cornbread-grubbing boy loved Cynthia.

This is the essence of graffiti: the invisible making something visible. Graffiti is a bomb and its shrapnel shoots out across a city.

It would be so goddamn cool if messages started appearing around town that read RUST LOVES METRO.

Metro, that's me. I share my bed with Rust.

RYEB

After I painted the *B*, I heard the faint clank again. It came from the direction of the old train station that had been closed for years. Sometimes on Sundays the deserted waiting room housed a flea market where people hawked stained mugs, yellowed books, and broken memories. The only trace of passengers was a sign saying how many child refugees had been sent off to Sweden during the war, in the years yadda yadda. A shitload. I didn't get how you could get to Sweden by train; there's a sea in the way. Maybe the kids had just been shipped off to the next town over and put to work in a margarine factory.

I didn't have a clear view of the brick station house from where I was working. Between me and the building there was a small overpass that had almost zero traffic in the middle of the night.

If you followed the tracks a mile north, you hit the Paimenportti station. It's the old boundary where the city's grazing lands used to start. Before the tracks were put down, a fence stood there, with a gate herders passed through with their baaing and mooing animals. To this day, broad pastures continue to spread out from Paimenportti, but now they're for trains, not sheep and cows. Just beyond the station, a half-mile stretch of north-south rail yard opens up where the State Railways, the SR, keep long chains of cars.

There were more tracks and fewer outside eyes at Paimenportti compared to the harbor, and more directions to run. We had painted there plenty of times.

Rats patrolled the place, but there were twenty tracks running side by side, and we could hide pretty easily among the trains as we worked. Even on light-filled summer nights, or in the wintry glare of floodlights intensified by snow. A dense forest rose to the west of the site, and we could plunge into its depths if it got dangerous. The forest led to rocks you could scramble up; the guards couldn't follow you in their cars. They had gym-pumped muscles that made them strong enough to lift their nasty hormone-heavy weights but not to run after us.

You didn't want to get caught. Then you'd get the crap beaten out of you and you'd be liable for all the graffiti that had been painted on train cars over the past few years. All of it, not just your own.

The Rats called our work smudges. They refused to say the word *graffiti*. Or *tags*. Or *stencils*. Or *stickers*. Or *murals*. Above all, they refused to talk about *art*.

Smudges.

Filthy smudges.

Goddamn filthy smudges made by faggot smudger-scum.

These same Rats hung needlepoint versions of *The Fighting Capercaillies* inherited from their grandmothers on their walls at home. Because, you know, two big grouses sizing up each other, that was real art.

Over the last year, the Paimenportti rail yard had become the venue where we played cat and mouse with the Rats. The Rats knew we went there regularly. They were on the constant lookout for us, and we were on the constant lookout for them.

But now it was fall, and as the evenings grew darker we flew south like migrating birds, toward the center of town. Tonight, that meant the rail yard fronting the harbor, which was smaller than the vast train-pastures of Paimenportti.

For a couple days, seven boxcars had been standing beneath the church tower, waiting for a little color. Let the Rats watch over Paimenportti. We were working here now.

JERE

Raittila pulled out a map of the harbor and showed us where we would be posted. The boss was wearing a hunter-green wool vest and a pocket watch on a chain, like he was on his way to some fancy nineteenth-century shindig. Whenever he joined us on night jobs he'd wear coveralls over his vest. According to a "true" story that circulated among us guards, he didn't even take off his vest and pocket watch when he fooled around with his wife.

Actually, Raittila didn't fool around with his wife. He politely asked her: May I penetrate your vagina with my penis tonight at eight o'clock on the dot? The rhythm he counted from a metronome.

He changed his shirt every day.

Raittila made sure that everyone knew where he was supposed to be. He kept a pen in his breast pocket and used it as a pointer as he reviewed the various locations on the map. We were going to wait them out. Eliminate every last escape route. Knock the legs out from under the swine.

"For once we have enough people," Raittila said, returning his pen to his pocket.

He introduced us to the guys the Lahti office had loaned us. It wasn't enough for us to just nod at each other. Raittila made us shake hands and introduce ourselves. For him, manners were what separated men from barbarians. The names of the guys from Lahti went in one ear and out the other, though they did have firm handshakes.

"The first thing we'll do is set up a perimeter broad enough to snare the Bacteria," Raittila continued. "Koivisto will be up in the crane all night acting as a lookout. He'll let us know when the Bacteria show up. Then, on my command, we'll tighten the noose. One thing that's going to make things a little easier is that the sea is guarding one of the longer flanks."

Evidently Koivisto was already up in the crane.

"How's he going to piss?" Hiililuoma asked.

"He's got his hat," I said.

Raittila glared at me. I shut my mouth.

"Some of us are better than others at holding it," he said drily. "The piss doesn't spray uncontrollably from their mouths."

Over the last couple of years, there had been a sixfold increase in incidents of smudging on trains and along the tracks. Last fall, the situation had gotten out of hand, and the SR hired us to catch the culprits. In addition to us security guards, Raittila was using a handwriting expert who claimed that the smudges were the work of four or five individuals, at most. Our job was to destroy this cell of smudger terrorists.

So far, the Bacteria had managed to avoid us. We had found them in the act along the tracks a few times. But every time they slipped off into the darkness before we could bag them. They were like agitated houseflies; getting close with a swatter was almost impossible. One time, Mattson, Hiililuoma, and I chased two Bacteria through ferns as tall as we were. We crashed through rasping stands of alder and clouds of mosquitoes; I was sure I saw one of the Bacteria's hoods bobbing right in front of me. Suddenly, we were standing in the sea, our socks and shoes soaking wet. There was no trace of the Bacteria. We trudged back in our squelching socks; a protruding branch had ripped Mattson's coveralls.

"We should be allowed to use dogs to hunt them down," Mattson had said, shoving a finger through the hole.

The moment we caught one, things would be easier. We could heap all the damages retroactively on his shoulders, which would be a big incentive for him to give up his partners in crime.

Plus, there were other ways to coax out the truth.

The summer had been quieter than March through May. We figured the Bacteria had come to the end of their natural lifespan. In August, Raittila had brought cake to our morning meeting and enthusiastically explained how at some point Bacteria inevitably moved away or had kids and started paying off mortgages and hated smudger-scum and felt ashamed of their own past. They became bourgeois, or headed off to Asia on extended vacations and got lost in a perma-high on the beaches of Goa or stung to death by jellyfish in the Indian Ocean. There had been several cases from other cities where an acute smudging epidemic had died off on its own. We dug into the strawberry cake and nodded.

But three weeks ago, eleven train cars had been painted in one night at Paimenportti. Raittila wasn't talking much about Goa or jellyfish or the bourgeois-ification of Bacteria anymore.

The SR had invited Raittila in for a chat. They called it an invitation, but it was clearly an order. When he returned from that meeting his face was red like burning-hot coals. He called in everyone for an emergency meeting, on duty or off duty. When we all arrived, Raittila ordered us to pile into cars so we could caravan out to a spot near Kyminlinna. We left the cars on the patch of sand that served as a parking lot.

Raittila led us through the spruces not saying a word, and, with a wave of his hand, ordered us to crawl the last fifty yards. No one protested, because Raittila, in his wool waistcoat and pinstripe trousers, had been the first to crawl through the wet moss. We had peered out from under the spruces at the deserted north-south rail line.

After fifteen minutes, a passenger train thundered northward up the track. It took an hour for the grumbling to begin. Raittila ordered every man to keep his gut on the ground and his trap shut; if anyone moved a muscle or if he heard a single consonant more, whoever it was would be fired. Effective immediately. The same fate awaited the guys lying to the left and the right of the crybaby, so the wimp wouldn't feel so lonely in line at the unemployment office.

Two hours of stakeout later, my clothes were completely soaked; the wet patch had spread from my stomach across my entire body. I was shivering uncontrollably, and there was no way I would have been able to pop up instantly even if I wanted to. My hands were full of red bites from black flies and goddamn midges; from the way my face was tingling I figured it looked like I had chicken pox. Someone nearby sneezed. Raittila hissed that the sneezer had better keep his fat mouth shut or get a job as a day-care lady where he could snort and snuffle as much as he wanted watching brats from morning till night. The entire time we were lying there, three passenger trains passed, plus a twenty-eight-car freight train. Two rabbits also crossed the tracks.

It wasn't until dusk fell that Raittila stiffly hauled himself up to his knees. He stepped out in front of us, pulled out his pen, and told us that we had just gotten a tiny taste of what Bacteria did night in, night out, without complaining. They had motivation, they had will-power, they had the patience to wait for the crucial moment, they had a burning passion for their work. Bacteria don't care about the cold, the wet, the wind, the sleet blowing in their faces, or, especially, the rules. That was the reason the Bacteria were succeeding and we weren't. This crew of baton-boy big shots was nothing but a bunch of lazy, comfort-loving, jiggling bellies who would rather spend their time lounging on the sofa watching TV than doing real work. If the snot-nosed, sniveling, double-chin-growing, beer-bellied couch potatoes stand-ing before him had even a quarter of the passion the Bacteria did, we would have caught the smudger-scum a year ago.

"Bacteria don't moan about eight-hour shifts, or overtime, or how much money they make. The Bacteria don't make any money. Bacteria don't demand overtime compensation or sick leave or days off because their wife is giving birth or little Ville is sick."

As he spoke, Raittila pointed his pen at each of us in turn. When he mentioned the birth and Ville, he pointed at me.

"I'd be better off if I fired you all and converted a few Bacteria. Everyone would save money: our company and the railways."

Raittila took off and left us wiping our noses in the spruce woods.

Now we would wait and spring our trap. After the briefing, we split up and headed toward the harbor in four-man teams. Hiililuoma and I climbed over the nearby chain-link fence with two other security offi-cers and advanced at a crouch past a long warehouse. Its wall was so pitted and peeling it looked like it had psoriasis. The rail yard was up ahead and to the left.

It was our team's job to make sure no one got away across the over-pass. The other teams would block anyone trying to run downtown or deeper into the harbor. Every escape route had to be cut off.

From his perch up in the crane, Koivisto reported that no illegal players had appeared on the pitch yet.

Of the four of us, only Hiililuoma and I had earbuds. We waited for our orders behind some Dumpsters near the warehouse. As we blackened each other's faces with the camo stick Raittila had handed out to us, the closest Dumpster gave off a sweet, rotten scent.

"Raittila picked this spot just to screw with us. He came here and planted a horse's head in that dumpster a week ago," Hiililuoma hissed.

"I can't see the trains," one of the other guards whispered behind him. "Where the fuck are the trains?"

This was one of the guys from Lahti. He was tapping his fingers against his knees. He barely looked old enough to vote; his face was dotted with pimples. If he was bored out of his skull after five minutes, he had a long night ahead of him.

METRO

A third clank flitted in my direction from the shadows of the overpass a hundred yards away. It didn't seem random anymore. It was like someone was announcing that, as of now, they were assuming control of our future.

This is what happens in this line of work. A single clink becomes a three-hundredpage book that you try to interpret and understand as you paint faster and faster.

If it was a Rat, then more were lurking nearby. Rats always traveled in packs.

I adjusted my hood, held my scarf up in front of my face. I didn't really need to. In the dark, a pale face glares brighter than a reflector. But I have dark skin. My dad is from the Congo; my mom is from Kouvola.

Love brought them together and my birth forced them apart. By the time I popped into the world, Mom and Dad had moved in together and spent two winters shivering in a wooden house where the curtains fluttered even when the windows were shut. Apparently I had been sick all the time, and things between my parents deteriorated with every illness. Because of me. By my third autumn, they had decided to decamp toward milder winters. Mom made it thirty-five miles south, to the shores of the Gulf of Finland. Dad kept going. The last time I got a card from him was five years ago, from Berlin.

The card told me to be a good girl and to listen to Mom, and then he asked me to send him a recent picture of myself. Underneath was the address where I hadn't felt the need to send a goddamn thing as a kid in junior high. Maybe a two-pound turd.

I felt differently now, at the age of nineteen, but I had burned the card after reading it. The only thing I remembered about the card was the picture on the front: a pink VW bug.

I took a look under the train car; I could see the legs of Rust's folding ladder. Bass pounded out from a car cruising on the other side of the red cliff.

"Rust," I whispered.

No answer.

A fourth clank.

September was the perfect time for painting. In August, people still lingered on restaurant patios and wandered around late, savoring the last velvety-soft nights of fleeing summer so they could make it through the cold months huffing and puffing around the corner.

Everything changes come September 1. That's when Joe Schmoe scurries indoors every evening regardless of the weather. He doesn't even like looking out the window until the blinding sun of February rolls around. As long as we stayed out of the halos of the streetlamps, no one noticed us.

That's why autumn is the ideal season for the graffiti artist. September, October, November: dark nights, empty streets. Winter: not so good. In the heart of winter, caps and paint freeze, and as the light increases in the spring, people start spending tons of time outside, which makes no sense. A warm September evening sends folks scampering inside to crawl under a throw, a much colder April night gets them all out into the streets, snorting with enthusiasm, coats unzipped as if the doors to the insane asylum had been thrown back. As spring went on, we had to move further and further from public spaces, to abandoned warehouses and buildings.

Finland's light-filled summer nights are a graffiti artist's worst enemy. Even a bigger problem than Rats.

But autumn. On autumn nights we can paint in the heart of the city, with the stars as our only companions.

I circled around to the other side of the train. My neck tingled, and I had the sensation that someone was creeping up behind me, on the verge of grabbing me in his steel fist and shaking me like a rag doll.

Again, I whispered, "Rust. Rust."

He had his back toward me and was completely absorbed in his work. He was also putting up RYEBREAD. We were both out tonight paying tribute to Cornbread.

Rust forgot the world around him when he painted. Only amateurs leave their iPods on and earbuds in when they write. That's why they're always the first to get caught. You need ears like a bat.

But it was different with Rust. When he got lost in painting, the bass started thumping in his head, then the drums and an electric guitar kicked in. He was at a concert while he painted. Sometimes he wouldn't even hear ambulance sirens, or pot lids clanging against each other.

I was his ears, his guardian angel.

I touched Rust's knee. He turned to look. He was just painting a crown over the *B* in RYEBREAD; Cornbread's tag had always included a crown.

A graffiti artist is the king of artists. The outdoor painters of old would be envious of us. They duplicated a slice of the landscape on their canvases. We change the landscape.

Rust's tribute covered the car end to end. Instead of flames, he had made it out of painted splotches of Rust. That was his signature style no matter what he was painting. Wherever Rust goes, Rust eats through the surface.

Rust never sleeps.

One time, Rust's letters looked so realistic that a Rat tried to kick through the hole of an *O* with his combat boot. Crunch. The guy tore his meniscus and was on crutches for the next few months. We knew this because Rust ran into the gimp-Rat at the post office. We recognize the Rats, but the Rats don't recognize us. Rust held the door politely as the Rat hobbled out on his crutches. Rust was sympathetic, asked what had happened. *Soccer injury*, the Rat lied.

We thought it was funny, and from that day on we called that Rat Lionel Messi.

"There's someone there," I whispered to Rust.

He looked where I was pointing, toward the pillars supporting the overpass, and went around to the other side of the train. He squatted down and turned his head. In the dark, you can see better out of the corner of your eye than you can head-on. Graffiti artists know to take their crew's paranoia seriously.

"I don't see anything," he said.

"Listen."

We pulled back between two cars.

Clink.

"That's not the wind, there's no fucking way," I said before Rust had time to suggest it.

My feet wanted to run. If I were alone, I would have been sprinting already, but Rust's calmness stopped my legs from moving.

He has looked after me ever since Mom stopped being up to the job. I moved in with him over two years ago.

"There's something moving over by the girders," I said, squeezing Rust's arm so hard he clenched his teeth. Now he could make out the movement, too, and he pulled me back to the furthest corner of the car. He started gathering up his stuff.

"I want to see," he whispered.

I was crouched; my bag was already on my back. I was ready to dash. Hell, sprinting was one thing I was good at, just ask the guys from the local sports club. Rust once told me that the crouch start was invented in Australia, from observing kangaroos. Now I was hoping I'd be able to move fast and hop over the tall chain-link fence in front of us without touching it.

Something emerged from the shadows of the bridge.

It was a rabbit, which broke out into a run, weaving between us and the overpass. Then a second flash.

"A fox," Rust said.

The animals zigzagged across the tracks toward the closest crane. The sea would cut off the rabbit in a second. The only escape was up the crane, and rabbits weren't so hot at climbing ladders.

You always have to have a getaway plan, Rust had taught me. *Lack of planning will kill you.* The rabbit didn't have a plan. The fox caught its meal as soon as the rabbit had no choice but to curve back from the edge of the pier. Under the pier, the fox violently shook its prey in its teeth until we heard the rabbit's neck snap.

"I only need a couple more minutes," Rust said behind me. "You cool with that?"

"I can finish, too. No panic."

I was embarrassed by how jumpy I'd been. When you're letting animals spook you, it's time to crawl into a sleeping bag and chill there for a couple of days, sucking on dime-store candy.

I went back to my side of the train. All kinds of things were spinning through my head: rabbits and foxes; the rabbit's squeal as the fox whipped it from side to side, its teeth sunk into the rabbit's neck; *CORNBREAD LOVES CYNTHIA; RUST LOVES METRO; I LOVE RUST.*

When I started painting the *E,* I concentrated on the final thought. *I LOVE RUST. I LOVE RUST.*

A final clank echoed from the overpass, louder than the rest, even though minutes had passed since the fox and the rabbit had run out. By the time I registered it, it was too late.

JERE

Two hours and fourteen minutes. That's how long we waited behind the reeking Dumpster. The young guy from Lahti had been flicking his fingers so long that they had to be at least an inch shorter. Then Raittila's voice crackled in my earbud.

"Bacteria on site."

"Roger."

"Are we finally advancing?" the young guard asked.

"What's your name?" I whispered.

"Salo."

"Salo, we'll advance when I give the order."

Salo continued flicking. I suspected his buddy from Lahti had fallen asleep; he had kept his trap shut unusually effectively the whole time. Hiililuoma had let out deep sighs at regular intervals, as if he were thinking about the summer that had just ended.

"Is anyone cold?" I asked.

"I am," Salo answered.

"If you're motivated, you're not cold."

Salo corrected himself. "I'm motivated."

"Isn't a motive a reason to take action, to move out?" Hiililuoma said. "How can we be motivated if we're not allowed to do anything except hide out back here?"

The fourth guy didn't say anything; he actually had fallen asleep.

We had to wait another half hour before Raittila gave us permission to spread out and advance toward the rail yard. He had wanted to be sure that no more Bacteria would show up.

"Two targets," Raittila's voice crackled in my earbud.

I took the left flank of our sector. Hiililuoma crawled to the right. Our reinforcements from Lahti, Salo and his pal, stayed in the middle.

I eventually learned the name of Salo's pal: Pippuri. Comatose Pippuri. He had snoozed away the majority of our wait. Either he had nerves of steel or narcolepsy. Or young kids who kept him up at night and then woke up early. Like me.

Hopefully the baby would be born in January, not December. I was born late in the year, and when it came to running and swimming I was never able to hold a candle to the boys born months earlier.

We hustled over to the concrete pillars supporting the overpass. I could make out one of the Bacteria a little over a hundred yards away. He had chosen his spot well. There were trains on two tracks, and the Bacteria was scribbling his filthy smudges in the gap between, making it impossible to see him from where we had been. It took me a minute to spot the second one. He was closer. Dressed in dark clothes, he melted into the shadow cast by the railcar.

"Ten minutes," Raittila announced.

I held up ten fingers. Over at the next pillar, Salo flashed ten fingers to let me know he'd seen my signal.

We had synced our watches after the briefing. Mattson joked about this becoming like some US Army black ops mission. It was like we were preparing to assassinate bin Laden.

Raittila glared at Mattson before saying, "You can quit playing PlayStation and focus on your job. Or you can quit this job and focus on your PlayStation. Which one is it going to be, Petri Mattson?"

Petri Mattson chose his job.

I stared at the railcars. Aside from us, ten more security officers had gathered invisibly along the fringes of the rail yard. Four men were stationed at the far end of the harbor; six to the right, near the cross streets leading into town. The sea took care of the left flank. Beyond the rail yard rose Vellamo, the wave-shaped building that housed the Maritime Museum. When you counted Koivisto high above in the crane, there were fifteen of us. Even though this was just a onetime operation, it was unusually large, and no doubt expensive.

The SR seriously wanted to catch these smudger-scum.

Either them, or Raittila.

I wasn't sure whose honor had suffered more from this prolonged wave of train-smudging: Raittila's or the railways'. I suspected Raittila's. He couldn't even stand to see scribbling in notebooks; he'd immediately rip out any pages doodled with circles and squiggles and tic-tac-toe.

There was a clank to my right; luckily it was so faint there was no way the smudger-scum would have heard it. Salo had shifted again. The guy seemed incapable of sitting still for more than two minutes at a time, as if he had fallen into a vat of energy drink when he was a baby. Salo probably walked around while he ate and compulsively did push-ups or rode his stationary bike while he watched television. The only one in Salo's household who used the sofa was his girlfriend. If he had a girlfriend. I couldn't imagine being able to stand such a fidgety guy. He probably twitched like a jackrabbit caught in an electric fence even while he was screwing.

"Five minutes," Raittila announced in my ear.

I indicated the timing to Salo. On the far side of the overpass, Hiililuoma communicated the same to Pippuri. But when I looked back toward the train cars I couldn't see anyone. I flinched as if someone had poured ice cubes down my back. I had only glanced away for a second, and both Bacteria had disappeared. Salo had also registered their disappearance, shooting me a questioning look.

"They're gone," I whispered into the mic. "They fucking disappeared."

"Both Bacteria have pulled back between the boxcars," Raittila answered. "They're staring in your direction. Don't move. Two minutes."

Suddenly I heard a squeal behind me. Luckily my legs were cramping; I normally would have bolted out of fright. I didn't have time to do anything but turn my stiff neck before a rabbit shot past me, followed by a fox. They dodged back and forth as they raced toward the train cars.

"Jesus," I gasped.

"What's happening?" Raittila's voice asked.

"Animal Planet just came to town. Are we moving?"

"Stay low. You guys are not going to screw this up. Do not move until I give the order. I repeat: do not move until I give the order."

The rabbit changed tack toward the sea. The fox didn't miss a beat, catching it near the crane.

The seconds felt as sticky as hours. Darkness dragged its heels across the rail yard. Eventually, a figure emerged from between the train cars. It climbed up some sort of ladder and faded into the shadow.

The Bacteria had resumed his work.

Salo waved that it was time. I gestured that we weren't going anywhere yet.

Another Bacteria came into view. He reached toward the roof of the car, his back to us.

Raittila's voice hissed in my ear. "Kalliola, Hiililuoma, Salo, Pippuri, go. Move in. Don't run until they see you. Catch those Bacteria."

I bent my stiff knees and stood. We moved forward at a half crouch, tightening the noose. I could hear Raittila in my ear, giving orders to the other security officers. For the moment their only responsibility was to make sure no one escaped. We had the best angle for advancing because we wouldn't be spotted until it was too late for them.

The smudger had his back to us and was concentrating on spraying; nabbing him was going to be a cinch. Only forty more yards to go.

Only thirty. I could already make out the mist of paint as it burst from the can's nozzle.

Then all of a sudden, the Bacteria turned toward us and started banging the side of the train with the can. Blows like gongs rang out across the rail yard. I started running. My left knee creaked. Salo huffed at my side like a rhinoceros; he was boiling with adrenaline.

The Bacteria dove between two train cars. Salo managed to grab his foot before he completely made it through to the other side.

"Here, puddy puddy," Salo yelped victoriously as he started pulling the Bacteria by its flailing legs.

METRO

CORNBREAD LOVES CYNTHIA. RUST LOVES METRO. I LOVE RUST.

I LOVE RUST. I LOVE RUST. The three words kept playing through my head over and over. I thought I was the one panting.

The Rat had managed to sneak up on me. The panting was coming from his mouth. I banged the side of the car with my can like a rabid junkyard owner. That was the warning Rust and I had agreed on.

As the bangs echoed, the Rat rushed me, crunching the gravel under his combat boots. I tossed my backpack over my shoulder and tried to dive between two cars. But the Rat sank his talons into my leg before I made it through. He was yanking at me, trying to get me back into his territory. I clung to the ladder running up the railcar.

"Here, puddy puddy," the Rat called out, and then he gave me one good hard wrench. I lost my grip, hit my shoulder on the coupling hook, and banged my temple against an iron loop.

Sprawled out on the gravel I was seeing the Rat double. I didn't realize that there actually were two of them until they started booting my ribs in stereo. They were blocking out the sky, but I was still seeing dazzling stars.

One of the Rats sank to his knees. Rust appeared behind him and clubbed the Rat in the back with his collapsible ladder. He started whaling on the other Rat too, but as he pulled the ladder back the one Rat grabbed the aluminum frame. The first Rat wobbled back up.

"A third Rat! Fuck, a fourth!" I shouted.

Rust glanced back. Two more guards were running toward us from the end of the train. A fifth was coming from the direction of downtown.

Rust dropped the ladder, grabbed my arm, and hauled me up from the gravel. Some of the Rats were cutting across the rail yard in front of us; they were heading us off so we couldn't escape to the harbor warehouses. We headed toward the quay and the sea. My legs gave way.

"You can do it," Rust said, half lifting, half dragging me.

"How many are there?" I groaned.

"A lot."

One of the Rats whistled like he had a duck call in his mouth. I glanced in the direction of the sound. More Rats had appeared from the direction of the warehouses. They were arcing around to surround us.

"Rats always travel in pairs," Rust panted. "In pairs. How the hell are there a hundred of them?"

He dragged me toward the pier. The fox had made off with its prey; all that remained was a puddle of blood and tufts of rabbit fur.

"C'mon, move those feet," Rust growled as I fell to my knees. He lifted me up and shoved me over the chain-link fence and half carried me to the edge of a high stone quay, where several yards below lapped the dark water. The quay was built of massive stone blocks onto which a narrow ladder had been installed. At the bottom of the ladder waited our means of escape: a rowboat.

We had used the boat on painting expeditions before; when a city's built on islands, a boat is a quiet, discreet way of getting around, especially at night.

"You first," Rust ordered. "Go, go, go. Hurry, hurry."

My head was spinning; my feet slipped on the wet ladder. I half slid down. One of my feet touched the bottom of the boat. As soon as I let go of the ladder I dropped and smacked my ribs against the bench. The pain cleared my grogginess.

I saw a school of herring swim past and realized a flashlight was shimmering across the water. The boat was fastened to the ladder's lowest rung with the same kind of knot Rust said bank robbers used to tie up their horses back in the Wild West. They could rush out of a bank, mount their horse, tug the rope loose with one hand, and ride off without having to stop.

The boat was our getaway horse.

But it was so dark I couldn't find the end of the rope. I tugged everything I could get my hands on. My fingers were slippery; I couldn't get a proper grip on anything. The car tire hanging from the quay as a boat bumper looked like the head of a Rat closing in on me. I kicked the rubber to free the boat.

Then suddenly I realized the boat was ten feet from the quay. And Rust wasn't in it.

He turned around on the ladder and saw what had happened. For a second it looked like he would jump into the water, but then he climbed back up to the top and started running. I couldn't see where he went.

Three Rats appeared at the edge of the quay.

"Stop," one of them yelled. They hesitated, considering whether to jump in after me. I was already four boat lengths out, and the dark water wasn't appealing. The Rats turned around and vanished.

I got a firmer grip on the oars and started rowing for the end of the old coal dock, along the black tires that bobbed against the wave-pummeled stone quay, past the cranes that rose above me like enormous storks.

A flashlight beamed out of one of the cranes and momentarily followed me. How had a Rat gotten up there?

They had been expecting us.

Like always, Rust and I had agreed on a backup plan. If one of us didn't make it to the boat, the other one would row to the tip of the old coal dock and wait.

I rowed along the long quay. Its stone edge ran high overhead and I couldn't see what was going on up there. The Rats were calling to each other. As long as their shouts kept moving, Rust was free.

Of the two of us, he was the faster runner; he had a chance of making it. That spring he had purposely goaded a Rat who had been chasing him at Paimenportti. Rust stumbled and randomly changed directions, giving the Rat a few chances to almost grab him by his hoodie. In the end, Rust outlasted the Rat, who was so exhausted and short of breath that an ambulance had to be called to cart him off.

I changed course, moving farther out into the channel so I could see what was happening up there. I could just make out the dark figures running around the rail yard.

At the edge of the old coal dock rose the Maritime Museum, a building shaped like a huge, thousand-foot-long wave. It was paneled in tinted panes of glass that were illuminated when it was dark; on autumn nights like this, they glowed green and blue like the Sargasso Sea. The building had originally been called Surge, but after the giant tsunami killed thousands in Thailand and Indonesia it was quickly renamed Vellamo, after the Finnish goddess of the seas. The city council was afraid that tourists wouldn't find a permanent monument to tidal waves appealing. My personal opinion on the matter was that a little honest whoring would boost my hometown's miserable trickle of tourists. They should have called it the Catastrophe Center, or the Tsunami Museum.

I could make out a lone dark figure running along the edge of the coal dock. It was Rust.

I let out a string of short whistles; that was our signal. I rowed the boat toward the end of the coal dock. Graffiti artists tend to have strong arms because the nature of our work means we end up rowing more than fishermen and climbing more than chimney sweeps.

Rust kept running. A group of Rats was following him at a distance but they were closing in.

I had to wipe away the blood that was dripping into my eyes. When I could see again, Rust had whirled around and was headed straight for his pursuers. What the hell was he doing?

Then I saw the reason for the sudden U-turn: two Rats had been waiting at the end of the coal dock. Now they were on his heels.

Rust was trapped: two Rats behind him, half a dozen in front of him. The facade of the Maritime Museum served as a blockade and on the other side there was nothing but a drop into the sea.

"Jump," I yelled. "Jump!"

I wrenched the rowboat closer so I could fish Rust out of the water once he jumped in. But he didn't choose the sea. He ran faster and faster, until he was almost right in front of the Rats. They steeled themselves to receive him, crouched down with their arms spread like goalies, wanting to make sure he wouldn't be able to crash through their line.

"Jump, goddammit," I wailed.

Just before the collision, Rust veered to the left, toward the wall of the Maritime Museum. Like a monkey, he pulled himself up the trusses and framing and scrambled up the fifteen-foot rise to the roof, a seven-hundred-foot ramp that you could climb in a wheelchair if you started at the very bottom. The Rats were forced to go back and circle around to the end, which gave Rust a head start of a few dozen yards. He ran up the ramp toward the top of the building. The ramp ended fifty feet above the ground in a crest of glass that hung over a small stage surrounded by concrete risers, where outdoor concerts were held in the summer.

I watched Rust's ascent from the channel.

He made it all the way up to the concrete theater. At least five Rats were halfway up the ramp. They weren't in a hurry anymore. Rust was trapped up top. The only ways out were back down the ramp or through the museum doors, which were locked.

One of the Rats was waving something in his hand. Another was banging the metal railing with a telescoping baton. Now I could make out more Rats at the bottom of the ramp. How many of the fuckers were there? Their black limbs intertwined; it was like a gigantic spider was climbing up the building.

Rust didn't hang around waiting to get his ass kicked. He scaled up the side wall of the auditorium to the highest peak of the building, to the crest of the breaker.

I rowed around the tip of the coal dock. A bitter breeze was blowing from the sea, but the sweat still dripped down my shoulders. I made it to the end of the quay, to the spot where the steeper slope of the building's crushing tidal wave rose to a height of a hundred feet. Rust was a silhouette advancing on his knees along the crest of the wave.

He stopped. Then he started descending the steeper slope, fitting his feet into the metal edges of the building's external framing. There was no ladder, just the trusses and the empty spaces in between. The actual wall dropped down behind the decorative grid.

Two Rats had appeared at the crest above Rust; they had shinnied up a hundred feet in pursuit of him. But the Rats on the roof wouldn't catch Rust. It was the bigger seething Rat pack below that he needed to worry about.

They had gathered there at the end of the old coal dock. One of the Rats from the pack started scaling the steeply angled rear wall toward

Rust. He was banging his baton against the decorative grid, as if he were chasing off crows.

Rust moved to the left to avoid him. But unlike the sloped front and rear of the building, the sides dropped down in vertical facades. The sheer wall was illuminated from inside, glowing bladder-wrack green and deep-sea blue. The thin metal framing crumpled beneath Rust as he crawled across the first few yards of the vertical wall, and then the rung he was reaching for came loose. He clung to a window frame, his legs swinging in the air. The tips of his shoes scrabbled for a toehold. The Rats below dispersed, as more and more of the metal framing clattered down.

"You're going to ruin this, too?" someone shouted. "Aren't the trains enough?"

"Jump," one of the Rats called from below.

The others joined the chorus.

"It's not far."

"Your knees will take the shock."

The Rat who was climbing up toward Rust didn't even try to follow him onto the vertical side wall. He stayed there at the corner to make sure Rust wouldn't be able to return to the steeply sloping end wall.

I could hear his taunting "Here, puddy puddy."

The Rat drew his nightstick across the decorative grid. The night echoed: rattattattattattattattat.

Rust glanced down at the waiting pack. He started cautiously climbing back up the vertical face toward the crest of the roof. Now and again a bit of framing came loose, windmilled through the air, and rattled to the asphalt. Right above Rust the heads of the two waiting Rats appeared at the edge of the wave's crest.

They all stared at each other. Rust dangling from the wall, the Rats waiting just a couple of yards above him.

From above, below, and the side Rust was surrounded.

"Jump," the Rat pack called out. "Don't be scared, we'll catch you. We promise."

The Rat from the end wall crooked a finger, beckoning. "Here, puddy puddy."

I could tell that Rust was getting tired, moving his feet and fingers, trying to find a more comfortable position. He was adjusting his grip more and more.

The Rat above him said something to him and offered him his hand.

"Climb up," I shouted.

Rust pulled himself up toward the two Rats who were on the roof. He extended his hand so the Rat could grab hold of it. For a second, they looked like Adam and God in that fresco that Michelangelo sprayed on the ceiling of the Sistine Chapel, creating the connection through which life flows into man. But the Rat God suddenly pulled back his hand and jabbed Rust in the chest with his baton.

That's when time stopped for me.

There on the wall, Rust tried to maintain his balance, slowly tipped backward, desperately holding on to the decorative window frame with one hand.

His other hand flapped in the air. He looked like a baby bird trying to practice flying with one wing.

The Rat whacked the hand that was still clinging to the wall. Now both of Rust's hands were free. He dropped backward, wildly flapping his featherless wings. The pack of Rats seventy feet below broke apart.

This I will remember. Even when I'm a demented ninetyyear-old lady and I don't remember my own name or which end the food goes in. I will remember Rust, who turned from a human into a bird and from a bird into a stone. I will remember the hand of the Rat reaching over the surging crest of the wave and waving good-bye. I will remember Rust frozen in midair, his wings flopping backward, unable to fly. I will remember the ring of Rats waiting down below.

Time stopped. The world ended, clocks stood still, waves petrified into granite, the brisk wind died down. Everything was surrealistically soundless, motionless, and eternal.

Then Rust slammed into the pavement.

JERE

I watched from above as the Bacteria flapped through the air. He looked like a baby bird that had left the nest too soon. The thud when he hit the ground was like the closing of a cellar door.

It had been my intention to pull the kid up.

He proved his agility when he ran away from us through the rail yard and down the quay. We managed to trip him and surround him once, but he popped up, lunged between Hiililuoma's legs, and zigzag-sprinted away. Stitched back and forth like a Singer.

I was sure we'd finally cornered him at the Maritime Museum. We were chasing him, and two other security officers came from around the corner. It looked like he was at a no-way-out dead end. He froze in place. I was positive his hands would go up in the air and we'd hear him say, *I surrender.*

Nope. Some people just don't know when to give up.

Totally unexpectedly, the kid bounded onto the wall and scaled it all the way up to the roof. We had to backtrack to the base of the ramp. It took a minute, but we surrounded him a second time up on the roof. Everyone was panting. Salo had fallen and busted open his elbow.

"Game over," Pippuri said, banging his nightstick against the railing.

Anything but. The Bacteria scurried up the wall like a lizard, up to the building's highest peak. I followed. Hiililuoma took off after me. The wind was gusting hard up above, and I was afraid I'd lose my balance and fall. Across the black water, the factory chimneys at Sunila were belching smoke. I flinched when a wing brushed near my ear. I didn't know if it was a gull or a bat from hell. That's what it felt like up there: hell in the sky.

I'd lost sight of the kid, so I crawled up to where the roof sloped down; Hiililuoma stopped behind me. He wouldn't come out to the edge. I looked down, thinking that if Hiililuoma wanted to shove me in the ass and knock me down, this was his chance. He could say I slipped. Hopefully he wasn't still pissed about Mirjami and me snagging from under his nose the lot where our house now stood. He hadn't said a word to me for a month afterward, aside from the obligatory grunts.

It took me a second to pinpoint the Bacteria's position. I could hear everyone else down below catcalling at him. One of our guys was climbing up the sloped rear wall.

Then I spotted the kid on the vertical side wall. He was moving about fifteen feet below me, inching along the framing. A piece broke off in his hand and whirled through the darkness. The lighting in the building's facade made his clothes glow blue and green; moving soundlessly the way he did, he reminded me of a deep-sea fish.

I wouldn't have dared to climb down the wall even if there was a ladder. I watched him from above without saying anything, saw him hesitate and eventually decide to climb back up toward the edge of the roof—and me. Someone from down below encouraged him to grow a pair and jump; they'd catch him. Bursts of laughter followed, like on an American sitcom.

The kid tilted his head. I could make out a tuft of sweat-dampened hair sticking out under his cap; his cheeks were full of freckles. Despite his exhaustion, he alertly surveyed his alternatives, seemingly oblivious to my colleagues' taunts.

"You can't escape," I suddenly said.

The Bacteria didn't answer; he didn't even look up at me.

"There's no point in you falling," I continued. "It's just paint. Vandalism. You didn't murder anyone. Don't pay any attention to what those guys are yelling."

The kid let go of the wall with his left hand, crooked his fatigued fingers. Someone was shouting to him from the sea, urging him to climb up to me.

"Give me your hand," I said. "I'll help you up. I promise I won't let go. I promise I'll protect you from those guys."

The Bacteria thought for a second, giving his right hand a rest, shaking out his fingers.

"Make him fall," a voice whispered behind me.

Raittila had appeared at the crest of the roof.

I shook my head no and held out my hand to the kid. He hesitated, thinking about his next move.

"Make him fall," Raittila whispered in my ear.

"No."

"Then get out of the way."

Raittila pulled me back. He nodded at Hiililuoma to join him at the edge of the roof and whispered something in his ear. Hiililuoma was kneeling and at first he shook his head but then he reached his hand over the edge.

The kid held out his hand and strained toward safety. Hiililuoma prodded him in the chest with the tip of his nightstick. He didn't even need to hit the kid. One nudge from the baton was enough, the kind of nudge you use to shut the refrigerator door.

The kid was still hanging from the building's decorative framing with his other hand, which Hiililuoma whacked with his baton.

I watched the Bacteria flap his arms and plummet through the air.

I heard a shriek from the sea. The rowboat was rocking a few dozen yards from shore; the other Bacteria in it was standing up in the boat, watching everything.

"Good job," Raittila said, squeezing Hiililuoma's shoulder.

METRO

I spent the next day in bed, not eating, not drinking, not sleeping. If I closed my eyes I saw Rust falling, over and over again. As I anticipated the fatal thud against the ground, he just kept falling down, down.

When I finally drifted off into an uneasy slumber, my love's freckled face came to me and said that he wouldn't have died if I'd waited for him in the rowboat instead of scrambling off in a panic. He illustrated his point with a diagram he threw up on the wall, in case I had trouble understanding.

It was an accident! I shouted. *I didn't mean to. I love you.*

If you loved me, you would have waited, Rust replied. Then he was falling, falling. First the freckles fell from his face in a red rain, and then he fell away.

They were blasting rock a couple blocks away. The intermittent explosions sounded like Rust's head bursting when it smashed against the pavement.

You saved your own skin, the fragments of his head said as they ricocheted around me. *Coward, coward, coward, coward.*

The only time I climbed out of bed was to go to the bathroom.

Someone came by and rang the doorbell; I didn't answer. It wasn't Rust's parents, that was for sure. They didn't even know where we lived. We were bunking in an apartment that belonged to a friend who had gone off to the Levant or the Orient for a year. The place was in his name, and so were the rent receipts. It was his name on the mailbox, not mine and not Rust's. The only address we had was a PO box, which Rust would check from time to time. We used prepaid burner phones and we opened the door only if we knew friends were coming over. Otherwise, if someone came to the door we didn't check to see who it was.

It was the perfect hideaway, impossible for the Rat machine to trace. There were only two times I had answered when the doorbell chimed unexpectedly. The first time it had been a pair of straight-backed Jehovah's Witnesses standing there, and the next time it had been a hunchbacked old lady trying to sell a pail full of lingonberries. Her face was more wrinkled than my fingertips after the sauna. She said she had already been to ten apartment buildings; I bought the entire pail. When Rust saw all the lingonberries in bowls and dishes scattered around our kitchen, he threw clothes hangers at the walls and raged all evening. Not about the berries, but because I had gone and opened the door without checking to see who was snooping around outside.

Rust had assured me that he'd be able to hide from the authorities if we just never opened the door. This was his primary guiding principle, which had been instilled in me as well.

He'd had other principles, too. You might even call them obsessions.

I had never been allowed to take a single photograph of Rust. He didn't want his face to be found on a single cell phone or camera. If someone shot a photo and Rust thought he was caught in the frame, he demanded the photographer delete the shot and stood there until it happened. One time at a playground he told a woman with braids to delete the pictures she had taken of her kids with her iPad, since he happened to have been standing in the background. Made a huge stink. It ended with the mother flinging sand on Rust with a plastic shovel while her kid shrieked at her side. *Mommy, no more patty-cake!* But the mother did delete the photos.

When I told Rust that his behavior aroused more attention than a photo ever would he laughed, saying, *People have such bad memories for faces that they can't tell the Queen of England from the old lady next door if they don't have a photo of the monarch in front of them.*

There was also the left foot thing! Rust always had to step in from outside with his left foot. He also had to circle any obstructions from the left, because the heart is on the left side. At first I didn't fucking get it at all. Now it seems totally sensible. If I ever took another step, I would always start with my left foot, because of Rust.

But I'm not going to.

The doorbell rang persistently a few times. I didn't check the door. There sure were a lot of Jehovah's Witnesses around these days. A lot of souls that refused to be saved.

I eventually had to crack open the door when someone kept kicking it for minutes on end. The blows sounded way too much like Rust's head crunching against the ground. For the thousandth time.

It was Baron.

He stepped in, shut the door, yelled at me for not opening the door and causing a disturbance. Me? I told him that Rust and I didn't open the door for anyone who didn't call and let us know they were coming by. Baron asked how the hell he was supposed to call her royal highness when she was unreachable by phone.

"Am not," I said.

He fumbled around in a heap of clothes for my cell phone and pulled it out. The battery was dead.

"Why aren't there any lights on in here? Have you gone blind?"

"I didn't notice they weren't on," I said.

"A blind person could see that, but not our sweet little Metro. It's dark as an elephant's asshole in here."

Baron pulled a handkerchief out of his pocket and said that the apartment also smelled like shit and death, and he didn't know which smelled worst, death, shit, or me, who had spent more than enough time wallowing in the other two. He retrieved the window crank from behind the black curtain and opened the apartment's only window.

"What's with this curtain?" Baron asked. "Do you think you're living in a coffin or something? Do you have fantasies of being buried alive?"

"I didn't realize there was a window there," I said, squinting from the sudden glare of light.

"Don't play dumb, it doesn't suit you."

It was difficult to tell when Baron was really angry. Usually he spoke almost formally, used the kind of language no one else in my circle of friends did.

"Why is your bed covered in blood? Are you snuggling up with a horse's head these days?"

"I don't know."

"What do you mean, you don't know? You're lying there like a dead horse yourself. Your face is all bloody, too."

"Leave me alone."

"Do you have a fever?"

"I killed Rust. Call the cops. I'm guilty."

"I don't know about guilty, but you look horrible. Zombies who have been gorging on guts look less gross than you do."

"I'm not some fucking zombie."

"No, you're right. I apologize. The comparison is offensive to zombies."

Baron pulled my bloody pants and shirt out of the tangle of clothes and held the brown splotches up to my face.

"Have you ever heard of a washing machine? Have you ever considered what sort of impression you're making, stalking down the catwalk of life in a gray bra?"

Baron looked like he'd prefer to handle my bra with a pair of work gloves on. He dangled the clothes at arm's length.

"I want to go to jail!" I shrieked.

Baron wrapped his arms around me, carried me across the room, and set me down. I didn't realize what he was doing until it was too late. Cold water pelted me.

"You don't get to go to jail. You get to take a shower."

I struggled for a moment but then I gave in. I huddled in the corner of the shower, letting the water stream over me. Baron adjusted the temperature until it became warm.

"Skin hygiene," he said, "is an important thing if you're not a zombie."

I stared at the water swirling down the drain and the crusted streaks of blood that were liquefying again. I felt my head and quivered. A big lump had appeared at my left temple and the water stung when it hit the skin surrounding it.

"It's not bleeding anymore," Baron said.

He spoke in the same tone that Dad had used when I was sick. Then Dad would hum strange songs from his homeland and stroke my hand.

I would have spent eternity in that shower but after a few minutes Baron twisted off the tap. He wrapped me in a towel and led me out of the bathroom. He didn't let me get back in bed. He said the sheets needed to be washed; they were bloody, too. Apparently it looked like a horned ram had been ritually sacrificed in my room. Baron brought me a chair and sat me down at the window. He went over and pulled up the dirty linen, made the bed with fresh sheets.

"You'll have good dreams tonight," he promised.

I mutely watched as people on the street walked past each other and crosswalk signs and bike racks and lampposts. The world had been cast into a sickly, totally random chaos. They should have always passed from the left.

"You and I are going out now," Baron said, handing me clean clothes from the closet.

"I don't want to."

Baron dressed me; I went totally limp. He finally managed to get shoes jammed onto my feet and tied the laces; I threw myself to the floor and lay there spread-eagled. Baron tugged at me for a while, then he got bored and left me lying on the rug. He disappeared out the front door. I was happy I would never have to see him again.

The sun shining in my face was bothering me, but I didn't have the energy to get up and shut the curtains. Was it sunrise or sunset? I didn't know which direction our window faced.

But what difference did it make?

No difference at all.

Baron came back. This time he didn't kick the door; he unlocked it. The shithead had taken my keys. He clattered around the kitchen, bent down next to me, and forced mashed bananas between my lips. I hadn't eaten them since I was a kid, when I had been laid up in bed with the measles, covered in red spots. Dad had fed me, the same Dad I hadn't heard anything from in years.

"You're acting like my Dad or something," I grumbled.

"OK," Baron replied.

"I hate mashed bananas. I hate my Dad."

"Then drag your big behind up and feed yourself. As long as you're lying there I'm going to feed you."

I got up, leaned against the table, and glared at Baron. He set the cup of mashed bananas down in front of me and unpacked the groceries. At the same time, he emptied most of what was already in the fridge into the garbage.

"What the fuck are you doing?"

"Everything in here is rotten."

"It's still totally edible."

Baron turned the carton of milk upside down over the sink. Nothing came out until he knocked it; thick, smelly paste slid from the carton.

"Rust would die of food poisoning if he ate your food. He'd die again. *Then* you could call yourself a murderer."

"Go to hell."

"That's where you're going to be soon if you don't eat. There are easier ways of killing yourself than dieting to death."

He dumped a pile of beady-eyed herring on the table and started nimbly cleaning them.

"I don't eat fish."

"These aren't for you. I'm eating this. I can't stand watching from the sidelines on an empty stomach while you cover yourself in ashes and drown in self-pity."

"This isn't self-pity. Rust is dead."

"I knew Rust longer than you did. He's the reason I'm eating. Rust would appreciate eating in someone's memory, not moaning and mucking around in misery."

"Go fuck yourself, Baron. Then cut off your dick."

Baron fried up the herring fillets and set down a stack in front of me. He sat down across the table, aimed a fork at one of the fillets on my plate, and crunched on it. My stomach growled.

"I'm not hungry," I burst out.

Baron shrugged, loosened his tie, and then attacked the next fillet. His musky aftershave mixed with the smoke from the frying. Baron had used the same aftershave for as long as I had known him, claimed that it reeled in both clients and the ladies. It didn't work on me.

"You reek like a muskrat's ass glands," I said.

"Musk ox," Baron retorted, spearing another fillet with his fork.

"Norovirus smells like violets compared to that."

"I more or less agree with you," Baron said. "But a kilogram of musk costs over fifty thousand euros. Even though you don't smell the money and prosperity I'm emanating, a lot of people do."

"That's the reason you drench yourself in that?"

"No one cares what you're like deep down inside. They care what you look like and how you smell."

I remembered the first time I met Baron. We had been on the roof of a six-story building, trying to paint down onto the wall. The only way to pull it off was to have one of us hang headfirst over the edge and use a roller with a telescoping handle. Two people had to hold the person painting by the feet so he wouldn't fall. Rust had asked Baron to join us because he didn't get dizzy easily. Instead of baggy pants and a hoodie, Baron had shown up in a dark suit, a striped tie, and a silver tie clip. He rolled out most of the text. When the blood went to his head at one point, he took a break, which he spent polishing his patent leather shoes with a goddamn cloth handkerchief. He sat on his poplin coat to make sure his suit wouldn't get dirty. When we split, his poplin coat was swinging from one arm, the belt blowing in the wind, as casually stylish as a Giorgio Armani ad.

Yeah, Rust and I ran. Baron didn't have to. He calmly strolled into the closest pub for a beer.

Baron didn't carry his spray cans, stencils, and tape in a backpack; he used a Cavalet satchel—timeless Scandinavian design. Whereas guards near rail yards stalked anyone wearing a backpack, Baron could walk hundreds of yards along train tracks, checking out promising spots to paint. One time the Rats even offered him a ride. He had introduced himself as an inspector from the Transportation Agency who had been sent out into the field to investigate problematic stretches of track. The Rats had driven Baron up and down the trackside road while giving him a precise account of their patrol schedules and routines.

"Let me get half a herring," I finally muttered as my stomach growled more and more belligerently.

I ate ten.

JERE

That night, after a short debriefing, Raittila sent the other guards on their way but asked me and Hiililuoma to stick around. Rain had started rumbling down when the ambulance and the police arrived on the scene.

Raittila reported to the police that during our rounds we had sighted smudgers in the rail yard. There had been two vandals, both of whom we attempted to detain. But they fled toward the sea, where they had a boat waiting. One of the vandals escaped in the boat and deserted his companion on shore. The one left behind panicked when the boat pulled out, ran up the ramp of the Maritime Museum, and climbed up to the roof's highest ridge. He attempted to descend the steeply sloped rear of the building. Unfortunately he had been startled by Hiililuoma, who had circled around to meet him at the foot of the back wall. The smudger had then moved around to the side wall, where he had slipped and fallen. The framing that had been knocked to the ground offered a pretty accurate reflection of his route. It wasn't our fault that he started climbing roofs and walls. It was an insane thing to do. But smudgers weren't totally sane, now, were they?

With the police we walked around and up the ramp of the Maritime Museum. By then it was a downpour. One of the policemen, a guy who was over six feet tall, climbed up to the peak of the roof. Because of his height he had no problem hoisting himself up, but once he was there he stumbled at least twice. He came back down at a crawl.

"You guys almost got to scrape up another body," he said.

He asked us to indicate how far we had pursued the deceased. Raittila said to the end of the roof ramp, no further. We stopped following once he started fooling around on the roof.

"How many of there were you?" asked the officer.

"Three. The three of us here," Raittila said. "The two of us were up top and Hiililuoma here was down below."

We walked back down the ramp. The police made a note of our personal information and said that the case looked perfectly clear. Not too long ago, a member of the same brotherhood had slipped while painting from a roof in Helsinki. He had had a safety line, but it had been so poorly fastened that it had slipped up halfway around his neck, strangling the guy.

The police also asked for any identifying marks of the vandal who had escaped. There wasn't much we could say. Dark hoodie, black jeans, fast feet. Managed to take his bag with him. Both scrambled away before we reached them. Plus, it was dark. Maybe they'd find something over at the train car they had been vandalizing.

"No one's going to miss this guy, that's for sure," the tall policeman growled, raising his collar against the downpour.

"It's still too bad," Raittila said.

The policeman nodded dutifully.

Raittila drove Hiililuoma and me to our cars. He reiterated that we'd better not deviate from the version he gave to the cop on the roof if the police came around with more questions. Keep it simple. It was only the three of us who had been at the scene. There was no point getting anyone else involved; this was nothing but an accident. He would prepare a written report of that night's shift that we could both read and sign.

It was still dark when I got home, but it felt like the night had lasted over twenty-four hours.

A dim night-light lit the entryway in case Ville woke up in the middle of the night. I waved my right hand in front of the mirror. I imagined the force with which Hiililuoma had whacked the smudger-scum on the hand. Not very hard. As strong as the sweep I used to brush the hair from my forehead. On level ground, there's no way any-one would classify that as excessive use of force. It wasn't our fault that the kid who fell was hanging from a nearly vertical wall. What did he think he was? A spider? Every profession has its risks, and the profes-sion of smudger has a lot more than most. When it comes down to it, it was a matter of career choice.

I slept deeply; I didn't wake up until lunchtime. I played Legos with Ville; Lego Jere continued his profoundly unlucky adventures. Ville was especially thrilled when Jere was catapulted into the air and fell from so high that his head popped off and rolled under the sofa.

"Uh-oh, Jere died. Pop!" he laughed.

I had to launch Lego Jere from the catapult dozens of times. The head didn't come off every time. I learned to attach the head loosely.

Pop. Pop.

Ville's joyful laughter always made me forget his long-lasting tan-trums. Mirjami appeared at the door to the nursery; she smiled at me and absentmindedly rubbed her belly.

Raittila called while we were playing. He said I could come into work a couple of hours late and I'd still get paid for the whole shift.

I threw myself onto the bed, read a Donald Duck book to Ville. Donald was a dogcatcher. Mirjami closed her eyes. Ville cared a lot less about the storyline than about my mimicking all sorts of dogs barking.

Once I came across a list of all the jobs Donald Duck had ever held. There were a couple hundred, from vacuum-cleaner salesman to locksmith, from repo man to demolition. In some odd way, I found Donald's entrepreneurial spirit consoling when I considered my own interrupted stint at college prep. For five years I had, like Donald, tried my hand at a bunch of odd jobs and training programs before I ended up subbing for someone on sick leave at Raittila's company. This was the longest time I had ever worked anywhere; it would be four years in November. During that time I had gotten married, built a house, and had a child, with another one on the way.

I had to read *Donald the Dogcatcher* out loud five times and bark louder and louder every time. In spite of that, Mirjami managed to nap at my side.

When I got to work, I was greeted by an empty changing room and two calendars. A *Hunks* calendar hung next to the girlie calendar; we had a couple of female employees and it had been determined that equality was important. Hiililuoma was already there; his coat hung from the rack, as creased as an accordion. The black-and-blue gym bag he usually carried with him was halfway unzipped on the bench.

I knocked on Raittila's door; he asked me to wait outside for a minute. I put on my uniform coveralls. Hiililuoma entered the dressing room in civilian clothes. We shook hands. It felt weird; we didn't normally shake hands. I asked if he was going to be headed out on patrol with me; Hiililuoma shook his head. A day off. He was going to go home to kick the ball around with his son.

Raittila poked his head out of his office and told me to take off my coveralls. He said he needed me in the office today, not the field.

When Raittila had called and instructed me to come into work later, I had expected to find the police there, thought they would want to hear more about what happened down at the tracks. But the only one in the office was Raittila. There were two maps on the wall: a map of the city and a map of the world, where Raittila put a thumbtack through every country he visited. About fifty of them. Raittila had said that pointing at the map was the best counterargument if some overly critical individual felt like accusing security company guards of being narrow-minded. Just the opposite. The more he had seen of the world, the more cultures he had encountered, the surer he was of one thing that unified all people around the globe, regardless of religion, race, gender, age, or profession: people craved security in their everyday lives, and we offered it to them.

Raittila showed me the report he had drafted of the previous night's events.

The report made no mention of the operation having involved well over a dozen security officers. There were only three of us left: Raittila, Hiililuoma, and me. According to the report, Raittila had joined us on our normal rounds because from time to time he liked to observe staff on their shifts. Raittila had written that I had noticed unusual movement near the trains as we were patrolling the rail yard. We had parked further off and tried to approach the smudgers without them seeing us. The rest was a repetition of what he'd told the police the previous night.

"How come the report says Hiililuoma is down below when the kid falls?" I asked. "Why am I on the roof?"

"I'm on the roof, too," Raittila snapped. "Neither one of us did anything. The least we can do is put Hiililuoma on the ground."

I put my name to the events as reported. There were two copies; Raittila said he'd deliver one to the police.

Then he asked me to wait in his office for just a moment longer. Raittila explained the way he assigned shifts and briefed me on the other employees, some of whom I knew. At the map he went over the areas the company patrolled and told me how many employees he preferred in each area and what the minimum coverage for any area should be.

"I'm going to have you spend a day at the office now and again," Raittila said, "so you can get trained in things other than legwork. That means you'll be getting a raise, starting today."

"How much?

"A little bonus."

"What about Hiililuoma?"

"When a man is prepared to shoulder responsibility he gets rewarded handsomely. As of today Hiililuoma is my new deputy. To be honest, you don't have the stomach for it. Completely understandable. Not all of us are able to make difficult decisions under pressure. But if you handle things intelligently and with a cool head from here on out you'll get a new position before long. It's a winwin situation for everyone. When I'm transferred to Helsinki within the year, the position of head of security services will open up for the most competent person. I recommend the most competent person. If it's Hiililuoma, as seems likely right now, you have a very good chance of becoming his deputy. You'll move ahead, taking slightly shorter steps than Hiililuoma, but in the same direction."

METRO

As I munched on the last herring Baron opened his satchel and spread some sheets of paper across the table.

"Time to get some fresh air."

"I don't feel like it," I snapped.

"You need to get some color on your face."

"What the fuck did you say, you racist?"

"I never would have believed a black person's face can be pale, but living proof of this aberration is sitting right here in front of me."

Baron leaned back in his chair and told me about his mother, whose hair had turned gray overnight after his father died. So it was perfectly possible that the tint of a person's skin could change permanently with the death of a loved one.

"OK, correction. Now you look red," Baron said. "Your pigments are going haywire."

I picked up my plate and hurled it at Baron. He ducked and it shattered against the wall. When I saw the shards I remembered that we only had two plates: mine and Rust's. And I had just broken Rust's plate. As I realized this, the tears finally came.

Baron wrapped his arms around me and I sobbed for a long time. "It's OK to cry over Rust."

"I'm crying over that plate," I howled.

My tears soaked Baron's suit, but he didn't push me away. Instead, once I had calmed down a little, he led me back to the shower. As I scraped away the dead skin, I imagined I was sloughing off the grief.

Baron waited for me to get dressed. I wanted to wear something that belonged to Rust. I pulled down his ski cap from the hat rack. It was so tight my forehead started to ache the second I put it on. When I went over to look in the mirror, the cap popped off. There was a groove circling my forehead where the edge had pressed into the skin. I had never realized my head was so much bigger than Rust's.

All the rest of Rust's clothes were too big for me and my feet swam in his shoes. How could a guy with such big shoes have such a tiny head?

I joined Baron back at the table and he explained all the papers to me. Each sheet was filled with dozens of little blue-and-yellow Chiquita banana stickers.

"We're moving on to bananas," Baron said.

"I don't get it."

"Three differences. What are they?" Baron asked, setting down a banana he had brought from the store.

It wasn't until I examined the labels side by side that I noticed how Baron's stickers differed.

"These say 'Chemical,' not 'Chiquita,'" I said. "What's up with these?"

The Chemical stickers were almost identical to the blue-and-yellow Chiquita ovals. Both featured the same lovely Latina in puffy sleeves carrying a basket of fruit on her head. But the smiling senorita in the Chemical stickers was holding a gas mask in front of her lips; the hand she was waving at consumers clutched a bottle of poison marked with a skull and bones.

"Almost all banana companies use deadly insecticides that cause cancer in their workers," Baron said. "Chiquita is one of the most notorious. It holds workers in an iron fist, bans labor unions, pays poorly, and terrorizes, abuses, oppresses, and fires workers who demand improved conditions. If a village gets too strident in its opposition to the company's actions, Chiquita calls in the militia and bulldozers raze the place. Companies cheerfully selling energizing vitamin C bombs from the tropics, like Dole and Del Monte, also use these methods. The very companies whose pineapple rings and preserved peaches Finnish supermarket chains sell with a smile and without the tiniest pang of conscience. Canned dreams."

"So?" I said. "Are we going to go paint in banana trees?"

"It'll do you good to get your mind off paint for a while and breathe some fresh, pesticide-laced supermarket air."

For the next two days, Baron and I made the rounds of the city's supermarkets. We'd hit the fruit departments, peeling the Chiquita labels off hundreds of bananas and replacing them with Baron's Chemical stickers. If an employee noticed us Baron would ask about avocado recipes other than guacamole, or inquire about the variety of chili peppers being sold. What about carambolas, this weird-looking star-shaped fruit? We're having a company party on Friday. What kind of punch would these work with?

When a helpless-looking man in a suit carrying a designer satchel asks for advice, the lady from the fruit department goes off and comes back with a thick folder and a colleague, and they start recommending recipes in tandem, and the quick-fingered girl hovering over the bananas becomes completely invisible.

I was standing outside the last store of the day, waiting for Baron to exit with a stack of recipes, a free ice cream, and the grocer's warm wishes to come back again soon.

"That guy you were just talking to banned me from this store once," I said.

"What happened?"

"I gave him a hard time for selling eggs from caged chickens. I told him it was the same thing as selling swastikas by the six-pack. He told me to get out of there and scrub my dirty mind; it was as black as the rest of me. I was barred for life."

"I guess 'for life' was shorter than you ever imagined."

"Then they go and roll out the red carpet for you." I slugged Baron's shoulder. "A suit can't make that much difference."

"I still don't think you really get how this works."

We walked to the beach and sat down on a bench bolted to the rocks. The autumn sun radiated warmth between strips of clouds; the empty sand curved around in front of the rock. You could still see footprints of bare feet, like petrified fossils, even though the sunbathers had been gone for at least a month.

"I lived in Stockholm for three years," Baron said. "When I moved there, I dressed the way you do."

"You wore a skirt?" I said.

"I painted train cars and warehouses and underpasses, like you."

"You still do, goddammit."

"Not seriously, just for fun. But you think graffiti actually makes you a force for change. Let me tell you: that's not how it works. You're not going to change the world with a couple of pieces. Rust was an idealist who flitted from cloud to cloud and trained you to wander around the clouds, too. In Stockholm I learned how to really, tangibly achieve something. To do that, the first thing you need is a long-term plan."

"Rust wasn't phony like you, you plastic suit-wearing whore."

"Rust begged to get caught. His biggest dream was to end up a martyr."

"Go jump in the sea."

I was furious, even though I knew Baron was just trying to prod me out of my coma. As far as he was concerned, it was better for me to hate him than to drown in sorrow.

He told me how he met this one Finnish guy in Stockholm named Sarge, and how they had painted together at all kinds of out-of-the-way spots. Sarge wasn't really a sergeant; he thought of himself as a backwoods guerilla fighting against a big, powerful enemy. "Another idealist" is how Baron described him. One night, the two of them encountered a guy among the shipping containers at some shitty little industrial area. He wore a suit. The guy in the suit and Sarge knew each other and the guy asked Sarge for help with a project the next night. Baron tagged along. That next night they took the metro to the Hallonbergen stop and ended up at a government office building inside of which immigrant affairs were handled.

"The guy in the suit glued palm-size stickers to the walls of the Immigration Board building; they were marked with the city's coat of arms and read GRAFFITI AND POSTERS ALLOWED ON THIS WALL."

"The walls were marked with the coat of arms?"

"The stickers," Baron said patiently. "They looked legit, like official notices from the city."

With Sarge's and Baron's help, the guy in the suit had put up these notices permitting graffiti in about a dozen spots near the government building. After that, they started painting on those walls. They bombed and did throwups in a bunch of different styles so the authorities would think that there had been dozens of graffiti artists, not just three.

"You could have tagged just as easily without the stickers," I said.

"The operation didn't end there," Baron said. "Next, the guy in the suit—"

"Does this guy have a name?"

"I promised I'd never tell it to anyone. Not his real name, and not his nickname either."

"Abba."

"Say what?"

"Let's call him Abba," I said, chucking pebbles into the water. "Favorite band of men who wear suits."

Baron pretended not to hear when I started humming "Money, Money, Money." He said that next, Abba sent a letter to the editor of a right-wing newspaper strongly condemning the graffiti that had appeared. The letter included his suspicion that the vandalism was the work of foreigners and called for tightening the immigration policy. He intentionally added a couple of spelling mistakes that luckily no one edited out of the version published in the newspaper. Abba was particularly pleased that his alter ego's nasty remark regarding "the primitive genetic disposition to vandalism that has no place in our civilized homeland" had been left in unabridged. As soon as the letter criticizing vandalism and immigrants was published in the paper, Abba, Sarge, and Baron made several thousand copies of it. They dropped them through mail slots, left them on windshields, attached them to bulletin boards at nearby schools and colleges, left stacks at coffeehouses.

"It was truly hilarious," Baron said, allowing himself a smile before he continued.

I rarely saw him smile.

The Immigration Board didn't even have time to release a statement before the newspapers started printing concerned comments from citizens about the racist policies and practices permeating the board and affecting everyday life in the city. Meanwhile, the trio led by Abba replaced the notices permitting the graffiti, which had been taken down, and threw up messages commenting on the racist letters to the editor. They painted one nearby wall halfway up with white paint then added a large "CAUTION! WET PAINT!" sign marked with the Immigration Board's logo to make it look like the board was trying to remove graffiti by painting over it. At the other end of the same wall, where some pieces were still visible, they added a notice in the city's name: GRAFFITI THAT DOES NOT MEET AESTHETIC CRITERIA WILL BE REMOVED BY THE AUTHORITIES.

"The idea being," Baron said, "that stylish works weren't a problem. So, conflicting messages."

"So what did the city do? Or the board?"

"They never had a chance to catch up."

Baron chuckled to himself; it was weird seeing a guy who was normally so serious giggling only a week after Rust's death.

Next, Abba and his helpers had written a supposedly official announcement on Immigration Board letterhead that read: IN THE FIGHT AGAINST VANDALISM, UNDER SUSPICIOUS CIRCUMSTANCES, ANY LOCAL RESIDENT OR EMPLOYEE MAY BE SUBJECTED TO A FULL-BODY SEARCH. They printed up as many copies of this notice as they did of the original letter to the editor and distributed it to the same colleges, homes, offices, stores, cars, and coffeehouses. They also attached notices to walls and lampposts, urging people to call the Immigration Board immediately if they observed any suspicious activity.

"At this point, Abba encouraged the two of us, me and Sarge, to get ourselves suits. We went to the local flea market. By now, the mood in the neighborhood was so tense and paranoid that you needed a suit to walk around freely. Anyone in a hoodie was suspicious. Abba carried his paints in a briefcase. I picked up my Cavalet at the flea market. Abba made us calling cards claiming we were consultants working for the city.

"The idea that the Immigration Board and the city were encouraging outrageous attitudes toward foreigners and students grew increasingly incendiary. References to *a police state* and *Orwell* kept popping up in the newspapers. In the right-wing papers, the city's no-tolerance graffiti policy received support; in the left-wing papers, it didn't. The talk shows on the local radio stations were overrun with people's furious and sometimes confused calls. Abba moved on to his plan's next phase. He disseminated notices inviting residents to a meeting called by the besieged Immigration Board and the City of Stockholm. The notice also said that there would be free drinks and food, and he ordered a hundred large pizzas in the city's name.

"So many people showed up that the auditorium was overflowing. People had to stand out in the lobby. Bewildered representatives from the city and the Immigration Board also showed up, having only found out about the meeting they had supposedly called at the last minute. We had set up chairs and tables on the stage. They gave awkward speeches apologizing for any potential confusion regarding the matter. Some of the speeches were interrupted by boos. The high school students who showed up did a commendable job of maintaining a raucous spirit."

What made the meeting especially rewarding, according to Baron, was the fact that at no point did the government officials have any idea how any of this started. Not even a year later. The city accused the board of taking rash measures and vice versa. People had brought the City of Stockholm and Immigration Board notices that they had torn down from all over town; the four stunned bureaucrats, two men and two women, tried to defend themselves against the accusations hurled at them.

The upshot was that graffiti was allowed in several specifically dedicated zones. The Immigration Board commissioned three full-wall murals to demonstrate their goodwill. The City of Stockholm promised to open a new activity center for local youth; the neighborhood had been asking for one for twenty years. The time it took to process immigration paperwork was at first cut by a third and then by a half of what it had been before.

"Think any of this would have happened if we had just sprayed a few tags without a plan?" Baron asked.

I shrugged, watching a tern hook and plunge into the troughs of waves. It wasn't until the bird's fourth try that it caught a tiny fish. But then the fish fell from the tern's beak, back into the sea. The tern screeched and started a new round of dives. Persistent bird.

"But the best moment," Baron continued, "was when the pizza arrived. The driver demanded that the Immigration Board pay."

The tern nabbed another minnow. In the background, a cargo ship slowly slid behind Varissaari Island. The ship's bridge rose higher than the tip of the island's tallest pine.

"I'm telling you this so you'll leave things be. Move on with your life."

"Have you ever loved anyone?" I asked.

"Resist secretly, resist strategically. Open conflict with those in power instantly throws up barriers. Play the mole, disrupt and dig tunnels through the system. It's the only way to bring about change."

"How the fuck can you act like such a grandpa? Is that tie cutting off the oxygen flow to your brain?"

"Don't avenge him." Baron lowered his hand to my shoulder.

The scent of musk enveloped me, fogging my thoughts. I shook my head and watched the tern wheel into the wind overhead, looking for another fish to eat. The cargo ship emerged from behind the island, splitting the sea before me in two. It took minutes before the waves it plowed up sloshed against the shore, and by then the ship had already disappeared behind the next island.

"Of course I'm going to avenge him," I said. "You're going to help me."

JERE

The dreams didn't start until a couple of weeks later. They always involved the sensation of falling; I would bolt awake right before my body broke against the earth's surface.

Once I woke up I couldn't fall back to sleep. I lay on my back in the sweaty bed. Mirjami was at my side, sleeping soundly, her blanket pushed onto me, smothering me under the double layer. I stared at the corner of the bedroom ceiling; a small dark splotch stared back at me, growing like a pupil in the darkness. On the third night of falling I decided I had to take a closer look. I was afraid of water damage.

I wandered around the gloomy house, opening cupboards and drawers looking for a flashlight. I finally found one in a closet, tucked in with cleaning supplies. The batteries were dead.

I took a floor lamp from the corner of the living room and plugged it into the bedroom outlet with an extension cord. I got a stepladder, turned on the lamp, and studied the corner of the ceiling. I touched the dark splotch and tasted my finger. Was it moisture or dirt? Or mold?

"What are you doing, Jere?"

"Nothing."

Mirjami sat up in bed, squinting as I stretched up to the ceiling.

"Is there something there?"

"Just a bug. I didn't want it biting you."

"Come here."

I went back to bed. Mirjami lowered a hand to my stomach. I listened as she rapidly dropped off, counted her exhalations to five hundred. Out on the road, the tires of a car crunched as it passed the house. The electric radiator murmured faintly. I tried to make out the sound of Ville's breathing.

I couldn't.

I turned onto my stomach. I was hotter than if I had been lying out under the July sun. I threw off the covers. Without the blanket, the darkness weighed more heavily on me. The pupil on the ceiling just kept dilating the more I thought about it. I wondered whether my son was still breathing. Maybe he'd shoved his face under his pillow and accidently suffocated himself.

I slipped out from under Mirjami's arm and crept into the nursery. On the way, I banged my leg on the edge of the dresser. Ville was clutching the stuffed crocodile we had bought him in Stockholm last summer, our first family trip abroad.

I went back to the bedroom, knowing I wouldn't be getting any more sleep. I couldn't turn on the light. If Mirjami woke up a second time to find me inspecting the ceiling she'd start thinking something was seriously off. Then she wouldn't be able to sleep, and she'd start worrying, and she'd get a migraine or something.

The mattress felt like a bed of nails but I forced myself to lie still. On the boat to Stockholm I had read a book to Ville about the fierce chariot races and gladiator fights of ancient Rome. The next day we walked through Old Town. On Drottninggatan, a guy who was nothing but skin and bones was lying facedown on a bed of jagged pieces of broken glass bottles. His dreadlocked girlfriend collected money in a paper cup, her feral eyes skittering across the crowd. *Was that a bloodthirsty gladiator?* Ville kept asking until I snapped, saying, *Nope, just your run-of-the-mill junkie.*

I crawled out of the bed and sat on the floor. I felt like going out for a run. But it was only three in the morning; one of the neighbors would see me and think I'd gone crazy. If Mirjami woke up to me coming in from a jog in the middle of the night, she'd start worrying about me working too much, and then she'd tell me to take a day off and rest.

It's easy to tell someone else to rest. But when you're resting you have a lot more time to think than when you're busy.

As a kid, I never had any problems falling asleep. Same was true when I was in the army. The best part of the army for me was that sleep always came instantaneously, regardless of the others sleeping, mumbling, and farting around me. It didn't matter how much rattling or muttering there was.

Now things were different.

A sudden downpour whipped raindrops against the window. I sat there with my eyes closed and patiently counted the taps.

METRO

Revenge is the most important human desire. Revenge keeps you alive.

My biology teacher from high school didn't think so. He said that people have three basic needs: food, sleep, and reproduction.

The theory had been tested for millennia of mammalian evolution. With 100 percent certainty. Food, sleep, and sex form the triangle in which humans exist. If one of the tips of that triangle disappears, humans will disappear, as well.

Without food or water, a person will die within a few days.

He'll die just as surely without sleep, slowly wasting away. A poor wretch punished by continuous lack of sleep will go crazy, have an accident, or be vulnerable to illness. The machine shuts down.

Without sex, a person won't die, but he won't have any descendants either. The line will die out when the person incapable of reproducing dies. Over the centuries, Darwinian natural selection had eliminated the most apathetic and laziest individuals from the group this way; they didn't have the energy to reproduce.

Eat, drink, sleep, and screw! Those were my biology teacher's parting words of wisdom to his graduating seniors. *All else is secondary in terms of perpetuating life.*

But my biology teacher failed to mention that the only real basic human need is revenge. A person can live without food, sleep, or sex if she has chosen revenge. Revenge provides her with sustenance, rest, and free orgasms.

Revenge is even stronger than love. When love dies, revenge remains.

I didn't say all of this to Baron. As far as he could tell I was mourning in silence. I met him at a local café where the guys at the next table were wearing fluorescent yellow construction vests, as if they were afraid they'd get run over when they stepped up to the counter to pour themselves a refill. Baron sure had complicated visions of how he was going to get rid of all the city's corrupt civil servants.

Up until Rust's funeral, I didn't paint. I delivered the papers early in the morning, came back to the empty apartment, and drew. Spring and my entrance exams loomed off in the distance.

Both of us had delivered papers. I had only done it for six months, Rust for almost ten years. First I met Rust, then he got me a job. He had enthusiastically explained that there was nothing more amazing than cycling through the city on a summer night. He was right. It was amazing in the spring and summer. But eight months out of the year, it was just cold.

We carried cans of spray paint in our postal service bags as we rode around town. We'd go straight from our nighttime painting gigs to delivering the morning paper.

No one ever searched postal service bags. Those of us who delivered the morning paper for the postal service were among the few people who could walk the streets in the middle of the night without getting attacked by Rats.

Sometimes I'd tag an electrical transformer while I was on my route: METRO, with a set of tracks above. Then I'd pedal on. Rust would go around in a T-shirt, even in November. He hadn't taken a single sick day in the last five years. He really was a star employee.

The first time I saw Rust it had been sleeting; he cruised past on his bike in a T-shirt and splashed water on my shoes. It wasn't exactly love at first sight.

That was two years ago.

Our first winter together, Rust convinced me to leave my parka at home and go out into a snow flurry in a sleeveless shirt. *You'll feel a lot better,* he promised. *You'll be rewarded. Your body will get used to it.*

I felt a hell of a lot better, all right. I was rewarded with two weeks in bed with a case of pneumonia.

Delivering the morning paper is a dream job for graffiti artists. Rust had been right about that. The ideal hours and locations. Unlike office workers, you were able to move around and check out spots you could paint later. No one thinks twice about a delivery person cruising around at night—not even the grumpiest, most sleep-deprived old fart standing at his kitchen window with a cigarette hanging out of his mouth because back pain and prostate trouble keep him up all night. The only time Rats stopped one of us was to try and wheedle a free paper. In return, the Rats looked out for our safety.

A paper is a small price to pay not to get your ass beaten by them. Plus it's the perfect cover in newsprint-patterned camouflage. Rust had figured out the best place to hide from Rats: right under their noses, in plain sight.

I went to the library to check out the newspapers from the last week and a half. One of them had a blurb about Rust's fall. It said it was an accident. A young man had fallen from the wall of the Maritime Museum while trespassing. Three nameless men from a security company were mentioned as eyewitnesses. Two days later, there was a slightly longer article about the incident. It also mentioned three eyewitnesses, and went on to review other deadly accidents involving graffiti artists in Finland and other Nordic countries, all of which were due to deficient safety measures. They interviewed a window washer, who presented his safety harness. He noted that vandals were often as indifferent about their own safety as they were about the appearance of their environment. The article ended by noting that, according to the police report, no crime was involved in the young man's death.

Three guards? What the hell? The harbor had been teeming with them.

I reached into my pocket and pulled out the pocketknife I always carried with me for cutting out images. I sliced out the articles, folded them up, and put them in my pocket.

The next day I showed the articles to Baron. He read them through a couple of times.

"The security guards filed an official report that the newspaper is using as its source."

"Why does it say there were only three of them?"

"It's simpler than a bunch of them. Ten or more starts sounding like an intentional chase."

"But it was!"

"My dear Metro, who cares if there were a dozen eyewitnesses or three?"

"I do! You do!"

"But nobody else. Nobody."

Baron handed the articles back to me. He apologized, said he had to get to a meeting. Seething with rage, I followed him around the corner, where his company car was waiting. The real estate company's logo was painted on the side: a smiling house. The windows were dimples.

"So the houses you sell smile?" I asked.

"Yes," he said.

I rode with him to Karhuvuori. Baron was showing a place there, and our apartment was in the same neighborhood. I mean *my* apartment. Karhuvuori was built up in the 1970s, evidently as cheaply as possible. The construction company crane had been brought in and erected, and as many buildings were slapped up out of prefab elements as could be done by rotating the boom. Apparently moving the crane had been needlessly expensive; they only did it a couple times. That was how the zoning plan for the area was created: by randomly spinning a boom.

The neighborhood had immediately earned itself a restless reputation and the nickname Kauhuvuori, Terror Hill. Plenty of bus riders claimed to have been on board when a blood-covered man with a knife sticking out of his back was crawling on the ground at the bus stop, waving for help, and the driver just hit the gas. Karhuvuori had received notoriety most recently when a national survey revealed it as the neighborhood with Finland's highest unemployment rate, almost 40 percent.

There was no bloody man crawling around the bus stop today; just a couple of old ladies in wheelchairs barking wearily at each other. The two old biddies looked like they had been bickering for the past forty years. They were starting to run out of steam.

The apartment building we were headed for seemed to be wincing like someone had just kicked it in the guts. The walls looked like they were about to crumble, and the big yellow stain on the building's beige backside made it look like it had bladder control problems. Baron set out a couple of open-house signs in the yard, unlocked the door to the third-floor apartment, and took a look around.

"Everything up to snuff?" I asked.

"Basically."

"Urban living at its best. Shoddy cardboard walls conceal a stylish shoebox inside. Neighbors create a never-ending sense of community day and especially night. The countless holes drilled and pounded into the walls create an exceptional sensation of space and light. If you're a woodpecker, you'll feel right at home. The speed freaks staggering around outside ensure you will get your daily exercise."

"It's a dream apartment for some lucky soul," Baron agreed.

"It might sell quicker if I painted something on the wall."

"No way in hell."

"C'mon. A smiling house?"

I sat on the kitchen counter and watched while Baron scrubbed the toilet. Even cleaning the bathroom looks elegant when you do it in a suit.

"I want to see the Rats' official report."

"Why?" Baron asked, toilet brush in hand. "It's not going to make you feel any better. You need to move on."

"I can't move on knowing that the Rats are hiding the truth."

Baron sighed and rose from his knees. He took off his rubber gloves. "You have to go. The open house is about to begin."

I walked home through the tall grass; the squabbling grannies were no longer at the bus stop. Evidently this driver had the balls to stop and pick up the locals. A deflated bright-red ball gleamed in the corner of the sandbox. I looked up at the dark windows surrounding me and tried to see if I could spot a child's face looking out longingly at her ball. My phone rang. I answered.

"Do you promise you'll drop this if I get you that report?" Baron asked.

"Yes," I lied.

I grabbed the flat ball out of the sandbox; maybe I could bring it back to life.

JERE

On Saturday, Raittila ordered me to join Hiililuoma on a special assignment. He told me to wear a black suit. We were going to attend the funeral of the young man who had fallen off the museum.

The young man who fell. I had silently repeated the phrase to myself. The young man fell. He was not knocked down.

Raittila said that our mission was only halfway finished. The deceased belonged to the crew of smudger-scum we were after, and it was likely that the rest of them would be sending off their comrade. The funeral would be the best time to bring in the entire crew and make them answer for their deeds.

"Humans are sentimental creatures," Raittila said, "prisoners to their instincts. Since the Stone Age, they've always wanted to say farewell to their fallen clansmen."

The funeral service was held that afternoon at the chapel in Parikka, a cemetery about five miles north of town. Hiililuoma and I pulled into the chapel parking lot early and stayed in Hiililuoma's Audi, watching the mourners dribble in.

"Grave garden," Hiililuoma said.

"Huh?"

"*Garden* and *yard* come from the same root word. So a graveyard is a grave garden."

Hiiliuoma liked to blurt out some pretty off-the-wall stuff sometimes. Evidently he picked it up from his girlfriend, who taught Finnish.

"I'm good with *graveyard*," I said.

Leaves were falling from a nearby maple; they twirled through the air and slowly blanketed the car's windshield and hood.

Hiiliuoma stayed at the wheel to keep an eye on things when I entered the chapel, the last guest to arrive. I took a seat in the back row and scanned the room. An elderly couple sat in the front pew, their shoulders slumped. At their side was a man with a layer of stubble covering his pale face. Further back, a couple of middle-aged women. A family with lots of kids. About thirty people in total.

A young woman and young man sitting near the aisle interested me the most. They looked a few years younger than me. The man was wearing a loose-fitting suit, probably borrowed. The woman had pulled her curly hair up into a bun. She leaned against the guy and was having a hard time looking at the coffin in front of her. She gnawed her fingernails and kept glancing at the walls.

On the casket's lid there was a framed photograph of a smiling teenage boy jumping spread-eagled into a lake.

The female pastor described the deceased, Markus, as a young man bursting with joy and energy, who had his whole life in front of him until sudden death cut it off. Markus had always been ready to plunge into new adventures; for him the world was full of unexplored realms, hundreds of places waiting to be discovered.

I couldn't help thinking about Ville, who was fascinated by our big atlas. He would open it up to a random page and want me to read him the names of the cities, rivers, and mountains. *I'm going to go there*, Ville always said, whether it was Annapurna or the Kalahari Desert.

The pastor fastidiously spread sand over the closed casket, as if she were sowing the last rye seeds from a starving farm. "For dust thou art, and unto dust shalt thou return," she uttered solemnly. I wondered how many times she had spoken those words.

A little girl in a black dress stepped up to play the violin. While she was playing, she started to cry, the tears snaking down her cheeks. When she was done, she managed to whimper that the song was for her big brother. I felt a pang and had to bite my cheek.

I imagined it was Adolf Hitler inside the coffin. That's what I always imagined at funerals these days, to keep the bawling in check. I made the mistake of revealing this trick to Mirjami at her grandmother's funeral, which is when I came up with the idea in the first place. She sulked for the next week.

Gran had a fine set of whiskers, a little like old Adolf. Now any time there was a documentary on television and Hitler's face flashed by, Mirjami would glare at me accusingly, and I had to try and pretend like I didn't notice. Movies set in World War II were banned in our home. As were the YouTube memes where Hitler blows up at his staff in the bunker for whatever reason: for learning that he's Jewish, or because the pizza he ordered came late.

I stepped out of the chapel before the service ended. I didn't want to hang around to shake hands with the family. I walked over to the car, brushed the maple leaves off the windshield.

"Anyone interesting?" Hiililuoma asked.

"Yup, this one couple."

Pallbearers carried out the casket and the mourners followed as it was loaded into a hearse. The girl with the violin stood there, legs crossed, chewing on her lip. The black-attired crowd stayed under the sloped roof of the chapel. A magpie landed on the roof, spun there like a weathervane. The roof reminded me of the one we had climbed while we were chasing the smudger. Only a lot lower, of course. If you fell from this roof, you'd only break a leg.

"The ones in back," I said.

The young couple didn't look like grown-ups anymore; they looked like stretched-out children. Standing in the doorway, the girl was bawling out loud, burying her face in the guy's chest. His curls puffed out in the wind. The suit's shoulder pads made his shoulders broader. In a field, he would have passed for a scarecrow.

The cars pulled out slowly. No one drives fast on cemetery lanes. The couple dawdled in front of the chapel. Our car was the only one left in the parking lot.

"What the hell are they doing?" Hiililuoma wondered.

"They're coming this way," I said.

"Should we give them a ride if they ask for one?"

"No way," I answered.

"Are you allowed to say no if someone asks for a ride at a funeral?"

"We'll say there's no room."

"The backseat's totally empty."

"Throw something back there."

Hiililuoma took a couple of road maps from the glove box and tossed them in the back. The seat still looked empty. The couple walked right past the car; they didn't even glance our way. The girl was still sobbing. They headed down the chapel road.

"Where are they going?" Hiililuoma asked.

"Wait here."

I climbed out of the car and circled to the right, around a row of gravestones. During the daytime, cemeteries look like airport luggage halls filled with black suitcases.

The grieving couple stopped to look at a scraggly-tailed squirrel that bounded out in front of them and scrambled up a birch tree. Then they turned out the gate. I went over to the same birch; the squirrel was nattering overhead.

I called Hiililuoma. "They're waiting at the bus stop."

"Don't they have a car?"

"Take a wild guess."

It took about twenty minutes before the bus came. The girl had calmed down a little. She was carrying a rose that she had been incapable of laying across the coffin. I called Hiililuoma and told him to come around. I jumped in at the gate and we followed the bus. The couple got off downtown. They both smoked a cigarette and then disappeared into a pub. We waited for them. Hiililuoma's girlfriend called for the third time; he had to explain why he was late for dinner.

"How long is this going to take?" Hiililuoma asked.

"As long as it takes."

"Those two could be in there until last call."

"Then we'll be here until last call, too."

I had met his girlfriend a couple of times. Johanna was a teacher and about a foot shorter than Hiililuoma, but she kept him in check. She always called repeatedly whenever we were out drinking at a sauna with the boys, so her man would remember to be among the first to come home.

When I met Johanna, I never would have believed she was such a drill sergeant. She was very flirty, hugging and kissing everyone, and at parties I'd get this feeling that she fell more and more deeply in love with every new person who entered the room.

To Hiililuoma's great joy, the two young mourners emerged from the corner pub less than an hour later. They had just popped in to raise a toast in memory of their friend. The woman was still carrying around the red rose. They walked past the church and climbed the hill next to the library. I had to jump out of the car again and follow them on foot. There was no cover on top of the hill, and I slipped on moss at the base of the steep slope while I was trying to keep an eye on them.

On the north side, the hill dropped off into a steep cliff; below was the rail yard where we had chased the smudgers. Between the rock face and the rail yard, there was a road that semis thundered down on a regular basis. The man and woman were standing at the cliff's edge.

He was leaning against the railing, gazing down at the rail yard and the building where his friend had fallen from the roof. She bent down and left the rose on the lip of the rock, high above where the smudged train cars had been.

"Caught you," I muttered.

I followed them as they continued past the antiaircraft cannon that had been at the crown of the rock since the war. The woman smoked a cigarette. They dropped down to the old longshoreman district built on the harbor slope. In the past, the area had been filled with long, low wooden houses containing one-room apartments, but now they had been replaced with brick apartment buildings.

The couple entered one.

I rushed after them and shoved my glove between the door and the jamb before the lock clicked shut. They were already in the elevator; I bounded up the stairwell as lightly as I could and listened. The elevator stopped on the third floor. I peered around from the stairwell, saw which door they entered, and went over to jot down the name that appeared on the mail slot. Two last names. It would have been too counterculture for a couple of anarchists to share a last name. There was a sticker on the door: NO JUNK MAIL!!!

Of course not.

I went down to the street and walked back to Hiililuoma's Audi. I told him what I had discovered. We high-fived. Hiililuoma dropped me off at the office, smirking at how he'd be home earlier than his girlfriend expected. Johanna would be pleased; Saturday evening was going to be unexpectedly warm-spirited. I felt like I had earned a couple of extra beers, too. I picked up my Skoda from the parking lot and drove home.

Mirjami and I usually shared a bottle of wine on Saturday nights; we'd set out a baguette and a few cheeses. Now that she was pregnant, I had switched to beer. Once I had carried home a three-liter box of wine from the liquor store, the kind where you could dribble out a glassful now and again and it would stay good for a while. Mirjami said it wasn't good for Ville to see such large quantities of booze at the dinner table.

When a pregnant woman announces her views, contradicting her is not a good idea. The agitation might make a vein in her head burst; circulation did weird things during pregnancy.

Ville fell asleep early. Mirjami and I took a sauna, just the two of us. Or actually the three of us.

Mirjami had picked up a movie for the night; a man and a woman were smiling at each other on the cover. Classic Mirjami selection. Every second week I got to pick, and on those days there was at least one gun on the cover, and we'd have to turn down the volume a few notches from the normal setting.

Within fifteen minutes, Mirjami had dozed off on the sofa. I finished watching the movie. It started with the woman and the man breaking up with other people, then they fell in love with each other, then they broke up, then they fell in love even harder than before. In the final scene, a child's swing swayed in the wind. As the credits rolled I mentally planned a swing for our yard. You wanted the rope to be long enough so you could go really fast. The problem in new residential areas was that it would be years before the trees grew tall enough and the branches sturdy enough to hang a swing. Let alone build a tree house. But I'd get a trampoline at least. First thing next summer.

When I turned off the tube, Mirjami snapped awake. I had noticed this before. My wife wasn't woken up by sudden noises, or by music, shouting, or explosions blaring from the television, but by silence. It wasn't the first time she had spent the majority of our movie night wheezing away in dreamland. It used to annoy me, but I'd come to understand it as a sign that she felt safe at my side.

There was no good reason we couldn't watch my action movies every week; Mirjami hadn't seen a single one of her selections all the way through in at least three months.

I tucked in Mirjami, looked out the window, and scanned the yard. I planned where I'd put the trampoline: on the side opposite the neighbors' greenhouse. It would be bad for everyone if a jump went wide and Ville crashed through the greenhouse and into Sorsasalo's vineyard.

Once Mirjami had asked me to turn off the yard lights at night so it would be easier to see the stars. I had stuck to my guns, though. Lighting does more to protect people, cities, and society from harm than the best alarms and surveillance cameras. Lighting spreads peace more effectively than the UN. This I knew.

What I didn't know was that this would be the last night I would be falling asleep in peace.

METRO

The attic was a long space broken up by big beams; it stretched the entire length of the apartment building. One end was strung with slack-hanging clotheslines; laundry drooped from a couple. A barricade of old cots dominated the opposite end. In between stood a row of locked chicken-wire coops, which served as storage for belongings that the residents had once considered important. Long-forgotten toy boxes, pails, skis, stacks of books, and computer monitors were heaped up in jumbles in these storage units.

I had no problem seeing into the closest cage.

The torn cardboard box was overflowing with footwear of various sizes, as if someone had punctured the stomach of a shoe-gobbling monster. Laces trailed down the sides like guts. An old humidifier gleamed at the top of the crooked stack of boxes next to it, looking like a white UFO. The impression of outer space was complemented by the deathbed beeping from the fire alarm warning that its batteries were on their last legs.

We were in the corner behind the pile of cots. There was an old rolltop desk back there, left behind by some previous resident, and a spinach-green sofa, its surface nothing but lumps and hollows.

The corner was our meeting place. No one came up to the attic regularly. The occasional laundry hangers were our only visitors, but so long as we were quiet down at our end, the cots kept them from realizing we were there.

There were four of us today. Besides me and Baron, Jack and Smew were present and accounted for.

Jack lived in the building and was the one who let us into the attic when we wanted to plan something in private. Jack wasn't Jack's real name. He got it from his grandpa, Jaska, who had been a painter. Old Jaska painted a lot of roofs in his day, and Jack still remembered the suntanned back that was crisscrossed by a big white overall X until the day Old Jaska died.

"The first tag I ever saw was my grandpa's back in the sauna," Jack liked to say. "The rest of his back was as red as his Communist ideals. Jaska used to read *Das Kapital* to me as a bedtime story."

Smew had a cowlick on top of his head that stuck up persistently, despite the occasional ferocious brushing. He got his name from the bird with the same hairdo. Rust was the one who had come up with the name.

Rust had been our bird expert. In truth, Rust had been our expert on just about everything. It used to be five of us who would gather in the corner of the attic, and Rust and Baron would be the ones who did most of the talking.

Now we were sitting there with nothing to say. Finally Jack mumbled how as a kid he used to ambush people who came up to collect their laundry, turning off the lights and yelling, "Fee fi fo fum, I smell the blood of an Englishman!"

"Why?" I asked.

"I don't know," Jack said.

We listened to the beeping fire alarm, waited for the UFO disguised as a humidifier to bring back Rust.

Baron broke the silence by saying that none of us could attend the funeral. The Rats would be there. They didn't know who we were now, but if we were spotted at the funeral we would be known entities.

I protested. I offered to pull a scarf over my head and hobble in on a cane like an old lady.

"You're not going," Baron said. "Or you'll be the next one to go down. If not from a roof, then into a spiral of lifelong debt. They'll blame you for every tag they find within ten miles of here."

"Isn't it enough for them that they got one of us?"

"That was an accident," Baron said. "Didn't you read the report?"

The Rats' report was the reason we had come up to the attic; Baron had set it on the desk. Smew had grabbed it and was reading it as we spoke. The word *report* was an overstatement; it was just two pages.

The way Baron told it, he had marched into the Rats' office, announced that he was a detective from the white-collar-crime division, shaken hands with the man standing there, and thanked him for the good work and the well-written report, which he had reviewed with his subordinates. Baron went on to inform the Rat that he would be needing another signed original. They would have to send the first original to the NBI in Helsinki; the National Bureau of Investigation was putting together a database of graffiti vandals for crime prevention purposes. They were taking the problem very seriously and were in regular contact with the police in other countries through Europol. At the European level, graffiti was being viewed as seriously as illegal immigration, drug trafficking, money laundering, and child pornography.

Head of Security Services Olavi Raittila had nodded and printed out a new report for Baron, to which Raittila had carefully appended his signature.

Some things are best handled in daylight, wearing a suit and carrying a briefcase.

Smew was outraged. "Head of security *services*?"

"Security is a service," Baron said. "I had to wait for the other two signatures for an hour. The fellas dropped by on their break."

Smew shifted his eyes back to the papers and huffed. He had the biggest hands and feet I had ever seen. His old man had noticed the same thing years earlier and encouraged his son to take up swimming since he had such obvious gifts. Unfortunately, Smew was terrified of water. This might have something to do with the fact that one day, his father, sick of his son's recalcitrance, had rowed Smew a hundred yards out from the shore, heaved him over the edge, and ordered him to swim back. It took divers over twenty minutes to retrieve the boy from the muddy bottom.

He basically died down there. Apparently the only reason they were able to revive Smew was because his father had decided to give him his swimming lesson in November. The freezing water had slowed his metabolism.

It would have felt like some consolation if Pops had been drunk when he tried to drown his son. But he hadn't been. He was stone-cold sober and a member of the town's athletic board.

The half-hour death had left its mark on Smew. Sometimes he'd get lost in his own world, come to a standstill while everything around him kept ticking on. For instance, he had spent ten minutes reading the first page of the report before snapping out of it. I had noticed that his eyes hadn't been moving at all.

Baron continued his story. "While we waited for the guards, the head of security services offered me coffee and Danishes. Olavi Raittila told me about his travel plans for the fall. Nice family guy, planning on traveling to Turkey with his wife. There's no sign of Greece's economic difficulties there; people are friendly, not bankrupt, jobless, and spiteful. Apparently the seawater in the inlets of the Mediterranean is warm at the end of October, not like the murky Baltic. And clear. Great snorkeling. Dolphins. Coral. Raittila's descriptions of underwater wonders didn't come to an end until two Rats appeared in the office and put their names to the report."

I wriggled in next to Smew on the sofa so I could read the report. On my other side, Baron was using his finger to draw in the dust collected on the desk. The gesture reminded me of Rust; he had never sketched on paper in public. He always drafted with his fingers, not pens. Sometimes he would lay out a design in the sand with a stick and then kick away the sketch. He didn't want to leave any trace of himself except on walls.

I flipped to the second page of the report for Smew. As I read, I began doubting myself: Had I really seen over a dozen guards in the darkness, or just imagined them? I had to close my eyes and remember the moment at the railcar; at the end, there were at least five guys chasing us. From the boat I had made out at least nine or ten at the museum.

"This is a lie," I said.

"If it's on paper, it's true," Baron said.

"Did you ask the Rats anything?"

Baron had reviewed the report at the office, asked which of the men had been on the roof with Raittila. The guy with freckles and an orange tint to his hair had lifted a finger. According to Baron he seemed like a nice guy, a little like an overgrown Dennis the Menace.

Baron told the three of us that as he was leaving the Rats' office he turned and said, *We know there were more guards present than just the three of you. We've had a couple of eyewitness accounts. But we're not looking for trouble. I just want to know off the record if there's anything else that you left out of the report.*

Carrot-top shook his head.

Head of Security Services Raittila cleared his throat, said that the train cars had been set out as bait in cooperation with the State Railways. There had been good cause to believe that the trap would be sprung that day, which is why more people than normal had been called in. They had wanted to be sure they could sever the acute cycle of vandalism with one blow. It hadn't gone exactly as planned, since despite the sizable force, one of the vandals got away and the other one died. They hadn't taken the sea into account as an escape route, or the possibility that the second vandal would try to escape from the highest roof. But there was no point getting all the boys mixed up in the incident. Accidents happen.

Baron fell silent, slipped the two sheets of paper back into his satchel. The pigeons were pattering on the metal roof.

"Which one of the Rats made Rust fall?" I asked.

"Raittila or Carrot-top. What was his name? Kalliola."

I reread the part of the report where it said that Head of Security Services Olavi Raittila and security officer Jere Kalliola had been on the roof of the Maritime Museum when the suspect fell. According to the report, security guard Petteri Hiililuoma had been down below.

Baron shrugged. "It says no one made him fall."

"You entered the Rats' nest and talked to them. You can see the guilt in people's fucking eyes."

"Metro, you're angry. You can't see a thing in anyone's eyes."

"Is anyone hungry?" Jack asked.

Smew popped up straight.

Jack maneuvered his way through the cots to an abandoned fridge. He reached in and pulled out a big jar of pickles; the expiration date had passed at least forty years ago. Evidently there was a whole shelf of them down in the basement. Baron tilted the jar. The pickles were floating in a cloudy sludge.

We didn't eat any.

On the day of the funeral, I pulled on my black dress. Baron wore his black suit and left his briefcase behind in the company car. It was easy to pick out the Rats in the chapel parking lot; they stayed in their car while everyone else greeted each other and went inside. Then one of them entered the chapel. Baron didn't want us to go any closer; he was afraid the Rats would recognize him. We monitored the situation through binoculars from behind a birch tree. When an old lady with a bad leg wheezed her way over to us to tend a nearby grave we moved to a different position.

Jack was reading the names from the gravestones half out loud: Sinkkonen, Parantainen, Repo, Aalto. He wondered why the gravestones weren't in alphabetical order.

"Do you think people die in alphabetical order?" I asked.

"Still," he grumbled.

Smew hadn't wanted to join us. As he saw it, he had already tasted a big enough slice of death. It was hard to argue with him.

"Have you noticed that the trees in cemeteries are exceptionally healthy?" Baron asked.

I shook my head.

"Thick trunks, lush crowns, even without the leaves," Baron continued. "They get a surplus of nutrients."

"Knock it off."

"I wonder if their sap is red?"

I covered my ears with my hands. I could see Baron's lips still moving. The musky odor he gave off reminded me of the dead people rotting underground.

After the funeral was over, the Rats didn't budge from the parking lot, even after everyone had dispersed. They had spotted someone else to follow instead of us. One of the Rats waited in the car while the other one circled through the graveyard, shadowing the couple. The Rat was spying on the couple; we were spying on the Rat.

A bus pulled up, and suddenly we were in a rush to get back to Baron's car so we could keep up our surveillance. We ran to the car, which he'd parked right outside the cemetery gates. The bus and the

Rats' Audi had disappeared by the time we made it to the bus stop. Luckily a route map was posted there. We headed for Hovinsaari. In the backseat, Jack was still going on and on about alphabetizing and how poorly organized cemeteries were. He kept going on about how people should be able to use GPS to find graves.

Rust and I had been to Jack's place, to his little room, once. Jack still lived with his mom. He got agitated when Rust set a handful of pens down on the desk; he fussed with them, spent minutes rearranging them before he calmed down. Jack hadn't let us lounge on his bed because he didn't want the bedspread to get wrinkled; we had been forced to sit on the floor. Rust had pulled a book from the shelf, flipped through it, and shoved it back. Jack had huffed and moved the book so its spine was in line with the rest of them.

Jack's mom hadn't been the least bit concerned about her son's neuroses. She was happy Jack kept the place tidy, wiped the television screen dozens of times a week, made sure the DVDs were in alphabetical order and her women's magazines were stacked neatly. He also dusted the photograph hanging over the TV of Grandpa Jaska carrying a red flag in the May Day parade. The whole time Jack did this, his mom kicked back on the sofa, watching TV, eating chips, and getting fat.

Baron parked his car near Hovinsaari School, a yellow art nouveau building that had a good view of the intersection where the bus would stop. Jack was drumming my headrest with his fingers, counting. He was up to five hundred.

"We missed it," Baron said.

"Yup." Jack drummed.

Then the bus emerged from around the corner and crossed the intersection. No one got off at the stop and I hoped that the couple hadn't already gotten off. But then the Rats' car appeared from around the curve at the top of the hill. They were leaving a big gap; they knew where all the stops were. All they had to do was maintain a visual on the bus so they could see when the man and woman exited the bus. We joined the team, picking up the tail.

The couple that the Rats were trailing got off downtown and went into a corner pub. The Rat Audi parked on the street. The wind was sending linden leaves somersaulting down the street; they looked like they were wrestling. We waited a block away, at the corner by a sculpture of two large steamer trunks and one suitcase. Baron told me that even though the luggage looked authentic, down to the fittings of the locks, they were made of concrete, not wood or leather.

His explanation was interrupted when the couple materialized from the pub. They headed up the hill with one of the Rats following them. We just waited near the Rats' car.

Less than half an hour later, the Rat returned to the Audi. We followed their car for a mile or two and stopped when we saw the security company's sign on a building.

"Is that where you went?" I asked.

"That would be it," Baron said.

"And are those the guys you met?"

Baron said that the one getting into the black Skoda was Jere Kalliola.

"Is that other one Raittila?" I asked.

"No. That's the third guy who was there that night, according to the report. Petteri Hiililuoma. He was down below, not on the roof."

I pointed at Kalliola's car. "Follow Carrot-top."

We drove across Mussalo Bridge. The sea-serpent silhouette of Suursaari Island shimmered out on the open sea to our left, over twenty-five miles away. On the other side of the bridge we ran into the semis headed for the new harbor outside of town, while a freight train clanked lazily past. Only one of the cars was painted.

"Whose work is that?" I asked.

"Hesburger's," Jack said. He carried an encyclopedia of Finland's graffiti artists in his head. When he said Hesburger, he wasn't referring to the fast-food chain; he was talking about a guy from Oulu. I'd never seen his work before.

"Over a hundred years old," Baron said, pointing out a row of wooden houses on the eastern shores of Mussalo. "The facades bask in the rising sun. Before the bridge was built the people who lived in those homes were just about the only mammals on Mussalo, aside from squirrels and moose. They used to row over to work downtown. Back then, the interior of Mussalo Island was nothing but thickets of deciduous forest. Now it's been devoured by a golf course and hundreds of homes. I'm selling lots like a never-ending string of pearls by conjuring up the golden glow of family life and the bliss of having your own yard."

"Looks like a fox farm to me," I said, pressing my nose against the window.

The Rat parked his car on the street. His house looked exactly like the other twenty houses surrounding it. Even the CIA would have had a tough time telling these shacks apart in an aerial photograph. Trampolines, gas grills, and baby birch trees filled the tiny lots in nearly identical layouts.

The mailbox in front of Kalliola's house was blue, while the next one over was red. Long live that minuscule difference!

I checked the house number with my binoculars. I also made a note of the Rat's license plate number.

"Got what you need?" Baron asked.

"Yup."

Baron cruised slowly down the streets lined with gleaming homes and garden gnomes.

"Houses are always coming on the market here," he said.

"Why?"

"More divorces than anywhere else in town. The dream shatters."

"Mussalo, Kotka's dreamland," Jack said from the backseat.

Baron dropped me off in Karhuvuori. Apartments almost never came up for sale here. Most were public housing.

That night, I rode my bike back to dreamland and spent ten minutes with the Rat's car. That's all it took.

JERE

My black Skoda had been defaced with yellow, orange, brown, and red paint. Sprayed to look like a huge hunk of rust. The driver's door looked like it had been peeled back, leaving a big, black, gaping hole. It wasn't until I tried shoving my finger into it that I realized the hole was painted, not real.

RUST NEVER SLEEPS had been scrawled across the hood.

An outline of a body was painted on the driveway in front of the car, like a chalk figure at the spot where they find the body in American police shows. This body was sprawled out spread-eagled, limbs contorted at the joints. A pool of blood had been painted around his head.

Before I could stop him, Ville bolted out of the house.

He circled the car, oohing over and over. Ville thought my rusty Skoda was the coolest car ever.

"I liked it better black," I said.

Ville remained in awe. I took him back inside and told Mirjami not to let him out. Ville started jabbering how Daddy had painted the car and it looked cool, like May Day.

"Like really, really cool. That stuff, what is it? What's that stuff you spray on May Day, Mom?"

"Silly String," Mirjami said.

"A Silly String car," Ville squealed.

Mirjami sat Ville down at the table and started making him some oatmeal. He dashed over to the window to check out what was going on with the car.

"Is it May Day?" he asked.

"It's fall now," Mirjami said. "May Day is a long way off."

"Can I have a balloon?" Ville asked.

I cursed myself for having built a carport instead of a garage. Sorsasalo had already wandered over from his greenhouse to gawk at the car. I explained we were currently waging an antivandalism campaign and we were breathing down their necks, had almost rooted them out. Someone was clearly frustrated and wanted revenge. Sorsasalo nodded, popped in to get his wife. She stepped over to snap some shots with her cell phone.

"Posting those probably isn't a good idea," I said.

Sorsasalo's wife shook her head. "I won't."

I got a tarp and covered the car, even though Sorsasalo's wife asked me to wait a minute. She wanted to take a few more shots of the hood. I didn't let her. I spread a second tarp over the body painted on the asphalt.

"You know whose record *Rust Never Sleeps* is?" Sorsasalo asked.

"No. And to be honest, I don't really care."

"Neil Young's. Maybe one of his fans did this."

"Isn't Neil Young some old has-been who fried his brains on drugs twenty years ago? His fans must be just as brain-dead, too."

"I like Neil Young," Sorsasalo said stiffly. "And Bob Dylan. You don't see artists like that anymore. 'Blowin' in the Wind' is one of the greatest songs ever written. It says everything relevant about humanity."

"I always thought it was about farting," I said.

Sorsasalo cleared his throat and stalked off, taking his wife with him. Exactly as I had hoped. As far as I was concerned, they could move away and take their greenhouse, their grapes, and their taste in music with them.

I called Hiililuoma, asked if his car had been vandalized. He lived in a row house over in Karhula. He said no. He usually pulled it into the garage at night but last night it had been parked on the street and it looked clean.

Of course.

I thought for a second, then I called Raittila and as soon as he answered asked if his car was all right. He didn't understand the question. I explained to him what had happened. Raittila said he'd check his Benz right away. I heard the hum of the elevator through the cell phone. A few moments later he said everything was OK.

"Unless you count fallen leaves as vandalism," Raittila added. "We're being terrorized by them around here."

"How the hell am I supposed to get to work?" I snapped.

"Don't you have two cars?"

"No."

"Don't get all worked up. I'll be over soon."

"Roger," I responded.

Mirjami brought Ville into the yard, announced that our son wouldn't stay inside any longer and she needed to take a shower. Ville immediately asked me to pull the tarp off the Skoda. When I said no, his lower lip started to quiver. Mirjami urged me to kick the ball around with the kid. As a father, I was supposed to know what little boys like to do. Then my wife vanished. Her dirty hair was more important than my car. Ville kicked the ball into the road on purpose. While I chased after it, he lifted up a corner of the tarp and examined the outline of the dead man.

"Superrrrcool," he said.

I yanked the tarp out of his hand and covered up the smudge. Ville started bawling again.

Raittila showed up before the police did. He was driving the company's Toyota and said I could use it until my car was repainted. He said there was no point making a big deal out of it. Clearly it was the work of the unbalanced smudger-scum we didn't catch.

"How would he know who I am?"

"He doesn't. Just a guess, or bad luck."

"It's by chance he vandalized my car? And drew a chalk figure of a dude looking like a dropped watermelon on my driveway?"

"Calm down and think for a minute," Raittila said quietly. "There's no way the second smudger could have recognized your face from the rowboat. You and I couldn't even see each other's faces, and we were three feet away from each other up on that roof."

Raittila started kicking around the ball with Ville. For some reason, Ville sent it right back with a solid knock. With me, Ville would nudge it so lazily that it always died between us on the grass.

"Someone's been talking," I said.

"I haven't said anything to anyone," Raittila said sharply. "You realize how that wouldn't be in my interest, don't you? All I want is for the whole incident to be forgotten."

"Then it was Hiililuoma."

"I can't speak for Hiililuoma." Raittila sent a header Ville's way. "But everyone is innocent until proven otherwise."

Ville begged for Raittila to throw the ball so that he could do a header, too. I had never been able to convince my son to try a header after the first time, when he took the ball on the nose and, once again, cried. I didn't understand why I had gotten such a crybaby for a son. I barely made a peep when I was a kid, even when I crashed going downhill on my bike and split open both knees. My mom had been the one tearing up while the doctor tweezed the sand out of my knees.

"None of us parked in the garage last night," I said. "Why only me?"

"Yeah, that is a little odd," Raittila admitted.

Our low-pitched conversation was interrupted when a police car drove up. Raittila encouraged me to tell the police about the couple we had followed home from the funeral. The most important thing was that we be as open as possible from here on out. Let the authorities do their job.

I reported the crime. The police took photographs of the Skoda; they didn't try to stop Sorsasalo's wife, who had reappeared with her phone. She bragged about how many likes she had gotten on Facebook within fifteen minutes of posting her picture of my car. *And you couldn't even see the message on the hood!*

I had a hard time keeping myself from grabbing the phone out of the witch's hand. There was a hole just big enough for it in the sewer grate. I restrained myself because of the police. Sorsasalo opened his living room window and started playing "Blowin' in the Wind."

But the toughest part was taking the car in to be repainted. I had to do that without the tarp. As I started the car, Sorsasalo's wife snapped a shot of the hood. Pedestrians smirked. I glanced in the rearview mirror to see if anyone was pointing at me.

Raittila followed me in the company car. It was like a circus making its way through town, with me the clown leading the parade.

At the body shop, a stubby little dude in overalls estimated that the job would cost a couple grand. A normal repaint would have been half as much, but the spray paint left an uneven surface and had to be sanded down first. The soonest he could promise the car would be ready was next week.

Back outside, I went off. "Why don't Bacteria paint something useful? Like cars, or houses?"

"One of them did paint a car."

"I'm not laughing," I said.

Raittila squeezed my shoulder. "You can't let them get under your skin. This is the first time they've made a personal attack, but it won't be the last. Guess how many dozens of threatening letters and deliveries of shit I've received as head of a security firm."

I shook my head.

"This is a battle of wills," Raittila said, "like ice hockey. You win by being smart, not by getting worked up. All this talk about the power of emotions and inner fire and momentum is total bullshit. The winner is the one who gives in to their feelings the least. Don't let them get inside your head even if they get inside your turf. This is a game you win by staying cool."

We drove back to my house so I could change my shirt. Despite the morning's coolness, my back was drenched with sweat. I understood that Raittila's perspective made sense. If you let yourself get distracted by the shit-talking, the door to the penalty box would start swinging and things would go badly for the team.

I climbed into the company car; Raittila was standing in my yard. I rolled down the driver's window.

"You need to build a garage," Raittila said, "and put up a surveillance camera under the eaves there."

"And how the hell am I supposed to cough up a garage?"

"I'll get a couple of guys to help you out. You just got a pay raise, remember? You're making enough for one measly garage. It can go right where the carport is."

I adjusted the front seat of the Toyota. This would be my family's car for at least a week. The floor was already dotted with crumbs and dried mud, the wheel felt sticky, the plug to the cigarette lighter was missing. I hated borrowed things. Library books had stains and creased pages; one time I found a dried slice of cheese in one. That was the last time I borrowed a book from the hallowed institution. These days when it came to bedtime stories, I only read Ville our own books.

Borrowing money from the bank is the only acceptable form of borrowing.

Raittila opened the passenger door and flopped down at my side. "Don't worry. This won't last. We'll catch them. Didn't you say you figured out who they were at the funeral?"

METRO

I was surprised to find pictures of the Rat car online before I had time to post them myself. I was at the library computer, so I added a comment: "Kalliola. My name is Jere Kalliola. I am full of shit."

Someone had extensively photographed Jere the Rat's car in the exact spot where I had painted it the night before. There were half a dozen shots of the Skoda blooming with rust. Unfortunately, the crushed man I had painted on the asphalt wasn't in any of them.

Rust would have been proud of my work. I had done my best to do the piece in his style. A dead man had come back to avenge himself.

Rust had struck.

From the library's computer, I sent photos of the painted Skoda to all the normal sites as well as Finnish and foreign newspapers and media outlets. I also added a caption: "Graffiti-loving Kotka resident and father Jere Kalliola decided to repaint his ride. Jere is a huge Neil Young fan."

I listened to the same songs over and over as I pedaled through town. I honored Rust by playing the record that had inspired his tag: Neil Young's *Rust Never Sleeps*.

Even though the album had been released almost twenty years before I'd been born, I knew it extremely well. Rust played it several times a week; for him, the recording was vital, a necessary ritual. The same as Rats needing to watch the messy crises and dirty bombs every night on the nightly news. Rust had the album on MP3, CD, and cassette but the version he loved most was an old vinyl that was as raspy as the post-op throat-cancer patient from upstairs.

Rust is raspy by nature, Rust had said.

Rust never sleeps. That described Rust to a T. He was always awake when I fell asleep, always awake when I woke up. I yawned all day long; Rust never did. It was annoying.

But now every night I longed for him to climb in next to me and read in the glare of the flashlight and rustle the pages while I tried to sleep. Even all those times we were forced to hide in bushes and wait for guards to leave, I'd never seen Rust doze off. From time to time we'd have to leave a piece halfway finished when a team of Rats suddenly appeared. You'd have to pull back into the shadows instantly and stay quiet. If you lost your nerve and started running, there was a greater chance you'd get caught. The safest thing was to keep still and wait. And wait. And wait. The Rats usually got bored first. I would feel the damp from the ground spread through my clothes to my stomach, shiver, and yawn. Rust didn't do either.

How could someone who never got tired or cold die?

I did some searching online and sniffed out the address of the other Rat mentioned in the report. Petteri Hiililuoma had posted pictures of his two-story home, playing the proud man of the house. One of the pictures was from last May Day. It looked like he was chopping a bottle of champagne in half with a saber. He wore streamers around his neck and next to him there was a woman holding out a red high-heel leather boot. The caption read: "The carnival comes to its climax as I open the bottle in the hussar fashion and prepare to drink it from my lady's boot."

What the fuck?

I invited Baron to join me but he refused, saying he had open houses, and asking in a sharp tone if I hadn't already gotten my revenge. *Work discreetly if you want to make an impact. Don't you remember my story from Stockholm?*

I tried Smew next. His voice was trembling with enthusiasm when he answered. He had stumbled across an old infirmary at an abandoned factory where he said no one had been in at least forty years.

"There's a paper here on the nurse's desk from 1966!" he cried. "You have to see this, Metro. No one has set foot in this place for half a century."

Jack was with him.

I promised to come by right after I took care of this one thing.

This Rat Hiililuoma was actually more of a country mouse. He lived outside my delivery area: Karhula.

I went downtown to check my PO box. A music magazine had arrived for Rust, nothing for me. No postcard from Dad. There was no way Dad could know my address, but sometimes I still had this crazy idea that if he really loved me he'd find a way to send a card to an anonymous metal box.

When evening fell, I crossed two bridges: Kivisilta Bridge, which separated downtown from Hovinsaari, and then a little later the bridge that crossed the tracks at Paimenportti. I stopped for a minute and leaned against the railing, scanned the rail yard opening up to the north. I had spent several nights there with Rust. I guess you could call them romantic, moonlit nights. Two rows of freight trains sat there. I felt like painting all of them rust colored.

I pedaled past the central hospital. To my right rose the water tower we had decorated once. To the left, the overpass we had bombed with candles after a friend of ours died in a car crash. Below it ran the highway. One time we had modified the signs for a good five miles, reducing the speed limit from 120 kph to 20 kph. Things were a little sleepy on the road the next morning. According to one right-wing city councilman, it was a heinous act of terrorism and an attack on civilized society.

Every mile I pedaled triggered memories of Rust.

I didn't know where his family had taken his ashes.

I hadn't dared to go to the spot where he had fallen.

Over the past year, Baron had been surveying the city, keeping tabs on which locations had the most surveillance cameras. He went so far as to create a map. There were dozens of external cameras in and around the center. He said a new one had just been put up near the spot where Rust fell.

Cities were filled with surveillance cameras. In urban areas you can follow people for miles without them having the slightest idea. We are being constantly stalked. There are thousands of cameras, at jobs, stores, parks, tunnels, jogging paths, street corners. It wouldn't do much good even if you rubbed off your fingerprints with sandpaper and got your ID number deleted from the databases. The cameras would still be following you. Every cough you make from the cradle to the grave is a click in the recorder.

I pedaled past the Jumalniemi shopping center, formerly horsefly-infested thickets, where grids of parking spaces now surrounded big-box stores. Just in this area Baron's map indicated more than fifty cameras. The worst part was that the real estate developers and the city and the police had outsourced surveillance operations to the Rats. In doing so, they washed their hands of responsibility. The Rats did whatever they wanted with the footage they collected. They didn't face the slightest punishment for misusing it, not even a finger wag or tsk-tsk from the city.

If you think the police watch over our cities you're delusional. Rats are the ones watching and controlling the cities with their cameras. The police only ask to see the recordings when a junkie stumbling around like an orc in some drug-addled Middle-earth robs five euros from a convenience store. But the tapes are allowed to collect dust and disintegrate and disappear when Rats stomp on a kid's leg because they don't like the look on his face and after an illegal search turns up a can of spray paint in his backpack. When that happens, the cops aren't interested.

If I had any extra money, I'd invest in companies that sell surveillance cameras and security services. They're the only companies that are doing really well in this recession-battered economy.

I'd use the profits to buy more paint.

I pedaled past the Rat Hiililuoma's house. It was one of half a dozen row houses. They all had garages and the Rat was keeping his car safe and sound, or he was still at work. I rode down to the stand of mailboxes and checked the address against the names. His was the third place from the left.

I left my bike at the rack outside the nearby grocery store, circled around back to the row of houses that included his. An iron ladder climbed up through the wild grapes to the roof, which connected all the houses. The street was empty and I scampered up the rungs without giving it a second thought. As soon as I got to the top of the ladder, I laid flat on my stomach and inched my way forward along the roof. The only one who noticed me was the magpie croaking in the branches of a nearby pine tree.

I stopped on top of the Rat's house. A humming ventilation duct rose next to my head. I was having a hard time deciding what to do.

According to the report, Hiiliuoma had been down below when they caused Rust to fall. So he wasn't guilty per se.

I considered dropping a pile of shit into the air conditioning. But I didn't have to go, so I abandoned that idea. A used Roman candle firework from last New Year's Eve sat a couple yards from my feet. Without the head, it looked naked, like it was lying on some nudist beach for rockets.

The last of the autumn sun filtered out of the sky and the black tar roof was warm from the heat it had been sucking up all day long. When I shut my eyes, it felt like summer and I was lying on the rocks at the beach. I rolled over on my side so I could sink into Rust's arms. But Rust wasn't there. My only companions on the roof were the humming air conditioning duct and the old firework.

For a second revenge felt futile. No matter what I did, I wouldn't get Rust back.

I thought about how I should focus on getting into university. I had been stuck in this little town too long. It was dangerous how I had lost all sense of time while the two of us cavorted around our urban jungle.

The spring I graduated from high school, I had applied to the School of the Arts in Helsinki; I had even done the preliminary assignments. I had decided there was no way I was going to be staying in this town that reeked of fish and wood processing; the playgrounds were populated by too many examples of high school girls a couple of years older than me who had gotten knocked up and popped out the beginnings of a big, snot-nosed family. The prospects for their future careers didn't extend beyond the register at the Robin Hood megamart.

But I was still here, almost twenty, lying on my back on a roof, watching the cold clouds, each of which reminded me of a white coffin. I had made it into the entrance exams, but didn't make it past the first round. I had been so confident about getting in that it didn't even register that I'd failed until I was halfway home. The black hole of the

Porvoo Cathedral bell tower stalked me for the rest of the bus ride back to Kotka. The building stayed behind, but the hole wouldn't let me go. *You're shit. You're shit. You're a stupid shitty nigger. Go back to Africa.*

By the time I stepped off the bus, my lower lip was quivering and I felt like the biggest loser east of Helsinki. I had already been envisioning living in a garret, and how from the window I'd be able to count the chimneys of Helsinki's skyline, how I'd be whisked from my student digs to school by metro. I had no idea where the School of the Arts was, or my apartment, but the metro was an essential element of the image. The metro meant tracks, breaking away, freedom, the big city.

When I got back, Rust held me for a long time and suggested that we paint a metro track on a wall somewhere. It would carry us far away.

That was the first time I ever went to the rail yard. Rust had been there before. The railcars looked amazing in the dead of night, especially after the apple-green tracks climbing upward appeared on them, emblazoned with METRO STRAIGHT TO HEAVEN.

But the State Railways didn't think so the next morning.

JERE

Hiililuoma wasn't at work. I was sure he was avoiding me. I did my rounds with Mattson instead. He told me how he and his wife had gone mushroom hunting, spending the day running through the brush in his ultralight trainers. He had been lucky enough to spot a moose. In the meantime, his old lady had picked a bucketful of funnel chanterelles.

"Now that's what I call natural hunting," Mattson said. "Chasing down a moose solo, with a rifle in your hand."

"Did you have a rifle in your hand?"

"No. I had a Fitbit. But wouldn't that have been cool if my wife came out of the forest with her mushrooms and I was waiting at the car with a moose in the trunk?"

"I don't think a moose would fit in the trunk."

"Not yours, maybe, but it would fit in mine."

I sent Hiililuoma a text message: *What's up? You sick?*

I didn't get a reply. Mattson's daydreaming had moved on from a rifle to a longbow.

Raittila stayed in his office all day. When my shift ended I dropped by to say hello. I stood there waiting in the doorway. An agitated housefly was bumping against the window. It was determined to get out of the stifling indoor air and cool off a little.

"I'm a little busy here," Raittila eventually said. He was tapping away at his computer in apparent concentration; in the reflection in the window I could see he was playing a game.

"About my car being vandalized."

"Are you still thinking about that? There's no point worrying about that," Raittila said. "The important thing is to prepare for the next time."

"How did you know that the Bacteria would be at the harbor that night?"

Raittila raised his gaze from the computer screen. GAME OVER glowed in the window glass in reverse.

"Don't you worry about that either, buddy," he said.

"I have to know if I'm training for deputy director."

"Hiililuoma is my deputy, not you."

"That's what I mean. I'm still learning the ropes."

"Learning how to be deputy director also means knowing when to keep your curiosity in check," Raittila said.

He turned back to his computer and started up a new game. He didn't lift his head again, even when I said good-bye.

The seat of the borrowed car was hurting my lower back. I called Hiililuoma; he answered. When I said hello there was a moment of silence at the other end. Then the line went dead.

"What the hell?" I muttered.

I dialed Hiililuoma's number again, and this time my call rang for a while until it went over to a robotic voice: *This is the voice mail of the person you are trying to reach blah blah blah.*

Instead of turning across Mussalo Bridge, I headed toward Karhula. Ten minutes later, I was pulling up in front of Hiililuoma's door. The last time I had been here was in May. Hiililuoma had invited Mirjami and me to celebrate May Day at their place. He had gotten himself a champagne saber and shot the bottleneck off the balcony into the street and drunk from his girlfriend's shoe. It had been my job to take pictures. Later that evening, I threatened to get a saber and drink nothing but champagne from here on out, rinse out my mouth with it after brushing my teeth, morning and night. The next morning, Mirjami had announced that no one in our house would be buying any sabers; I could use the money for a new washing machine and a tube of Pepsodent.

I leaned on the doorbell. Hiililuoma's girlfriend answered— Johanna the brunette, who liked to wear red and black and reminded me of a flamenco dancer. Every time she opened the door she was as radiant as if she never found anything there except birthday cakes and gifts wrapped in gold paper.

"Is Petteri around?" I asked.

"He sure is, come in."

As if it were May Day and she had just laid out a smorgasbord with a bottle of bubbly waiting to be popped. Even though she turned her head away, her breasts continued to jut firmly in my direction.

I cleared my throat, not entering the house. "Do you mind asking him to step out here?"

Mild disappointment flickered across Johanna's face. I didn't know if I really was a welcome guest. Or did she act this way with everyone? Mirjami had privately predicted that they would never last. Johanna wouldn't be able to stand him for long; she was like a flame, fluttering and scorching those around her. But Mirjami frequently felt that the relationships of friends and acquaintances were a lot unhappier than ours.

Hiililuoma appeared at the door, rubbing his eyes. I asked him why he had answered the phone but hung up as soon as he heard my voice. He croaked that he was asleep when the phone rang and fumbled with the keypad. The call must have gotten cut off by accident. He claimed to have the flu. He didn't look sick to me.

"You weren't too concerned about my car," I said.

Hiililuoma scratched his neck and glanced at his feet. Then he stared at me. Classic reaction. When a person has something to hide he never looks you in the eye right away; he gazes down at his toes and off into the branches of the nearby birches. Then a second later he starts ogling you like he can't believe what he's looking at, like he's got two full moons shining in his face instead of eyes. That's how he tries to maintain his credibility. Just like Hiililuoma now.

"What are you insinuating?" Hiililuoma asked.

I mentioned the report he was perfectly familiar with and that was signed by him, yours truly, and Raittila. I said that the more I thought about it, the more mind-boggling I found it that my car was the only one that had been vandalized, even though all three of our cars had been outside.

"And?"

"Why my car?"

"How the hell would I know?"

"Have you leaked something?"

"You gotta be fucking kidding me."

"It wasn't Raittila. It wasn't me. Of the three of us, you're the only one left."

My voice cracked. I had always hated that about myself; whenever I was agitated, my voice would rise and break.

"Hey, think about how many people were there. How many people saw?" Hiililuoma's fist tapped my chest in time to his words.

"We were the only three on the roof."

"What the hell are you going on about?"

"I didn't do anything. But I'm the only one who has been targeted."

"Jere, I have nothing to do with your goddamn car. I do agree that smudging it was a shitty thing to do. But you can save your irritation for the smudger-scum. Don't blame me, goddammit. I've never ratted on anyone. Never. Ever. Fucking ever. I've been accused of things that my friends have done, and I've taken the blame. I was expelled from motherfucking school because my classmate went and pissed in front of the principal's office and I got blamed for it. The other guy got a scholarship that spring!"

Hiililuoma stopped talking. He stared wildly, opened his mouth a couple of times as if there were more to come. But all that came out was thick breath that smelled of sleep. He had vomited up everything he had to say. He slammed the door in my face. Johanna was looking at me from the upstairs window, and when she noticed me looking back she waved cheerfully.

METRO

I waited quietly on the Rat's roof waiting for him to drive off in his tin can. I wished I could have heard everything they were arguing about. Something about the Skoda I had painted.

The other Rat, Hiililuoma, emerged from his Rat's nest again to wrench a stump out of the ground in the corner of the yard. He had a crowbar, and as he heaved, red-faced, the long root writhed under the grass like a viper. The root reached across the entire yard; its shuddering tip was breaking the surface of the ground over by the grill.

"You're ruining the yard," a woman shouted from the window.

The Rat glared up at the window, got an axe from the garage, and started hacking away at the root to sever it. If I had any luck, he'd sever his own foot.

"Knock it off," the woman shouted.

I climbed down the ladder and retrieved my bike. For a second I thought I'd take the long way back, past the Korkeakoski power plant, but curiosity got the better of me. I wheeled my bike around and slowly cruised past the Rat's house.

He was still focused on his axe work; the whacks against the root sounded through the entire neighborhood. Some of the blows were missing the root and sinking into the lawn. A dark-haired woman had appeared at the door.

"You're ruining the whole yard," she said.

"You're the one who wanted a fucking flowerbed here. Now you're getting your flowerbed."

Just as I passed the Rat, he raised his eyes and gave me a piercing stare. Then he buried his axe even deeper.

Smew came to meet me at the rusty chain-link fence. He told me to leave the bike in an overgrown rosebush nearby; there was no way anyone who came past would notice it under there. Then he plunged into the same rosebush, telling me to cover my face. I crawled behind him. Rosehips lined our thorny route like tiny, bright-red lanterns. The bushes formed a dense barrier that reached all the way to the steel mesh. Smew had lifted up the bottom edge by jamming bricks between the ground and the fence.

"We climbed over and I gashed my hand. It's easier this way."

I squirmed under the fence. The tip of one of the fat steel strands scratched my back.

"We're pretty sure the nearby buildings are abandoned, but you still probably want to be quiet," Smew said. "We haven't seen any dogs."

He indicated I should follow the gentle slope down toward the riverbank. We passed an old machine shop; most of the windowpanes were broken. Smew peered in one of the holes.

"This looks cool, too. Some of the old machines are still in there."

Smew waved me toward a low building surrounded by yews. Its roof was topped with a wig of green moss. A long crack rippled across the yellowish stucco wall like a line of dunes. I instantly had the urge to paint a caravan of camels crossing the desert.

"You'll have time to do your thing later," Smew said when he noticed I'd stopped. He could tell when I'd gotten an idea. "Let's go in."

The guys had pried open one of the windows. I crawled through the hole, dropped to the floor, and brushed off my clothes.

We were in a small infirmary. There were six beds that still had mattresses and gray blankets. When I ran my palm across the nearest bed, blue-and-white-checked fabric was revealed under the heavy crust of dust.

Rectangular nightstands stood next to the beds. The newspaper from November 1966 that Smew had mentioned over the phone lay open on the nearest one. According to the front-page story, four people had died in an explosion at the Sulfuric Acid Ltd. dynamite factory. A glass of water stood on the next nightstand. The liquid had evaporated; the glass still held a pair of dentures.

"Whose are those?" I asked.

"God only knows," Smew said.

Tracks ran across the ceiling, where curtains could be drawn around the beds for privacy. The curtains were like gauze, they were so badly eaten by moths and other insects.

A pair of pajamas lay folded on one of the pillows. The fabric shell had disintegrated from the pillow on the next bed over; a pile of down was all that remained at the head of the bed.

Smew had moved on to the doorway that yawned at the end of the ward. He gestured for me to follow.

The next room was smaller. There was a huge light fixture on the ceiling; under it, in the middle of the floor, stood an examination table. An old advertisement for Jaffa soda hung on the wall, with orange slices bursting out of a bottle to form an orange palm tree. Next to that was a big drawing of a naked, skinless man, his muscles gleaming bright red despite decades of dust. Some of his internal organs had disappeared along with shreds of the poster. He looked like a victim of illegal organ harvesting.

Smew had pulled up a doctor's chair in one corner; its springs complained. He started pulling open the drawers of a desk. When he got to the bottom drawer he crowed and lifted out a skull. He blew the dust out of the eye sockets.

"To be in a hella cool place or not to be," he said to the skull.

Rust and I had preferred painting outside. Baron was more into complex projects to try to drive society in the direction he wanted. But Smew's thing was abandoned buildings. He had snuck into deserted factories, schools, train stations, churches, army barracks, and movie theaters. He didn't paint the walls. Instead of aerosol cans, he carried a camera. He wanted to create a photographic record of the kinds of places that history had passed by and that you'd never find in textbooks.

A lot of times, Smew would leave some token of himself on his way out, a little wink at the next person who might come by. In a clothing store that had gone bankrupt he had contorted two naked mannequins into a passionate embrace in the storeroom. Then he had hung a sign around one of their necks: *Together at last*.

He thought dilapidated spaces were a lot more photogenic than the same places when they were bustling with life. Wrinkles made people beautiful; dust and degeneration and decay put the crowning touches on homes and workplaces.

Of the five of us, Smew had the biggest reputation outside Finland. His photos of rooms crumbling in the fists of time had been published online as well as in several foreign photography books showcasing the allure of abandoned places.

For Smew, the banks of the Kymijoki River offered the perfect environment to work in. During the last decade, a bunch of old factories along the river had gone under. Their shuttering had sparked a chain reaction: the area had fallen into recession, and unemployment rates were now the highest in Finland. Numerous schools, libraries, post offices, banks, and stores, not to mention medical facilities, had closed their doors. People had been forced to abandon their homes and move to other parts of the country.

The province of Kymenlaakso was full of abandoned, decaying buildings and industrial areas. The more deserted it became, the more love Smew had for the place.

One time up in our attic hideaway he told us he couldn't wait for the day when the entire stretch of riverside had emptied into a long string of ghost towns, like the Klondike when the gold rush died out. But the place Smew wanted to visit most in the world was a lot closer than Alaska.

The dream he had nursed for years was to climb through windows in the Ukrainian city of Pripyat and photograph the frozen life inside the sentient buildings there. Stopped wall clocks, the unmoving Ferris wheel in the background. Pripyat had been a city the size of Kotka when Reactor 4 at the Chernobyl nuclear power plant had exploded in April 1986. The entire population had been evacuated in a few hours, but not until after the catastrophe had been hidden from residents for a day and a half, during which time the people had bathed in radiation.

Guided tours of Pripyat had been arranged from southern Kiev for several years now. But the tours stuck to predefined routes that were interrupted by checkpoints. You could view the reactor from a couple hundred yards away. The tours took visitors to the kindergarten in downtown Pripyat, where children's drawings of elephants, lions, and balloons still hung on the walls and a toy car still stood on the floor. But independent tourists were threatened with imprisonment and any number of cancers. Entering buildings on your own was absolutely forbidden. The moss that had grown on the wallpaper and the insulation in the apartment buildings' walls had absorbed radioactivity, turning into wet bombs with gamma radiation levels over thirty times higher than the average radiation in Pripyat. It was over two thousand microroentgens in places. A hundred kilometers away, in Kiev, people went insane if radiation levels in the city climbed over fifty microroentgens.

Luckily, a steel shell had been built over the collapsed nuclear reactor. Before it was built, radiation levels in the vicinity of the reactor were over a thousand times higher than current peaks.

Smew wanted to spend days on end shooting in Pripyat, not just a few hours like the guided tourists. A Russian photographer friend, Vorkuta, had promised to acquire enough army-grade protective gear and radiation gauges for a five-person team. Vorkuta and Smew and three other explorers intended on sneaking past the checkpoints by way of the Pripyat River; no one guarded the water access. Next spring, when the leaves were just coming in, Smew was planning on bunking in some abandoned apartment in this ghost town and entering as many forbidden buildings as possible to capture former human habitations that had been taken over by moss, brush, and wild animals. Nuclear accidents don't destroy nature, he liked to say, they just destroy people.

"Apparently there's an operating theater in Pripyat that has an oak tree growing in it," Smew said, skull still nestled in his palm. "In the spring, tons of songbirds nest in the tree. Lots of bird species that were presumed extinct have returned to the area."

"Do they have three feet and two heads?" I asked.

"We should be fine," Smew said, eyes flashing. "Vorkuta's been there four times. Last time he did see a fox with two tails, and he says the mosquitoes and wasps are bigger than normal."

We went back to the ward. Jack had been working away this whole time, hunched over next to a wall. His fingers moved as quickly as a pianist's; colorful ribbons dangled from both palms, which he snatched and fixed to the wall.

Jack's passion was taping. It suited his meticulous nature. At home, he treated dust bunnies and disorderly belongings as if they were undisciplined recruits and he was the drill sergeant. He and Smew hung out a lot together. While Smew hauled around his camera and tripods, Jack hauled around rolls of colored tape and patiently cut and constructed images in these abandoned spaces.

In addition to the rolls, his shoulder bag contained a book as thick as a brick on ancient architecture and sculpture. Lately Jack had been creating images of statues on the walls, from *Nike of Samothrace* to *The Dying Slave*.

Taping was slow; it took hours, sometimes days. There weren't many people who stumbled across Jack's finished works to marvel at them in situ. We were the only ones who knew where they were, and he had sworn us to secrecy.

Jack had done two *Venus de Milo*s: one in a classroom at a school that had been shut down because of mold, the other at a deserted bowling alley, lane four. In these temples, the taped Venuses would be gazing upon the world around them in silence until the bowling alley's roof collapsed or the wrecking ball smashed through the walls of the school slated for demolition.

Jack made fleeting art in mausoleums of broken dreams.

But as long as the walls still stood, Michelangelo's *David* would stand thoughtfully in this little former infirmary amid anemic beds and ownerless dentures in a glass.

The blue-skinned David of transparent tape, thousands of strips of it on the wall, looked hesitant and a little chilly. He stared at the Goliath who could not be vanquished with a sling: time's brutal march over mankind's puny lives.

"Jack should do another *David* at Pripyat," Smew said. "I've been trying to get him to come, too. Reactor 4 would make an excellent Goliath for David to stare down."

Jack grunted, didn't turn around. His fingers started seaming tape even faster.

Smew placed the skull on the pile of down that had once been a fluffy pillow, then he placed the newspaper that had been printed half a century ago on the bed in front of the skull. It looked like the dead man had been reading when he died. Above the headline about the dynamite factory explosion, Smew had written in marker: SMEW WAS HERE 2014.

JERE

When I pulled into the driveway Mirjami was standing at the door, waiting for me. She was scratching her wrist. That's what she did when she was upset. She interrogated me as to where I'd been; I should have been home hours ago. Ville was late for his swimming lesson. When was I going to stop staring at my own belly button and start taking responsibility for my family?

Ville was standing there at Mirjami's side, holding a plastic supermarket bag in his hand. Tears had dried into pale trails on his cheeks.

I stammered that I had been forced to do a little overtime. Mirjami interrupted me, told me that Tuesday evenings were dedicated to Ville, and reminded me that we'd agreed that I wouldn't do any overtime on Tuesdays. It was the only thing in my calendar set in stone.

She was right.

I got Ville into the passenger seat. He wanted his car seat so he could see out the window. It was only now that I remembered that the car seat was still in the Skoda. I buckled the seat belt. It rubbed against his neck and I promised that we'd come up with a better solution on the way home.

Ville complained the whole trip, *I'm choking and I can't see out the window, and I'm gonna throw up, Dad, it makes me throw up when I can't see out the window.*

At the swimming pool parking lot, he immediately sank to his knees to hack. A real drama queen.

I hustled him into the locker room, told him that he'd still have plenty of time for his swimming lesson if he was as quick as a fox. I climbed the bleachers and said hello to the other parents, all of whom had taken off their jackets and were enjoying the warmth of the upper deck. The kids were splashing around the little pool, practicing floating on their stomachs. *Head down,* the swimming teacher encouraged them. When Ville finally appeared, swimming lessons were just ending. The kids who wanted to got to jump from the starting blocks into the big pool. Headfirst or feetfirst. Ville didn't go and jump, he just quietly stood there in the cold, like a sparrow caught under the eaves in the rain. When the other kids took off Ville was left shivering alone. The bleachers emptied of heat-radiating parents. A woman edging past me was huffing, said she always forgot during the week how hot it was at the pool.

Hard to believe when you looked down at the trembling Ville.

I called down to him and told him not to go anywhere. My voice echoed in the cavernous space. I climbed down to floor level and waved him over from the dressing room stairs. It took a while before he heard me. I hurried over to the cashier and asked if they had a pair of swim trunks to lend me. I was handed a black pair with SWIMMING POOL stamped across the butt in big white letters.

Ville was waiting, lips blue, when I made it out of the locker room. The first thing I did was take him into the sauna to warm up. I scooped water on the rocks and Ville immediately moved down to the lower bench. I told him he'd get warmer faster if he came back up.

He didn't.

"We'll have our own swimming lesson," I told him.

"It's cool being here together," I said.

"You like swimming?" I asked.

My son sat there with his legs bent, knees in his mouth, not saying a word.

Eventually I coaxed him out of the sauna and into the kiddie pool. Ville took so long putting on his goggles that he started complaining he was getting cold again. To me the water was so warm that you sweat instead of getting wet.

"Show me how you float on your tummy," I said.

Ville had his goggles on, but he still tried to float with his head above the water. I encouraged him to put his head underwater like his swimming teacher had taught him. Apparently this was a no-go. As soon as he did, his goggles filled with water. I tightened the straps for him. Ville floated again, and this time he almost made it from one end of the pool to the other. I encouraged him to keep at it.

Then he showed me his breaststroke and backstroke and dog paddle and crawl. In the end, he even demoed a couple flutters of butterfly. It looked more like a cabbage moth than a monarch.

"It sure is cool being here together," I said.

I had him jump into the big pool, too. I plopped in first and promised to help him if he couldn't make it back to the ladder by himself. Ville jumped once, feetfirst, legs and body rigid. He wanted to go again, and then one more time. He jumped six, seven times. In the end, he wanted to swim the twenty-five-meter trip to the other end of the big pool. I told him to grab hold of the lane line immediately if he started getting tired. He made it all the way to the other end without stopping.

We went back into the sauna. This time I got him to sit with me on the upper bench a little longer. An older man was sitting at the other end of the bench.

"Is he going to become a swimmer?" he asked.

"He's fast, that's for sure," I said.

"I can see that, he's got fins instead of feet," the man said.

Ville lowered his head, but I could see he was smiling with pride.

When we got home, Ville rushed into Mirjami's arms and said how much fun he had. He enthusiastically jabbered how he and I had agreed that we'd go swimming together once a week, plus his swimming lessons.

Mirjami managed to work up a little smile for me, too.

We sat at the kitchen table after Ville fell asleep. Mirjami said that we needed another car. Then she could take Ville if something came up for me at the last minute.

I said that was fine with me, as soon as we got a little money stashed away. Which now we would be able to do since I'd just received a small raise. We'd probably be able to get one by around the time the second child was born. But we weren't going to get some used junker; it had to be safe for the kids.

Mirjami reached across the table and took my hand. She asked if I wanted a beer. She had no interest in making my life taste like tar. She squeezed my hand. We planned what kind of yard we wanted when the second kid was born and the renovations we would do to the house.

At first the baby would sleep in our room, but a little later Ville would give up his room for her. I would remodel the unfinished room upstairs, and Ville would move up there. He'd probably like being able to live up so high since he liked pirates and old sailing ships. We could even make the room a little like a crow's nest, or a captain's cabin. We could get Ville a telescope; then he could look out from his nest to see what was happening on the horizon. He could be the vigilant guardian of our happiness.

I continued enthusiastically envisioning the décor of Ville's future room. Mirjami lowered a fingertip to my lips. She took the bottle of beer from my hand and led me firmly toward the bed.

"Stop talking," she said. "I want you now."

METRO

I crawled into the warehouse through the little window. Judging by the thick layer of dust, no one had used the place for at least ten years. It was located in the half-deserted industrial area between the oil harbor and the Vaasa Mills bakery, where you were more likely to spot hares and flocks of crows than people. Fishermen were the only ones who frequented these shores on a regular basis.

Surprise, surprise—Smew had found this place, too. He had explored the empty buildings dotting this scrubby wasteland, photographed them from inside. He had climbed up the ladder to the roof of the Hankkija silo that stood nearby, said it was the best vantage point in Kotka, though very windy.

We had checked the warehouse; there wasn't a single surveillance camera there. A narrow catwalk circled the interior fifteen feet above. A steep flight of iron stairs led up to it but half the treads were missing. From the landing you could access ceiling tracks, hooks, and cables that had been used to move heavy goods within the warehouse. We had attached a rope to one of the hooks so we could swing from it or climb up to the ceiling.

Parts of the catwalk had collapsed and there were about a dozen of these gaps along the wall. The longest chasm was over six feet wide.

At one point we had tested which one of us could circle the catwalk the quickest. Rust had won hands down. He leapt across the collapsed sections like a gibbon.

The first time we had come here the floor had been strewn with the white skeletons of pigeons. The birds had entered through a broken upper window and been unable to find their way out again. A couple of fresher pigeon carcasses had been decomposing there among them. Rust had climbed up and covered the window with cardboard. We buried the pigeons in the bushes outside.

As a hideout, the warehouse had some superb features. At one end, there had been a small apartment for a watchman; the flimsy dividing walls had toppled over. But the former bathroom remained, with a tub and a faucet that still worked. The water tasted like rust and stayed ice cold no matter how long we let it run, but it was drinkable. Plus the electricity worked, too. Lightbulbs hung from the ceiling at the ends of long wires. They swayed there in the wind.

According to Smew, stuff was still being stored in the building next door, the one with the corrugated metal roof. We hadn't even tried to get in there. The last time we had been here a black van with its headlights off had pulled up in front of the next-door building in the middle of the night. We hit the floor and caught the scent of tobacco writhing in through a broken window. We had stayed on our side with the lights off and not saying a word, as the men loaded up their van, speaking tersely to each other.

"Stolen goods," Rust said once the van left.

Rust and I had planned on painting all of Kotka inside our warehouse. Not rushing, taking our time. A 360-degree panorama that would cover the walls. Then we would tip off the media. It would be a piece that no one could fault. Or of course someone would. For some folks, rusted corrugated metal or yellow brick soured to the shade of piss is always more stylish than the modern *Mona Lisa* painted on top of it.

But tonight I wasn't planning a city. There was no Rust. I had a different reason for being at the warehouse.

I headed for the fire extinguisher attached to one of the walls. This extinguisher had more important things to be doing than guarding an empty building. I threw it out the window; Baron was waiting on the other side to catch the heavy red cylinder.

"Are you sure about this?" he asked.

"Yup."

Using his company car he drove me to one of the war-era bunkers at Jumalniemi. We had spent some time there the previous summer, when the nights cast too much light on the streets. We turned the place into a Finnish version of a Stone Age cave, painting the walls with moose and bears and lynx among our tags. The mosquitoes from the nearby spruce woods gathered at the bunker and we spent many nights that summer in our concrete cave working by the light of citronella candles flickering on the floor.

One time a bearded local historian showed up, stood at the mouth of the bunker, and told us what a comfortable lair we had. He praised our paintings and told us stories from his scouting days, showed us how to build a campfire in front of the bunker. *Remember to light the fire from above, not below.* Then afterward he had raised a huge stink in the papers about vandals destroying our cultural heritage. That bunker had been abandoned in those shitty mosquito-choked woods for decades. I'm positive that back in the day the soldiers would have been thrilled if someone had bothered to throw up a little color on their walls.

But no. The Rats started coming by the bunker on their patrols. One time they pinched Jack's buddy Speedy and beat the crap out of him, broke his nose and jawbone and three of his ribs. So much for our forest refuge.

We hadn't been back since. A recent rainstorm had left a large pool of water in front of the doorway, and there was some cardboard in the corner. It looked like a hobo's bed. Not smart if the Rats were still patrolling the place.

I sprayed the fire extinguisher into the bunker until it was empty. The place filled with foam. Then we went back to the car and I got the rest of my supplies out of the trunk. Rust had left me a little inheritance: a small toolbox containing all the implements a working woman could need.

With a wrench I unscrewed the top of the fire extinguisher's empty tank. Then I cut off the bottom of an empty plastic bottle with my knife, turned it upside down, and used the bottle as a funnel. I poured a can of pink paint into the fire extinguisher.

Baron rubbed his forehead and asked, "Are you sure you know what you're doing?"

"Concept or execution?"

"Both."

"Just keep an eye out and make sure no one shows up."

Once the can of paint was emptied I filled the rest of the fire extinguisher's tank with water and then screwed the top back on. Baron gave it the final twist and then we sloshed it back and forth.

"More," I said. "The paint has to mix properly."

The foam had seeped out from the mouth of the bunker. It looked like a dense volcanic cloud erupting from the earth. A foam volcano.

We headed toward Jylppy and stopped at the gas station, where we had to wait for a couple of kids to fill their mountain bikes' tires. When they were done Baron backed up next to the air hose. The hose was long enough that all I had to do was open the trunk, which saved me from having to lift the heavy fire extinguisher, and more importantly, from anyone seeing what I was doing. I opened the valve at the bottom of the operating lever, the same kind of valve you find on bikes and cars. Then I let pressurized air into the tank. The paint inside the tank gurgled the way Rust did when he rinsed out his mouth after brushing his teeth. Rust had taught me how to turn a fire extinguisher into a weapon for urban guerillas.

My best teacher ever.

My phone told me when I'd been filling the tank for three minutes. I didn't dare fill it any longer. The pressure resistance of extinguishers is generally tested with water, a hydraulic pump, and a pressure gauge. But that's when we're talking about the pressure produced by water alone. If a crack or hole forms during testing, the water will drip and spray out. But when you fill an extinguisher with air, the tiniest crack changes the nature of the extinguisher, and its metal shell becomes a shrapnel-slinging explosive. It becomes a bomb.

Rust had done this twice and said to use extinguishers only in dire circumstances. This was my first time.

There were three parts to the mixture: paint, water, and pressurized air. The more paint and water there was in relation to air, the tighter the jet would be. The more air, the broader the spraying paint would fan out but it also used up the charge instantly. With higher pressure, on the other hand, you could direct the paint to go as high as fifteen feet and still paint a design.

Ever wonder how graffiti artists cover entire walls of buildings several stories high? From the ground to six feet up is obvious. Hanging from the roof only gets you about six feet, up where the swallows roost. But there's usually a hell of a lot of wall space left in between. It's hard to paint no matter what, but especially if you are in a rush. Unless you have a paint-filled fire extinguisher.

Trial and error would have taught me the best proportions for my mix. But I didn't have the time or the inclination to run any tests. An extinguisher is not a portraitist's ermine-hair brush, not some precision instrument. It's a coarse, crude bulldozer.

It wasn't normal paint I poured into the tank, either; it was glo-paint, which glows and shimmers in the dark. Rust had left some in our basement storage closet: Martian green, vivid turquoise, gaudy pink. Special colors, he had said. Meant for war, not for peace.

Rust and I had two alarm clocks: a battery-powered one, and one that you wound by hand. I had needed them to get up on time to deliver papers. Not Rust; he had the ability to wake up at the minute click right before the beeping and rattling would begin. It's a trait you envy when you're bumping into doors, still half asleep, trying to shut off the shrieking contraptions from hell.

On this night I woke up right away. I had slept with the clocks under Rust's pillow so the neighbors wouldn't wake up with me, but one of them was already moving around. I lay in bed for a moment, pinching my cheeks, and listened as the throat cancer patient one floor up flushed the toilet.

I had slept in my clothes, the way I always did whenever there was a nighttime gig. I glanced in the mirror. The brass button from my coat sleeve had left an impression in my cheek. Baron was waiting in his car up the block from my building.

Some woman in a denim jacket was leaning against the side of the bus stop with both hands, like she was trying to hold it up. She was singing karaoke to a nonexistent crowd.

"If I'm leaning against that stop five years from now, please put me out of my misery," I said to Baron.

"Huh?"

We headed toward Mussalo, stopping for a minute on a side road to shake the extinguisher. The valve was letting out a low, constant whine. Baron backed up a step and shook the extinguisher with his arms held straight out. As if a safety gap of six extra inches would make any difference if the thing exploded.

Baron didn't like the idea of using his company car for this mission but it was the only option. I wasn't strong enough to carry the extinguisher myself. Smew had a driver's license, but his mom wouldn't let him drive her beater Volvo because she knew he could sink into one of his comas at the wheel. Smew got around on the old 125cc he had used since he was a teenager. Jack had one, too.

The Mussalo fox farm was fast asleep. Five doors down from the Rat there was only one house in which a honey-yellow light glowed in a window. Baron parked on the street behind a van. I climbed out.

From a graffiti artist's perspective, the unfortunate thing about new residential areas is that there aren't many places to hide. The hedges haven't grown yet, and the apple trees planted as symbols of eternal bliss are scrappy, stunted saplings that rabbits and moles and puppies strip bare in the winter.

I circled around through two backyards to the windowless end of the Rat's house and peeked around the corner, spotting the surveillance camera right away. The Rat had attached it low enough under the eaves that he could change the battery from the house's fire escape.

Big mistake.

You should always place spy cams in spots you can't reach without bringing in equipment, like a tall ladder or a truck-mounted crane.

I tightened my hood around my face, scrambled up the ladder, and sprayed the lens of the camera with black paint. The gadget kept humming faintly to itself as it started recording the depths of the coal mine I had just plastered on its lens.

I crept over to the windows and peered in from the bottom corners. There was a sliver of light gleaming underneath one of the closed doors. It wasn't the Rat couple's bedroom, because at the next window I could make out the heads of a man and a woman and the contours of their bodies bulging under the covers. I could feel Jere Kalliola's snoring rattle the glass. I backed up to the previous window, checked the pale strip gleaming under the door. I decided it was the bathroom light. I counted to five hundred and waited; no one came out. They had just forgotten to turn off the light.

I went back to the car. Baron unrolled the window a hand's width. His musk flooded out so pungently that my eyes started to sting. Baron refused to join me. He said he'd satisfy himself with the role of driver. I didn't bother arguing with him. I checked to make sure that my hood was good, then I lifted out the extinguisher. The fifteen-pound cylinder felt like it weighed at least twice as much. After carrying it a few meters I wanted to roll it along the ground. But I was afraid that it would detonate in my face if it went over a single unplanned bump, plus it would make noise.

It wasn't too long before I was back at the Rat's house. The blinded surveillance camera whirred in the darkness like a nightjar.

I was caught off guard when the bathroom door opened. A little boy stumbled out; he disappeared into the darkness, rubbing his eyes. The pale strip remained glimmering under the door. They kept a light on in the john all night because of the kid.

I checked the Rat's bedroom window one more time. The couple was still lying there, buried under the blanket that sheltered them from the world's wrongs. Thanks to you, Mr. Rat, I don't have a pair of arms to rest in anymore. I pressed my ear to the glass; the snoring tickled my earlobe. I remembered how Dad used to tickle the soles of my feet with an eagle feather. *This is how you turn a sparrow into an eagle,* he had said.

Shitheads have shitty stories.

I took a couple steps backward, pulled out the pin, and pressed the lever. The paint sprayed all the way to the roof. I eased off on the pressure so the tank wouldn't empty immediately. I started writing and by the time I got to the third letter I had a handle on it. For a minute I was afraid I wouldn't have enough paint for the entire message, but there was plenty. I even managed to paint three big hearts at the end.

There they hung, dripping pink blood. Part of the message ran across the windows, obscuring my view into the bedroom.

Since I'd released the pressurized air I started dragging the metal tank across the lawns. I didn't want the Rat family to realize how the painting had been done. A magician never reveals her secrets.

A dog started barking somewhere nearby, startling me. Its slobbery chomp tore holes in the darkness, making it easier to spot me.

When I was little, a dog bit me. I still had the marks on my calf. With a straight face the owner had explained to my mom that her poor dog had been scared because he had never seen a black person before. A delicate pedigree pooch, lots of dog-show prizes. In the end, Mom had apologized to the dog.

I counted the number of barks: thirteen.

No one opened any windows or doors. The one light that had been on in the nearby house had gone out. Of course it was possible that someone was watching me from a darkened room, capturing this all on a recording he intended to turn over to the police. Anything was possible.

Except Rust coming back to life.

I pulled down my hood more tightly around my face and crouched down, moving along a hedge that had shed its leaves. When I made it to the car I heaved the extinguisher into the trunk. We had lined the trunk with plastic to keep the car from getting dirty. Tufts of grass and dead leaves clung to the surface of the extinguisher, plus one fat, mashed snail.

"Wait a sec," I said to Baron.

I slipped back out in front of the house to snap a few shots of the big, pink, glowing letters: JERE LOVES GRAFFITI.

JERE

When Raittila saw the text painted on the front of my house he burst out laughing.

"Sorry," he said, growing serious. "But you do have to admit."

"What do I have to admit?" I asked, teeth clenched.

A saw-toothed vein somewhere in my forehead was pounding harder and harder by the minute, and my head was splitting.

"That it's kind of funny," Raittila said.

"Funny?"

"Totally reprehensible, of course," he added. "But whoever it was could have made an uglier mark. Squirted a wall full of random smudges."

"To me that is a random smudge."

I glanced at my watch. The painters were late. They had promised to come almost an hour ago. I had already called twice to ask where they were and sworn in front of Ville. I needed a tarp covering up this mess immediately.

"Don't let them get under your skin," Raittila crooned, like some tawdry love song.

He always wanted to finish up company Christmas parties at the karaoke bar. His claim to fame was the tango "Silver Moon."

"Easy for you to say," I answered. "Your skin has been unscathed here."

"How's Mirjami?"

"She's inside with Ville, watching cartoons. She hasn't let him outside. I told her not to."

"Good call," Raittila said encouragingly. "The kid doesn't need to know anything about this. Cut off the flow of information. Contain the damage."

"You think he doesn't know?" I barked. "There are stripes of paint running across windows. The rooms are tinted pink! The inside of my house looks like some pervy Barbie bordello. Ville's bitching inside because we won't let him out to see what it's all about. He's spending more time staring at the windows than he is at the TV."

"Don't worry. We'll handle this together. All for one and one for all."

The whole time he was talking, Raittila was taking pictures of my house. The police had already left. The claims rep from the insurance company told me to prepare my claim carefully; she couldn't say offhand whether our home insurance covered anonymous vandalism, since it was on the surface coat of an exterior wall. *Are you sure it wasn't some friendly prank?* she had asked, emphasis on the word *prank*. After my lengthy, detailed explanations she wanted to confirm whether the text JERE LOVES GRAFFITI covered a patch of wall about ten square feet. I roared into the phone, *It's covering the entire goddamn wall!*

That's when the headache had kicked in. It felt like someone had started sawing against my frontal lobes with a rusty blade.

"A good reason to live in an apartment building," Raittila said, pointing at the surveillance camera. "Apartment buildings are easier to monitor. If you live on the top floors, there's no way anyone can get at you. You can easily set up a camera in the stairwell that records everyone who enters the building."

"I had a camera. The lens is black now."

"You can think of the corridor and elevator of an apartment building like the security check at an airport: everyone registers. The only part of your home anyone can get at is the front door, and you can always change the lock."

"The camera is exactly where you told me to put it."

"Single-family homes are vulnerable."

"There's no way I'm moving. Your advice is useless."

"These are facts. This isn't advice."

Raittila stopped photographing, waved at Ville, whose nose was pressed up against the living room window. Ville waved back; he had pulled on Mirjami's pink wool hat and was taking turns poking at the pink paint and the pink hat. Raittila gave him the thumbs-up; Ville gave it right back.

"Why the hell are you encouraging him to approve of vandalism?" I snapped.

"He's a kid. He doesn't understand," Raittila said.

"You have any kids?"

Raittila didn't answer. I was sure he didn't. To him, kids worked like electronic gadgets: press a button and you always got the same factory-programmed reaction. When you grew tired of that, you just turned off the kid. In Raittila's case, this meant that he'd remove himself from the presence of his acquaintances' bawling, shrieking kids for a week to a year, until the next time he showed up offering child-rearing advice.

"I called Hiililuoma," I said. "Nothing happened to his house. Or car. Both of mine have been totally ruined."

"They're not totally ruined," Raittila said soothingly. "A little surface work is all they need. That's life, from the day you're born until the day you die. Women call it putting on your makeup."

"So why don't you or Hiililuoma have to slap makeup on your fucking houses and I do?"

Raittila didn't answer, preferring to study my chewed-up lawn. Dozens of footprints had been sunk into it as the police and neighbors had walked across to gape at the pink mess. By this point the yard was more clay than grass. Raittila speculated on how many Bacteria had participated in the vandalism and how they had pulled it off. The police had wondered the same thing; they couldn't think of any other cases in the area that targeted a private home. They had all marveled at how the painter had managed to paint the two-story wall from end to end, all the way up to the roofline. Normally you'd need scaffolding or a good ladder. The police had looked for ladder marks in the lawn but they hadn't found any. The number of vandals also remained a mystery: it was impossible to pick out their footprints from among the dozens made by gawkers who managed to trudge across my yard before I made it out myself.

The web was probably full of photos of my smudged house. *Kotka's most photographed home.* Just a couple of weeks ago the thought would have made me proud.

Jere loves graffiti. Fuck me. To top it off, the hearts. The saw blade was ripping across the front of my skull again. Serrated spots danced in front of my eyes.

"The kids need a yard to play in," I managed to say somehow. "A home that quiets down at night. I don't need some upstairs neighbor grinding away on his stationary bike while I'm trying to sleep. Or a home theater next door blaring until midnight. I want to live in a house. Fresh air and my own yard on the other side of the wall. Not a neighbor. This is the house I want to live in."

"I haven't had any long-term problems with my neighbors in the building," Raittila said. "I always let them know right away what I think about any disturbances."

We watched as the painters' truck headed down my street. They didn't have to guess which house was mine. The driver opened the window.

"Hey. I've been waiting for you," I said.

Before the driver responded, he took a picture of my house.

"Kids get a bright idea, huh?" the painter asked, scratching his scruffy chin. "Got to keep those paint cans out of reach."

"No, goddammit. My son will never do anything like this if he knows what's good for him."

The guy with the stubble and his buddy started setting up scaffolding. Over an hour late, and he hadn't even had time to shave. They didn't bother going around and walking across the paving stones; the pipes they dragged cut deep grooves into the lawn. I wondered if lawns were covered by home insurance. I looked into the back of the truck.

"Where's the tarp?" I asked.

"What tarp?"

"I specifically asked you to bring a tarp to cover the house."

"You mean to keep people from seeing it?" the scruffy guy asked.

"Yes, yes."

"This'll go a lot more quickly without a tarp," he said. "A couple of days, max."

Two weeks later I wished I had recorded our initial conversation. All conversations need to be recorded, even if you're just having them in line at the supermarket.

Only a quarter of the painting was done by then, and some Russian tour buses had started showing up to ogle my home. Some saucy Slavic women in high heels had handed me their cameras and asked me to capture their puckered lips in front of the gigantic pink hearts.

"Lahvely design," they said, thanking me.

METRO

I was mixing paste for tonight. Each of us has their own recipe; making it yourself is a matter of honor. A lot of people might have mistaken it for normal cooking. I put a cup of water on to boil. In the meantime, I put three tablespoons of wheat flour in a mixing bowl and added ten teaspoons of cold water.

Rust had sometimes used potato flour instead of wheat flour, but I found that potato-flour paste didn't stick as well to uneven surfaces. Plus it was too easy for the mixture to get lumpy while making it. Some people used rice flour, but at this latitude and on this continent that was trying a little too hard.

Respect to our Chinese colleagues who use rice flour. They're forced to live even more paranoid lives than we are. In China, artists working outside the system don't get much respect. It's the penitentiary for the artists themselves, and a labor camp for re-educating the family.

Wheat flour is perfect for our conditions. It's cheap, buying it from the store doesn't arouse any suspicions, and it makes an effective glue. Making the perfect glue demands a soft wrist, like an ice hockey player with a deadly accurate wrist shot.

I watched the tiny bubbles form at the bottom of the pot, listening to *Rust Never Sleeps*. *"And once you're gone, you can never come back."*

Food is not a basic human need. There are better uses for a pot than making pasta.

Sleep is not a basic human need.

You can always sleep less. You should always sleep less.

While the rest of the world is asleep, it's my time.

When the water came to a rolling boil, I slowly poured the flour into the pot, stirring the whole time. With a soft wrist I whipped that wooden spoon, with a wrist that the NHL would pay millions for. If I were a man, and if I played hockey.

The paste foamed as it boiled. I had to keep stirring so it wouldn't get lumpy. I kept an eye on the timer and after two minutes I took the pot off the burner and set it on a trivet. Finally, I added three teaspoons of sugar to improve adhesion.

Once the paste cooled I poured it into tin cans disguised with labels for canned peaches and fruit cocktail. I kept a collection of lidless fruit cans with different labels. Del Monte and Pirkka protected me from the Rats. If they stopped me to search my bag, the only thing they'd think was that I'd been grocery shopping. The little lady likes canned fruit? Yeah, I sure do. We eat fruit salad at home every day; as an athlete, I have to avoid fat.

I moved over to the can sealer. Paste sealed with a sealer lasts longer than paste kept in a container with a removable lid. The latter starts to smell after two days. Sometimes I added copper sulfate to increase the life span. Can sealers were advertised at hunting supply stores like the latest cars: CNC-precision machined, nitrated spindles with two permanently lubricated, grooved ball bearings. Exceptionally low rolling resistance, custom articulation, drift-free axle. But instead of the Benz of can sealers, we had a Lada. It was slow getting up to speed, the bearings rattled, and it clanked as it sealed. Not beautiful, but reliable.

Rust had snagged it from his uncle after he died; his uncle had hunted moose in the fall and used it to can the meat for winter.

This batch of paste filled three sealed cans.

Paste is part of the work. An essential part.

The stack of paper and my roller with the telescoping handle were already stuffed into the bottom of my gym bag. On top of my materials I heaped clothes that reeked of sweat, a towel, a couple of bananas, and my can of peaches filled with paste. The brush for spreading the paste was hidden inside the towel. Little Miss Metro headed to the gym. I always like to get an extra-early start.

A gym bag is good cover, which is something I learned before I began to paint. If you have black skin you get a break in the Rats' eyes if you're training and want to run or jump Finland back onto the world map. Mom came up with the idea by accident, when she forced me as a little girl to go to the Hippo Games at Karhula track, where some big beast with swollen cheeks was staggering around in the middle of the field. It was a hippopotamus, according to the blond girl with pigtails who appeared at my side to stretch. *You should know since you're from Africa,* she'd said. Pigtails thought that hippos were as common in Africa as mosquitoes in Northern Europe.

To me the creature looked like a squirrel with a case of the mumps that needed to find a blanket to crawl under and rest, instead of stumbling around out there. I had been sent to bed when I had the mumps. I hadn't been vaccinated against it, because Mom and Dad had gotten into an argument with the clinic and refused to let them touch me. Somewhere there is an extensive series of photos of me with fat cheeks.

The children who participated in the Hippo Games wanted a photo of themselves with the mumpy squirrel. I had to get in the photo, too, even though I didn't want to. Pigtails said that the hippo and I made a really good pair. Then she said oink oink. She thought that hippos and black girls say oink oink. She was the one with pigtails.

Pigtails's dad kept coming over and telling her how to warm up. *Fifteen minutes to go. Now just a light jog over there and back. Stretch your hamstrings. Remember to stretch when you exhale. Rotate your arms vigorously. Your arms are what give you the momentum for the critical yards.* Pigtails's dad also appeared later at the long jump, chased the rest of us off from the approach so his daughter could practice stepping up to the foul line before her turn. He rubbed Pigtails's shoulder blades and offered her some sports drink.

I was wearing jeans and jumped half a yard longer than Pigtails. In the fifty-meter dash I had time to wave back at Mom before Pigtails made it to the finish line.

Pigtails and her friends called me Hippopotamus for the next two years. *Go back to Zambezi. Oink oink oink!* But the teasing eased off in other ways. One time a group of rowdy drunks fell silent when I walked past them in the park. They said hi and gave me the thumbs-up; they thought it was cool that a local girl showed promise on the track.

When I quit the club, I kept on hauling around my gym bag.

I tooled around downtown on my bicycle. I kept my gym bag open on the handlebars so I didn't even have to climb off my bike. At the first stop, I popped open the can and glued a Jere-themed flyer to the wall using my paste.

My instincts told me that of the three guys mentioned in the report, Jere Kalliola was the one who killed Rust. I didn't believe that Raittila, head of security services, had been directly involved. Bosses never do the dirty work. They just stand off to the side and nod their approval.

I thought it was so goddamn wrong that Jere the Rat still had a face full of freckles and Rust's freckles were nothing but a heap of ash.

When getting up with wheat paste, if you know what you're doing it only takes a few seconds to slap up one flyer. You have to have really shitty luck for someone to step around the corner right then and catch you, especially if it's night.

I had a ton of flyers with me so I made a lot of stops. I put up a few of them while I was delivering newspapers, too. A mailbag and a gym bag: a graffiti artist's treasure chests.

After the flyers were up and the papers delivered, I headed toward the harbor. I hadn't yet dared to visit the place where Rust fell. There were too many spots around the harbor watched over by cameras. Plus if the Rats started chasing me again there was nowhere to run except the sea. I didn't want to risk using the rowboat anymore. The Rats might follow me in a motorboat.

But now it was time to return to the spot where my world ended.

I parked my bike at the rack in the courtyard of a building on Vuorikatu. I climbed over the chain-link fence and cut across the tracks. I skirted the big warehouses so I would approach the Maritime Museum's enormous wave from the direction of the paper factory's stacks of lumber. I hoped that the surveillance cameras at the Museum would be aimed toward the city.

As an extra precaution I had pulled on Rust's parka, which was too big for me. I held the hood in front of my face and crouched like a hunchbacked dwarf. In reality I was five-foot-eleven, and from behind, if I were wearing a loose coat, a lot of people mistook me for a man.

I took the roll of paper from my gym bag and pasted pieces on the shed across from where Rust fell. The telescoping handle proved useful. The roll of paper contained the images of the Rat's house that I had enlarged into a huge image. I had made a collage with the house cut up and many photographs of it arranged both right side up and upside down. The entire piece was huge. The top of the piece glowed with the same pink text I had painted on the Rat's house: JERE LOVES GRAFFITI. On the bottom of the piece, growing down like roots from the houses turned upside down the text was black: JERE KILLS GRAFFITI ARTISTS. In place of the hearts that I had left on the original message, three skulls accompanied the new text.

I had spread the same image across town in over a hundred smaller flyers.

JERE

I was waiting at the corner in my car when the couple walked out of the apartment building. The woman was talking and waving her hands around and the man was chuckling.

I followed them in my car and watched them go into the same corner pub they had visited to knock back a pint after the funeral. The woman's hands were waving around the whole time. To my eyes it looked like she was describing the graffiti she had done. Now she was drawing a heart in the air.

The police disagreed. They had checked out my tip and according to Raittila they were sure that the couple didn't have anything to do with the smudging of the train cars. Not to mention vandalizing my car and house.

Yeah, sure, right.

I was certain that the police hadn't asked the couple a single thing, or at least not the right things.

When I had reported the flyers slandering me that had been spread all over town, the authorities said they would investigate. That's what they said whenever they had no intention of doing anything.

Besides, the flyer could be targeted at anyone named Jere, the female officer had consoled me. Since the early 1980s, ten thousand Jeres had been born and christened in Finland.

The insurance company claimed that I had to pay a supplementary deductible for repainting the vandalized wall of my house. Our home insurance fully covered the damage caused by lightning strikes, windstorms, fires, and even goddamn wild animals, but there was no mention in the contract of hearts being painted on the front of the house. They might be able to reconsider if the message on the wall could be viewed as hostile. But pink hearts? Could they be considered vandalism with 100 percent certainty? In terms of intent, the message could be read as fundamentally positive, or even constructive. The claims rep from the insurance company said that just between her and me, one of the insurance investigators suspected that in this era of viral social media it was a promotional stunt on my part to get attention for me and my family. The rep stressed that she didn't want to discount the unpleasant experience I had gone through. Then she started going on about increases in insurance fraud. Whenever the latest iPhone version came out, an unbelievable number of the old phones started to break. All supposedly by accident. It was hard to trust people.

That's when I hung up.

Raittila had said that we needed to be patient. We needed to think of Bacteria like chickenshit big mouths at the hockey rink who couldn't skate and didn't know how to hold a stick. Their skill was heckling. The Bacteria tried to prod and goad the other side into rash action. I had to calm down. We would consider our reactions in light of every man's stomach for them. If the problems continued we'd give the matter more weight.

It was easy for Raittila to be so calm about it. His car and house hadn't been tagged. His name hadn't been spread around town in flyers accusing him of murder.

If Raittila was comparing Bacteria to hockey players, then by that logic he should have been comparing us to them, too. Raittila was the coach and I was the innocent stooge who was the only player on the team to pay for a team penalty, by his orders. Who had given the order on the roof of Vellamo? Raittila. The man who at this very moment was watching TV in his unvandalized apartment, satisfied, in his smoking jacket and tasseled slippers. Who was the one who had knocked the kid down? Hiililuoma. As a reward for his deed he had gotten a promotion and, according to office gossip, was planning a Christmas trip to the Seychelles with Johanna thanks to his bump in cash flow. Hiililuoma hadn't said a peep about his travel plans to me. He hadn't even said he was sorry my home got tagged. His place and Audi out front sparkled in gleaming, tip-top condition, of course. I noticed that he had gotten a new set of gunmetal rims.

Hiililuoma had been avoiding me ever since I paid him that visit. He'd throw me a quick hello when I ran into him but whenever I suggested we grab a beer, he'd mumble something about taking his son to practice or doing yard work. He was lying. Hiililuoma had always had plenty of time to stop for a beer and bullshit.

But bullshitting with a friend is totally different from trying to bullshit that friend.

I waited across the intersection in my loaner Toyota while the couple enjoyed themselves in the bar. Hiililuoma and I had spent plenty of time in this very bar. They had stolen it from us.

The Toyota still smelled weird, like strangers screwed in the backseat every time I parked it. I wondered how many other people had keys to this car.

After eleven o'clock, the couple emerged from the pub. The curly-haired young woman exited first; she swayed on the sidewalk, tried to hold herself up by shoving her hands more deeply into her coat pockets. Her intoxication made her look like a little girl trying to stay up on a new pair of skates. The man paused on the bar's front steps, lit up a smoke. Now that he wasn't wearing a suit coat with shoulder pads, like at the funeral, his shoulders looked narrower. The adult had turned into an adolescent. He was tall. He could have gotten a summer job as a high-jump stand. Or a rain gutter.

When they started walking I got out of the car and followed them on foot from the other side of Kirkkokatu. Each clock on the church tower showed a different time. It had been like that for years. The sexton clearly hadn't been on very good terms with the clockmaker.

Dozens of jackdaws were sleeping in the branches of a now-leafless linden. In autumn, the trees of downtown Kotka served as tenements for the black-feathered birds.

The couple stopped at the corner of Sibelius Park to argue; I continued on through the park. I knew where they were headed.

I waited for them a couple blocks down the street. They weren't in any hurry to get home. The girl meandered into the road and swayed there with her arms spread wide, as if she were doing a rain dance.

Raittila had concurred with my theory that the smudger crew that had messed up my house included a girl, because of the pink hearts.

The guy stepped out into the road to hustle the girl to safety when a pair of headlights started approaching rapidly up Kirkkokatu. She struggled in his grip, giggling; she seemed to have an irresistible impulse to dive out in front of the car. I continued on toward their place, walking in front of them.

I had chosen my spot in advance. There was a bike storage closet next to the entrance to their building. I had entered the locked room three hours earlier, when a plump-cheeked old lady brought her three-speed in for the night. I had greeted her cheerfully and followed her in. She relaxed her suspicion when I bent down to pump up the rear tire of a hybrid in the corner. I ended up topping off both tires before the old lady locked her bike and left. After that, I pressed in the tongue of the latch so that when the door closed it didn't lock.

Now I hurried the last two blocks under the streetlamps' yellowish pools of light and checked whether the storage room was still unlocked. It was. I sat down on a wooden garden swing that stood at the end of the apartment building and waited for the couple.

Even small cities grow at night. A one-block trip takes two or three times longer than it does during the daytime. At first I heard the noises: the clang of the rainspout, the clatter of the tin can against the asphalt, the shattering of glass, giggling. Apparently one of them was kicking everything within reach.

As the couple turned the corner, I sat motionless in the swing. Humans have a hard time noticing an elephant in the dark if the elephant doesn't move. But we immediately spot the mouse scurrying down the elephant's back.

They walked past me, poking at each other; the guy had a bunch of keys in his hand. He was humming a percussive song. The girl was tittering as if someone were tickling her armpits. She'd been feeling good ever since they stepped out of the bar. But that smile was about to drop to her ass.

I pulled on a ski mask and got up from the swing. I popped the girl in the back of the head with my baton and she dropped to her knees. The guy thought she had stumbled because she was drunk and came back to help her up. He didn't even realize there was a third person there until I gave him a good whack on the side of the head. A howl escaped his lips; only one of his legs gave way. I hit him again, this time on his thigh. The strength went out of his legs and he dropped instantly. I grabbed him by the collar and dragged him into the bike storage and gave him a third whack so he'd settle down, like his girl.

I went back out to get her and then closed the door. I didn't turn on the ceiling light; I set a flashlight down on the handlebars of a bike in the corner and aimed the light at the couple. I duct-taped the girl's wrists to the frame of a nearby mountain bike and drew a strip of tape across her mouth. I duct-taped the guy's wrists to the rear fork of a bike hanging from the wall. I left his mouth untaped.

"Can you hear me?" I asked.

"What?" he groaned.

The girl writhed and whimpered a couple bikes away.

"Confess what you did to my house."

"We don't have any money."

"I don't care about your money. What did you do to my house?"

"What house? I don't know where you live."

"Don't you know that you're supposed to respect other people's property?"

"I do respect people's property."

"You're full of shit."

I hit the kid's back. Tears welled up in his eyes. The girl looked on, eyes wide.

"What the fuck did you do?"

"What did I do?" the boy cried.

"I'll give you three clues. Car. House. Flyers."

"I don't know what you're talking about."

"Stop lying!"

I hit him again on the lower back.

"I'm not lying," he managed to gasp.

"Do you want me to do something to that bitch of yours there?"

"No."

"Which one of you paints? Or do you both?"

"Annaleena paints."

"What does that cunt paint? Trains? Houses? Cars?"

"Landscapes."

"Landscapes! You call painting a wall full of shit a landscape? Spraying tags on top of tags."

"No more hitting." The kid had slid to the concrete floor, his taped arms rising over his head like the horns of a cow. The girl shook her head wildly.

I bent down next to her and ripped the tape from her mouth.

"You want to contribute to this conversation? You want to confess, you fucking slut?"

"You don't understand. I don't paint walls."

The girl's breathing was choppy. Blood dripped from her lips as she spoke.

"So what the fuck do you paint, then?"

"Paintings. I'm in the art club at the community college."

"Stop fucking lying to me! You know what a home is? It's a sacred place. I draw the line when someone violates my home."

The boy had managed to sit up. He shook his head.

"I didn't do anything. Nothing," he insisted.

Their backtalk and lies were infuriating. I grabbed the bike that the boy's wrists were attached to and gave the rear wheel a good spin. It started rotating ferociously and the kid's fingers were crushed backward between the front fork and the spokes. He screamed louder than I've ever heard anyone scream before, even Mom when she found Dad hanging in the basement. I was sure that his shrieks carried all the way up to the attic. I hit him again so he'd shut up.

"You didn't do anything?" I asked, his scream still ringing in my ears. "You want me to spin it again? Is that what you want, goddammit?"

He was sobbing quietly in front of me. I couldn't look at the fingers of his right hand. They were bent back from the knuckles.

"You're going to talk now or I'll do the same thing to you," I hissed at the girl. "Which one of you painted my car and my house? Which one of you is raping my home?"

"I only paint watercolors," the girl stammered. "Bouquets. Landscapes. Seascapes, Sailboats."

I raised the baton; she sniveled and curled up into a ball.

"Birch trees. Wildflowers. Chickadees. Stormy skies," she said. "Those are the only things I paint. I won't even paint them if you don't want me to."

The bones of the kid's broken fingers had pushed through the skin. He was dangling from the bike as if crucified. I pulled my knife out of my pocket. The girl started shaking uncontrollably. She was jabbering over and over about wildflowers and watercolors.

"I won't paint, I won't paint."

I cut the tape to free their hands. When the boy's hands hit the floor, he started howling again. I heard the elevator machine room rumble on the other side of the wall. Someone was coming down.

"Leave me alone," I said to them. "I didn't do anything. I'm innocent."

I left them in the bike cellar and ran out.

My shoes clopped in the street, echoing above the city like drumbeats. I had to get away from the asphalt, away from the drumming. I headed up the slope at Palotorninvuori Hill. The grass was soaking wet with fallen leaves and dew, and I slipped as I climbed. I was sweating when I made it up to the cliff, to the spot where the couple had paused to leave a rose on their way home from the Bacteria's funeral.

I pulled the ski mask from my head. I wasn't so sure that they were guilty.

I stood there above the harbor. My mouth tasted like rusty metal. I had bit my tongue in the bike cellar. I knew that I had to hurry back to my car and get out of there before anyone could follow me. No one could find out about this.

But my legs wouldn't move. I could hear heavy panting nearby, approaching, growing louder. Someone was already climbing the slope. I was sure that the cops were after me; there was no point trying to run.

"I didn't do anything," I roared into the darkness.

I waited to be knocked to the ground and handcuffed.

"I'm innocent."

A moment later, I realized that no one was going to emerge from the slope's darkness. The heavy, harried panting was coming from my own mouth.

METRO

The four-block walk from my apartment took more effort than any other trip I had to make that fall. The flat ground felt like a glass mountainside, like in that fairy tale where rival princes try to ride up to rescue the princess. I would have rather run a marathon.

I was still hesitating on the stairs. I dawdled so long on the third-floor landing that a guy had time to walk his dog and come back in. The dog had pine needles in its coat and smelled like wild mushrooms.

But I eventually pressed the doorbell. I had no choice. Unless I wanted my phone to be flooded with more and more calls starting tomorrow.

A woman with orange hair opened the door; on her forefinger she wore a big ring set with a rock. It was a special rock. It radiated energy through power impulses. That's what she had explained to me in the spring, which was the last time I had seen her. To me it looked like most of the rocks you'd find at a gravel pit.

Orange hair. Great. She immediately reminded me of a female Jere the Rat. Hair wasn't the only thing orange about this woman. She was dressed in blazing orange: a batik dress made of the same fabric as the orange curtain hanging in the window. The last time I was here the curtain was turquoise, as were the dress and the hair band and the dried flowers in the vase. The hair had been streaked with turquoise stripes.

The woman was my mother.

"Darling," she said, hugging me.

"Turquoise is out, huh?" I said, trying to squirm free.

"It is no longer the season of the sea."

My mother had set out a cake and teacups. She had baked the cake herself, piled it high with whipped cream and sunk satsuma slices into it. Clunky round earrings dangled from her ears.

"Oh you noticed," she said in delight, stroking her earlobe. "Guess what the color of new life is?"

"Black," I ventured.

"Silly pill. Happy birthday! You're a big girl now."

As she poured us tea she reminisced about how I had learned to walk with the help of this very dining table.

"You'd grab hold of the edge, prop yourself up on your tiny little feet, and try to walk all the way to the wall. You'd tumble over, sweet-pea, oopsy-daisy. But you never gave up. You'd try again, oopsy-daisy."

"Face-plant, oopsy-daisy," I said.

When I had finally made it three steps without falling, Mom and Dad had moved the table further from the wall. Four steps. Five steps.

"I've heard that story a hell of a lot of times."

"It's a story you have to hear every birthday," Mom said. "A feel-good story."

"Is orange a feel-good color?"

"The color orange is a ray of sunlight that opens you up to pos-sibilities. Every morning is a possibility. Every morning is, without fail, the first morning of the rest of your life. How are you going to use it, sweetheart?"

Luckily the phone rang, and Mom wasn't able to answer her own question. She did answer her cell phone, though: "Mademoiselle

Miranda, how may I be of service?" When my mother spoke as Mademoiselle she changed her pronunciation. She tried to sound French. When I had commented that spring that her gargled *r*'s made her sound more like a Mongolian throat singer than a Parisian fortune-teller, she locked herself in the bathroom until I left.

The bad part about Mom being offended was that, after catching her breath, she terrorized me with phone calls and tried to make me a better person.

I had already lost one battle. When I moved out of the house I had been forced to give her a phone number where she could reach me. She had threatened to report me to the police as missing if I didn't give her some way of maintaining contact. She was good at coercion with a smile.

I hadn't given her my address. I told her that I lived in Kouvola. She would never head up there to look for me. She said the boxlike buildings there stifled her energy flows. In truth, she was just too lazy to heave her fat ass off the bed and haul it up to Kouvola. In my child-hood photos she is as slender as a stalk of summer grass, and now her presence made the kitchen feel cramped. She didn't like going any far-ther than the corner store; she ordered her new crap online and had it delivered to the front door.

Suited me.

If Mom had known that for the past two years I lived a few build-ings away she would have been coming over all the time. I didn't shop at the local supermarket so I wouldn't bump into Mom by accident. I had seen her at the bus stop a few times, and when I did I pedaled in the opposite direction.

I tasted a piece of the cake that Mom had jammed twenty candles into. She was busy explaining into the phone how she could tell that the gentleman calling was sensitive and gifted and how he had a bril-liant future in front of him. He shouldn't allow a single setback to get him down. Mom said she could see from today's cards that he would be meeting an important person in the very near future, someone who would change the direction of his life. This person would be wearing red.

Ten minutes of this.

Mom had two phones. One was in her name and it was free to call. Dialing Mademoiselle Miranda's number cost €7.99 a minute.

"So what are these fucking cards you use to read the future?" I asked when she hung up. "The postcards on your fridge?"

"I sincerely wish you wouldn't swear so much. Swearing has control over you the moment you're no longer in control of your swearing."

"I just asked a simple question. Where are the fucking cards you read to dispense your incredible wisdom?"

Mom poured me more tea, even though I didn't ask for any. It was some acidic health chai that was supposed to be gentle on your stomach, but it just made me fart, like all of Mom's herbal teas. This one was called Waft from the Tropics.

"I tell my clients that I read from cards because it puts them at ease."

"So you lie to them."

"No I don't. I don't need cards to read their fortunes. But I don't want to waste their valuable time explaining why not."

"I don't see a crystal ball around here, either."

"A good fortune-teller doesn't need any aids. Think about it now, sweetheart. Does the power lie in cards? Or coffee grounds? Or a prism of some sort? No. You either have the gift of divination, or you don't."

"You don't have to feed me that Mademoiselle Miranda garbage you feed your clients. You don't have any gift of divination. You've just come up with a good way of making money. Of course it's better than the phone-sex calls you used to take when I was still living here. It was hard to sleep with you panting and moaning into the receiver at midnight and saying you were a sweet little thing with a tiny waist and a ghetto booty."

Mom opened her mouth to respond but luckily the phone rang, and she turned back into Mademoiselle Miranda. Whenever someone called Mom she started up her digital timer, the kind normal people use in the kitchen so they don't overcook the pasta. Mom kept glancing over at her clock to see how long the call was lasting. Stretching out the therapeutic babble just long enough that the person needing help wouldn't get irritated was a talent in and of itself. The important thing was to leave a cliffhanger at the end of the session like they did on TV, so the person would call back and ask for more advice from the marvelous Miranda. "Call me again if something unexpected happens in your life next Tuesday. *Bien sûr.*" Of course it would if you were eagerly anticipating it. Seeing a bulldozer at a stoplight would seem unexpected.

"*Excuse moi*, it's been a busy day," Mom said when the call ended.

"It's cool," I said. "I need to head out soon anyway."

"You're not leaving yet. How have you been?"

"Fine."

"Are you still working at that shoe store?"

"Yup. It's going fine."

"You should apply for managerial training. They can always get rid of employees, but not managers."

I had told Mom that I was working at Express, an enormous shopping mall on the outskirts of Kouvola. I was sure that she would never turn up there. She didn't have a car and there was no other way to get to this particular shopping hell. It was about thirty miles from Kotka. Whenever she expressed a desire to see more of me I'd plead the irregular shifts that our completely unpredictable boss scheduled for us. People with families always took priority when shifts were assigned. Mom would have spazzed out if she had known that instead of slaving away at a shoe store I had dropped a hell of a lot of newspapers through her mail slot over the past year. Sometimes for kicks I delivered her a free copy of the Swedish-language *Hufvudstadsbladet.* I knew she didn't know Swedish very well. I always got a laugh from the thought of her mouthing the Swedish-language comics at the breakfast table.

"Are you seeing anyone?"

"Nope."

"It would be good for you to find a soul mate."

"I'm not getting married. I'm not going to have kids so I can abandon them."

"I didn't abandon you, darling, and you've always had your father."

"I've had more than my share of fathers. The only real one disappeared years ago, unfortunately."

Mom fell silent. There had been a revolving door of boyfriends after Dad disappeared. The worst one had been the bald geography teacher who wanted to walk me to school every morning. One time he told me to drop by his classroom at the end of my day and he'd give me money for a burger. It wasn't until I was in the room that I realized that day's lesson was about Africa. *They speak the same language we do,* he cheerfully announced to the class. *We're all the same!*

"I'm done trying to shove a new dad down your throat," Mom said, after she ended another call. "All my time goes to this. I'm an entrepreneur."

"You're living on unemployment."

"Unemployment is an essential part of my career as an entrepreneur. I might lose my gift of divination if I dedicated my life entirely to business."

"For Christ's sake."

"I pray every night, darling. To my Higher Power. I pray that you will find happiness in your life the way I have."

"Goddammit, have you become religious, too?"

"I've always believed in a Higher Power. With a big *H* and a big *P*. A little like the Indians. Or pagan people."

With Mom it always got to a point where I couldn't think of anything else to say. She lived in her own little realm where she was the queen. The Sun Queen. The majority of my comments rolled off her like water off a duck's back. It didn't faze her in the least if I called her an ex-boozer, a fat mastodon who had devoured a layer of fat as insulation against the world, or the Courtesan from Karhuvuori, who wasn't satisfied with phone sex calls but had decided one winter to be Kotka's only two-hundred-pound pole dancer. Her career came to an end when the pole snapped, followed immediately by her leg when she fell off the stage. Her response was always the same. *In life you have to trust your instincts.* Then all of a sudden she might be offended by something totally trivial, something I had meant as a joke, like the quip about the Mongolian throat singer.

"Your father called a week ago," Mom suddenly said.

"Which one?"

"Dad."

"Where from?"

"Berlin. He remembers your birthday every year. He asked what he could give you as a present."

"Nothing."

"Your father would really love to hear from you."

"You can tell him that I'm a fortune-teller these days, too. I can see him headed to Australia on the next cargo ship to become a kangaroo farmer."

Mom leaned her chubby cheek in her palm and looked me in the eye. I had to turn away. She stroked my hair.

"It's already puffy enough," I said.

"I have a present for you, sweetheart. Today's your birthday, after all."

Mom handed me a soft package. I muttered a thank-you and fingered open the tape. I could feel my mom's steel-heavy gaze on my neck.

"You're chewing your nails again," she said softly. "What's wrong?"

"Nothing."

I reached into the wrapping paper and pulled out a blazing orange fabric decorated with an amoebic yellow pattern. It was the ugliest thing I'd seen in a long time.

"I dyed it myself. I've taken up batik dyeing. My best work to date. A tablecloth for you. Whenever you eat breakfast or have your evening tea you'll get strength from its rays and remember your mother. You and me, children of the sun, darling."

JERE

The kid's name was Joakim Salmi. The kid whose fingers I had broken. Joakim Salmi had played the piano since he was four years old and was in his third year of studies at the Sibelius Academy in Helsinki. He had put off school this autumn, however, because his brother Markus Salmi had died in an accidental fall from the roof of the Vellamo Maritime Museum. Joakim had wanted to stay in Kotka and support his sister. He had temporarily moved into her one-bedroom flat.

Joakim's sister, Annaleena Salmi, was the girl I had dragged into the bike cellar with him. She worked as a nurse's assistant in a nursing home. She sang in the parish choir and grieved over the golden crucifix that had fallen from her neck the night she and her brother had been assaulted by an unknown assailant.

Annaleena Salmi was particularly shocked by the incident because it had taken place the first evening the siblings had been able to laugh since their brother's death. They had been sure the worst was behind them and they would be able to go on with their lives. She had told her brother that he could go back to his studies at the Sibelius Academy the following week. She would be fine.

Then I changed all that, right at their front door.

It was hard to say whether the brother's fingers would ever be fully functional again. The nerve damage was extensive. *Well, if I'm not a classical pianist I can always plunk away at some bar,* Joakim had remarked bitterly from his hospital bed. In the newspaper photo, both his hands had been swathed in heavy, mitten-like bandages.

They suspected that the attacker was some junkie who had randomly targeted them. The sister said how sometimes it's even hard for a religious person to believe that there's a purpose to everything. Her big brother had died two months ago, and now her other brother was disabled, apparently permanently.

I folded up the paper. Across the table, Ville was explaining something about the giraffe with the longest neck in the world. I hadn't heard the beginning of the story and didn't understand the end. Everything was off. We now had to keep the lights on in our kitchen during the day because the tarp I had requested weeks ago had finally showed up, right when the repainting was almost finished. Mirjami was glaring at me from the armchair, displeased.

"You can't just shut yourself off in your own world," she said.

"I'm sorry, what did you say?"

"What are we going to take to the Raittilas as a gift?"

"A bottle."

"Bottles always end up getting emptied. I'm not going to sit there watching you all get drunk."

"So let's take flowers, then."

"The first time we go to your boss's house we have to bring something more than flowers."

In the end, we brought a little candleholder in addition to the flowers. The Raittilas' door had a brass plate etched with curlicue letters and an old-fashioned doorbell, the kind you twisted. Raittila's wife opened the door. Her face was curtained by long, blond hair, behind which she eyed our cellophane-wrapped gift a few seconds too long before thanking us and saying how nice it was.

"It was designed by Alvar Aalto," Mirjami said.

"It's nice," Raittila's wife said again.

Raittila looked for a tea light to put inside the candleholder; nothing bigger would fit. He lit the candle and we watched the stubby flame flicker in the amoeba-shaped glass.

"World-class design," Raittila said.

Raittila's wife looked familiar; I didn't have the nerve to ask where I'd seen her. Maybe television.

They lived in an apartment building that had been built in the 1920s. Raittila said that any building that had been built almost a hundred years ago and was still standing would stay standing for the next hundred years. Nowadays folks were building homes where the predicted lifespan was a couple of decades, at most.

"I don't mean your house personally," Raittila said.

At the Raittilas', the living room was called the salon, and the floor wasn't full of toys like at our place. Two hundred-year-old pillars framed the door to the salon. *Neoclassic architecture,* Raittila's wife explained. *Doric capitals.* I could understand about every third word she said.

The dining table was dark wood, and the surface showed no sign of the stains that had permanently seeped into the varnish of our dining table, despite persistent polishing.

We ate moose. Raittila's dad belonged to a hunting club. Some years his little group had so many permits that every member took home the meat from a whole animal.

"Things are getting a little tight at Dad's place. He doesn't have room for a new storage freezer every year," Raittila said.

"Gee, that's a shame," I said, when the silence grew awkward.

"We all have our trials and tribulations." Raittila spread his arms like an evangelist standing at the podium of a Pentecostal church. "Dad, me, you."

The center of the dining table was dominated by a five-branched candelabra; tall, cream-colored candles rose regally from it. Raittila's wife had relegated the gift we had brought to a small side table.

"It's really cute," she said when she noticed Mirjami glancing over at it.

We drank our coffee from rose-patterned cups: Raittila's wife's grandmother's china. They were Meissen porcelain; each one was worth three hundred euros. I noticed the hand Mirjami was using to hold her cup start to tremble.

"So, not your average Moomin mugs," she managed to say.

"Moomin mugs are butt-ugly," Raittila's wife said.

Mirjami laughed and glanced at me. Both of us were thinking about our kitchen cabinets, which contained a dozen different Moomin mugs that we drank our coffee from every day. Mirjami's favorite was the mug with the Groke on it; in the morning, Mirjami's puffy eyes and shock of hair didn't bug her as much if she compared her reflection to the Groke.

There was a view from the Raittilas' salon down to Sibelius Park. Raittila and I were standing there at the window once we finished our coffee; he had poured me a glass of Cognac. The women were sitting in a room where the walls were circled by glass-fronted bookcases. Raittila's wife called it her *bibliothèque* and she was showing Mirjami a book big enough to serve as a TV stand.

"Everything all right?" Raittila asked.

"Yup."

"No new incidents?"

"Nope."

"Didn't I say all you had to do was get a grip on your nerves? Bacteria exhaust themselves. They have their life spans. Cheers."

We clinked glasses.

"We still don't know who defaced my car and my house," I said.

"Does the patient always need to know what caused the disease? Isn't it enough just to get better?"

"Is it possible to find out?"

"Everything is possible if you have the stomach for it. Do you?"

I grunted in response, because I couldn't think of anything to say. I tossed back my drink and grimaced.

"How do you like the Cognac?" Raittila asked.

"Burns a little. Maybe I could have a little soda water or something with the next shot?"

"Soda water?"

"Vichy."

Raittila pointed at a round glass bottle filled halfway with brown liquid.

"What does the shape of the bottle remind you of?" he asked. "Be honest."

"A glass sausage."

"You must be kidding."

"Well, that's what it reminds me of."

"That is a replica of a flask found on the battlefield after the Battle of Jarnac, among the bodies of the noblemen. In 1569. The Huguenot Wars. It's a sun disk. The glass cork is a fleur-de-lis."

"OK."

"The Cognac is Louis XIII. Made from a thousand different distillations, the oldest of which are over a hundred years old. One bottle costs 2,300 euros."

"What?"

"And you're asking for a refill cut with Vichy water. That gulp you just took already cost two hundred euros."

"Goddamn."

"But yeah, let's go ahead have another. With Vichy. You know what? I'll bet you'll like it better with Coke. Wait a sec, I'll get a can from the fridge."

Raittila started heading for the kitchen.

"Hey, don't go," I called after him. "This is really damn good. Amazing. I don't need any more."

Raittila didn't stop, so I rushed into the kitchen after him. He was already rummaging through the cabinets with a can of Coke in his hand.

"Shall I pour you a full glass? A big water glass like this? No wait, I'll just fill it halfway. We'll top it off with Coke."

"Olavi, I didn't mean it."

Raittila pushed past me into the living room carrying the water glass and splashed in three fingers of Cognac from the glass bottle. He topped it off with Coke from the can.

"There you go. For the man who appreciates the finer things in life."

"I can't drink that."

"If you don't empty your glass I'm going to pour it out," Raittila said. "There goes five hundred euros down the drain."

I could feel my ears burning. I had suffered from shyness since child-hood. When I would give the wrong answer back then my face would almost always blaze bright crimson. Once, the teacher had remarked that both in terms of comprehension and coloring I reminded her of a turkey, and the nickname had stuck for years. Now it felt like those school years had returned. The Turkey emptied his water glass with a few gulps.

"Drink, boy, drink," Raittila urged. "You only live once."

Raittila got his camera and took a photo of me as I emptied my glass. After checking the shot from the screen he burst out laughing and slapped me on the back.

"Get a look at yourself," he chuckled. "Even the bums in the park aren't that red in the face."

"I'm not laughing."

"Oh come on, don't take it so seriously, man. You think I'd really serve you Louis XIII? That's one-star Jallu in that decanter."

Raittila explained that he had acquired the decanter during a cruise from Stockholm; a group of Japanese men at the bar had been spotting each other drinks of the exceedingly pricy beverage. The bartender had asked for five euros for the empty bottle; Raittila filled it with Finnish Cognac at home. He said I wasn't the first guest he had fooled.

"But your picture is by far the best," Raittila said, complimenting me. "If I had kept you going a little longer I wouldn't be able to tell you apart from a tomato."

"Pretty funny," I said.

"Wasn't it, though?"

Raittila insisted on offering one more round. His hand was pressing down on my shoulder. We watched a dark figure run across Sibelius Park.

"He won't be running long with a heavy tread like that," Raittila noted.

Another figure ran across the park in the same direction as the first one.

"A lot lighter on his feet," Raittila said. "He's going to catch up. Hopefully they're friends. At least we are. Comrades in arms."

"How the hell would you be able to figure out the name of the Bacteria who fucked up my house?" I asked, my voice rising into an annoying squeak again.

"I have an informant."

"Huh?"

"Someone close to the Bacteria. How else do you think I found out that they'd be scribbling away in the rail yard the very night we were there? You think it was luck that we went out with such a big crew? Not the day before? Or the day after? Pure chance? You think relying on chance is the way to live life?"

"Why don't you catch them, then?"

"Law of supply and demand. We have to make sure we have enough work to do. The more we're seen as necessary, the more we'll get paid. No Bacteria, no us. We have no interest in bringing this urban warfare to an end. Of course we need the occasional effective, successful interim operation to convince the moneymen. Which is where your bonus came from, by the way."

Raittila slapped me on the back and led me over to the women and the bookcases. I spent the rest of the evening eyeing him and trying to digest what he had told me. Raittila's wife was reporting on their trip to both sides of the Pyrenees the previous summer, and Raittila tossed in comments as he nipped at his Cognac. They had spent their days hiking through emerald-green mountain pastures and admiring the horizon beyond the Bay of Biscay, and their evenings gathering around oak tables surrounded by vineyards.

We had taken a cruise to Stockholm with Ville in July and spent most of it at the kids' ball pit. The buffet had featured all-you-can-eat shrimp and all-you-can-drink wine.

I hadn't heard Raittila's wife's first name when we were introduced, and the evening was so far along I didn't have the nerve to ask it now. Right before we were leaving, the shots of Finnish Cognac gave me the courage to ask were I'd seen her before. Had she been on some television program? Or in an ad?

"I work at the bank. I handled the mortgage for your house," she said.

"Right. Sorry. I have a bad memory for faces. I was sure we had met before."

"Olavi recommended you," Raittila's wife said. "Otherwise there was no way you would have qualified for that sort of loan."

"No need to thank me," Raittila cut in. "Or just bring me a bottle Louis XIII some time as a token of your appreciation."

I couldn't tell from Raittila's voice if he was serious or not.

We said good-bye and took a taxi home; the driver hummed along to the tango swaying from the radio with his cigarette-roughened bass. We had left Ville with the neighbors for the night. Our yard was dark, even though I remembered leaving the yard lights on when we left. I stopped for a second to check the lamp in the glow of my cell phone. Mirjami called for me to come in.

"The lightbulb's gone," I said.

"Come on."

I went in to get a flashlight and then moved the beam across the yard. The tarp was still where it had been when we left. Ville's little wheelbarrow was in the same spot, and so was the pile of leaves he had heaped up.

I went in. Mirjami had already taken off her blouse and was brushing her teeth in her bra.

"Cold, Raittila's wife," I said.

"I thought she was nice," Mirjami said.

"Pretty snooty."

"No she wasn't."

"Pyrenees and mountain meadows."

"I'd also like to go somewhere besides Stockholm on our next trip."

"What's wrong with Stockholm?"

I lowered a hand to Mirjami's naked belly, felt the baby kick my palm.

"This one's going to be a soccer player," I said.

"That's what you said about Ville, too."

"Ville didn't kick anywhere near this vigorously."

Mirjami moved my hand away, saying she'd gotten sweaty at the Raittilas' and that she wanted to get into bed feeling fresh. She drew the shower curtain. I prolonged my toothbrushing, enjoying the curves of her silhouette as it faded in and out of view through the dotted plastic fabric. It was beautiful even when she was pregnant. You never knew what kind of treasures awaited behind curtains.

Then it hit me.

I grabbed the flashlight and ran outside, stumbled into the front yard barefoot, and yanked back the tarp covering the front of our house. The wall was filled with a glowing text, this time painted in screaming orange: JERE THE MURDERER LOVES GRAFFITI FOREVER. Instead of hearts, the wall had been smudged with big orange suns shooting out rays in every direction, like one of Ville's drawings.

The whole fucking wall was ruined. Just when we had gotten it repainted.

I should have kept my cool, but I couldn't stop myself from letting out a howl. I howled so long that the lights came on at the neighbors'. Doors opened and people came out.

Ours was the only door that remained firmly shut.

Inside I found Mirjami, who had panicked and rushed out of the shower when she heard me yelling. She had slipped on the wet bathroom floor and gashed her head open. Whorls of blood mingled with water still spraying from the shower, tinting the tile red.

METRO

My coffee had cooled down. The orange patterned tablecloth Mom had given me was spread out across the table. I traced the ovals with my fingertip.

My suns were cooler than Mom's amoebas, but Mom had picked a good color. It had inspired me to go to the basement on a scavenger hunt. In the corner of the basement closet, behind all the cans of paint, there was some orange glo-paint that was brighter than the sun. I knew just what to do with it.

Baron had refused to drive me back to the bunker for another fire extinguisher. He said painting the Rat's house once was enough. The words of someone who has never loved anyone so fucking much that a splotch of rust on a building's gutter still shattered her heart into pieces. That simple sight brings back everything associated with Rust, with the violent rush of a tsunami crashing through a dam. And the whole time you have to pretend like there's nothing wrong, because no one except for a few friends knows that you've been in love. I can't even visit the grave because a surveillance cam has been set up there, too.

Fuck.

Ten extinguishers wouldn't be enough. A hundred.

Smew had come to my aid. He defied his driving ban and snuck off with his mom's ancient Volvo. I promised Smew I'd shake him awake if it looked like he was falling asleep at the wheel. Smew told me not to worry; he and Jack went out cruising sometimes so he wouldn't forget how to drive. Smew assured me that he was a better-than-average driver.

That was a little hard to believe. The Volvo had shuddered to a stop about a dozen times on our way to the old infirmary in Karhula. We had also driven half a mile down the road with our emergency lights blinking before Smew remembered how to turn them off.

We had finally made it to our destination. We scrambled through the rosebushes to the old industrial area. Since my last visit, Smew had further investigated the deserted buildings and photographed them. He had also located an unused extinguisher left behind on the wall of the machine shop. We took the extinguisher and emptied it in the bunker, and I filled the tank with a mixture of orange glo-paint and water and pressurized air just like I had done before. Though I did do one thing differently. This time, at the gas station I bumped up the pressure in the tank way past the safety limit Rust had used. I wanted the paint to spray out from the nozzle all at once and make a gigantic octopus blotch on the Rat's house.

We kept the extinguisher in the backseat on top of a blanket rather than let it clank around in the trunk. It was making this low, complaining groan. Smew said the ship's frame had made the same sound in the movie *Titanic* when the ship ran into the iceberg. We freaked out at every pothole and every time the car died. We drove toward the Rat's neighborhood at a crawl. I walked the rest of the way through the tall grasses at the side of the road, to make sure the coast was clear.

There was a tarp hanging in front of Jere the Rat's house. I wouldn't be able to use the extinguisher, meaning I was going to have to work up close. The tarp did provide one advantage: I would be able to work behind it, out of sight, as long as the Rat and his family were gone or deep asleep.

Once I'd checked out the house we drove to Kotkansaari. We carried the fire extinguisher to the old warehouse at the edge of the harbor, the one where I had found the first extinguisher. Together we lifted it into the old tub in the watchman's apartment for safekeeping, putting a blanket under the metal cylinder so it would rest on something soft.

The next night I returned to Mussalo on my bike, with what remained of the orange glo-paint in a can. The Rat's house was dark; I had slipped under the tarp and started to paint, this time with a brush. After many peeks through the windows I was convinced that there was no one home. I'd occasionally hear people in the street, and when I did I stopped and waited. I worked on my sun-splash masterpiece without anyone bothering me.

Still, I almost got caught. Just as I was finishing, the Rat couple returned. Jere Kalliola was drunk and braying loudly. Despite his intoxication, the Rat wondered why the yard was dark; he came back out with a flashlight to check out his home turf. It didn't take him long to realize that I had taken the bulb out of the yard light. I hid on the scaffolding as he swept the beam of his flashlight back and forth across the tarp. When the Rat gave up and went inside I quickly snuck out of the yard.

I didn't hear the wailing howl of the wounded animal until I was saddled up on my bike the next block over. It never crossed my mind that the Rat would discover what I'd done that night. Otherwise I would have stuck around to witness it. I would have loved to have recorded his cry and sent it in to the radio for the nature sound of the week. *This is what a murderer who has been kicked in the balls sounds like.*

***

I rinsed out my cold coffee and checked the web. No photos of the tangerine-colored house had appeared yet. I had an irresistible urge to ride out and take a look in person.

It was already dark. I put on my trainers and sweats, but instead of heading to the Rat's house I hit the running trail. They had started lighting the course again with the onset of winter. I wore my fanny pack but instead of an energy bar and a water bottle, it contained a can of spray paint.

Sometimes you'd run into people at the Karhuvuori running track who were creepier than the *Halloween* movies. I didn't mind the beer guzzlers, but last summer I got the shit scared out of me by heavy panting bearing down on me a couple of curves back. I beat a quick retreat into the wild raspberries and watched as a bald guy wearing camouflage pants and a bulletproof vest over his T-shirt pounded the trail. His vest wasn't lightweight Kevlar, but an army-green version with iron plates that looked like he got it from his grandpa. Cue-ball's footfalls left deep prints in the dust like dinosaur tracks. Between pants he was roaring, *You can do it! Push yourself, faggot, push yourself!* as he slapped himself on the cheeks.

So it helped to be faster than the other joggers.

On this night, after my second lap, I headed off the trail and up the hill. There was a dead pine tree there where I practiced climbing sometimes. I scrambled up to the top tonight and pulled the can of spray paint out of my fanny pack, painted green pine needles on a dried branch fifty feet off the ground, a little life for a dead tree. I could see all the way to downtown Kotka from here. So many windowless facades begging for murals.

I yearned to be able to paint an entire wall legally. I admired Belgian artist Roa, who painted pigs, rabbits, birds, and deer. He only used black and white and painted the animals so meticulously that they looked like gigantic ink drawings. Rust had shown me photos of a mural Roa had done on the windowless end wall of a six-story building in Berlin. He had transformed the wall into a hunter's meat locker. A dead rabbit and roe deer were strung up by their back legs to ropes hanging from the roof, an equally dead heron at their side. Below them lay an enormous, lifeless, stiff-bristled boar; a heavy-horned mouflon that had been bagged sprawled across it. Roa had visited the wall once a month. The dead animals gradually decomposed, until in the last image of the series, only skeletons were left on the wall. Above the vault of the pig's ribs the curly-horned mouflon skull was turned toward the sun. Its spine looked like a ridge of snow-covered peaks.

There was no way I could make murals like that in this local Rat-run zoo. Here you had to paint on the fly while you kept one ear listening for the crunch of gravel and panting.

Blu was another artist I really admired. He had done an amazing mural in Berlin where the naked body of former DDR leader Erich Honecker filled up the whole facade of a building. The pink body was formed from the thousands of naked citizens that Honecker ground up in his teeth, one at a time. Driven by his bottomless hunger for power, the piece showed a dictator devouring his countrymen, and at the same time he was eating himself alive, hunk of flesh by hunk of flesh.

Both Blu and Roa worked alone. They would park a small crane at the site and use it as needed. Blu didn't even sketch. He had been able to create the dictator-ogre in one go, painting directly onto the wall. It was so detailed it left Michelangelo and the Sistine Chapel in the dust.

And it was all legal. They got to work legally.

If I brought a crane to some wall in Kotka and started painting, the Rats would be there in five minutes, as soon as I had gotten myself off the ground. By the next morning, the sanitation department would be hosing away the smear that had once been Metro.

***

I finished my final lap around the 5K trail sprinting as hard as I could. Some speed freaks shouted encouragement from the bushes. When my knees started to give way I forced myself to run another hundred yards, and then another hundred. I imagined the Rats were after me. And then I fell. I lay there in the middle of the trail for a long time. I felt like throwing up.

I went back home. One of the neighbors was watching television so loudly that the foyer was reverberating. "Shhh, the baby's sleeping. It's so nice when the little one's asleep," someone on TV was whispering at a volume of eighty decibels. The upstairs neighbor was banging something heavy on his floor, yelling, "Quiet!" The person next door started twanging his electric guitar. Evenings sure were homey in Karhuvuori. Rust and I had gotten used to wearing earplugs when the noise got out of hand.

I had made it all the way to my apartment door before I realized what was wrong.

I backtracked down the stairs, walked around the corner, took a quick glance over my shoulder, and picked up the pace. I circled the neighboring building and the next one, too, before I dared to hook back toward my building.

The lights in my apartment were off now. I was almost 100 percent sure that there had been a light on in there a second ago. I always turned off the lights when I went out.

I called Baron, explained the situation to him, and told him that I needed to spend the night in one of the apartments he was selling.

"You can't just waltz into them."

"Hey, come on, I need a place to stay. I've just been running. I'm freezing out here."

"Are you sure there was a light on in the apartment?"

"Yup."

"And now there's not?"

"Nope."

"Maybe it was the reflection from the streetlamp."

"Yeah, or a helicopter. Or a comet."

He remained silent and I was afraid he had hung up.

"I'm only trying to help," Baron finally said grumpily. "Maybe the bulb burned out. Or the fuse."

"I'm not going back to check. There's someone in there."

"You've been running hard. Sometimes I see stars when I've been running."

"Baron, I'm going to catch pneumonia while we sit here shooting the shit."

"No one outside our crew knows about your apartment."

"I'm not sleeping there tonight."

Emptiness echoed in my phone, as if the sea wind were blowing through it. A dog walker packed into a parka walked past. The little pooch was panting and drooling; he wanted to chomp my leg for dinner.

Baron sighed in my ear. "I'll be there in fifteen minutes."

JERE

Lying there in her hospital bed, Mirjami reminded me of the waxwing that had flown into our window. I had been sitting with Ville in our living room right after the move. There were no rugs or furniture in our just-finished home. We were waiting for the sofa we'd ordered from Sotka. There was just the shiny new parquet floor, and a skyscraper-like stack of unpacked banana boxes next to the wall. I was rolling a Matchbox car across the floor with Ville and wondering if the car was rolling a little too easily in my direction. Was the floor crooked?

Then there was a thump at the window, and when we looked out we saw a tuft-headed bird on the ground, wings limp. The bird had a black eye, as if it had taken a blow. Ville burst into inconsolable tears. I carried in the flaccid pile of feathers and placed it on the floor.

"Death, death," Ville repeated hysterically.

I didn't know where he'd heard the word.

Mirjami had been at the grocery store, so it was just me crouched next to the dead bird, helpless. Its lemon-yellow tail was the same color as Ville's favorite toy car.

"Do something," Ville wailed.

"I'll try."

"Death is coming," Ville cried.

I tried to remember packing a shovel. I had to get this bird buried as soon as possible. Kids forget what they can't see. I lifted the bird's leg; it felt as slack as a rubber band. Did we even have a shovel? During my panicked rummage through the boxes all I found at all resembling a shovel were spoons and ladles.

"It's alive," Ville exclaimed.

I hurried back into the living room and saw that the waxwing had turned over. The tip of its yellow tail was quivering weakly. Then the head started to twitch. A bright red drop formed on the bird's beak.

"Blood, blood," screamed a scared Ville.

The drop grew and plopped to the floor. Another red ball beaded up on the beak.

"It's dying," Ville squealed. "It's dying again."

The bird vomited three rowanberries onto the parquet. After that, the waxwing picked itself up and rocked there on its feet, half stunned. I carried it outside. It stumbled around the frozen clay for a second and then flew off. Ville squeezed my hand all evening. I was his hero.

"Dad saved a bird," Ville told Mirjami.

At Ville's request I told and retold the story of how I had resuscitated the waxwing by lifting its legs up and down.

Now, Mirjami moaned in bed. Her head was wrapped in a bandage that made her head twice its normal size. A tube snaked into her hand; I couldn't look at the spot where it entered the skin. I had always hated everything about hospitals. My father had turned into a completely different person after one week in the hospital. At home, Dad had always known without hesitating what everyone should do; he would give strict orders accentuated with a wave of the hand or a glare that even my big brother never argued with. But when he ended up in the hospital, Dad turned into a tentative stutterer; the direct gaze of his eyes faded into a blank stare. The doctors spoke about cancer, but for me cancer was just the hospital's code word for the fact that the place sucked all the fight out of a man, and then his life.

The first night after Dad had been sent home from the hospital, he hanged himself in the basement.

"Jere," Mirjami groaned, her eyes cracking open.

"You're fine," I said immediately. "Everything's fine."

"What happened?"

"You slipped."

"How's our child?"

"Your mother's looking after Ville."

"No, the baby."

I bit my lip.

"I guess everything's fine."

"You guess?"

"Goddammit, I can't understand anything these doctors tell me. You lost a lot of blood. But that shouldn't affect the baby, I guess."

"You guess?"

"I don't know."

"Jere, please go get someone who does know and bring them here." Mirjami closed her eyes.

I left the room. The corridor was so full of fire extinguishers I started suspecting that the building was full of pyromaniacs, not patients. Instead of nurses and doctors, the only person I saw was a dark-skinned janitor pushing a cart lined with a black garbage bag. Before I became a security guard, I worked for the sanitation department. It was our job to pull out all the junk that got caught in the city's grates and gutters. We found fetuses every week; people flushed them down the toilet at home and imagined they were gone for good. At first we had buried the fetuses in margarine tubs near the smoking area; a colleague would give a short speech and we would fold our hands and smoke a quiet cigarette in memory of the deceased. One guy had made crosses out of twigs. Once our boss had showed up in the middle of one of these funerals. He cursed and kicked over the cross and brought us a black garbage bag and swore that if he ever again suspected us of playing priest, by God, we'd be fired on the spot, with a kick to the kidneys as severance.

I followed the janitor to the elevator and out the side door of the hospital. I watched him cart the garbage bag over to a huge Dumpster. I didn't get why foreigners who did shitty work were always smiling like they were lounging poolside in Rimini, with a Bacardi and Coke in hand. Didn't they understand they were getting screwed?

The guy said hello. He had a funny accent.

I waited for him to go back inside and then rushed over and opened the lid of the Dumpster. Using my pocketknife I cut a long slit into the side of the garbage bag. Crumpled, used paper towels, cardboard toilet paper rolls, and used maxi pads tumbled out—no fetuses.

I took a deep breath.

I had to put a stop to this ordeal. As long as the Bacteria were on the loose, my family wasn't safe. We'd all end up in the hospital, and after that it wouldn't be long until the black garbage bags.

I called Raittila. I told him I was ready for anything to make this go away. I had the stomach for it now.

METRO

I waited for Baron for an hour near the Karhuvuori shopping center. It had started to rain, and I was shivering and numb in my T-shirt, even though I had popped off some squat-jumps and darted into the convenience store to warm up. The clerk had glared at my scrappy appearance, but she let me skulk in the corner by the dirty magazines for ten minutes. Then she announced it was closing time and that I'd better start looking for a wet T-shirt contest somewhere else, like at the bar next door, Barbaari. I might get lucky there.

When Baron finally arrived he nudged open the passenger door and before I had time to put on my seat belt he said, "Do you know what this is called? An excess of caution."

"I never thought I'd hear you bitching to me about being too careful."

"I can go check your apartment," Baron said. "Give me your keys."

"Then they'll see you."

"They?"

"Him. I don't know how many there are."

"If there are," Baron said, looking at me the way a kindergarten teacher looks at a kid who claims to have seen a witch and a pumpkin up in a tree.

"Neither one of us is going in there. I need to take a shower. I'm freezing. What the hell took you so long?"

"You think it's easy for me to just arrange a place for you to stay? I had to figure out which one of the apartments we're selling is definitely empty and pick up the keys from the office."

Baron headed downtown. My nose to the glass, I gazed out at the warm orange lights of the power plant and the metal stairs that criss-crossed its exterior, climbing like the stairs to a castle tower. The old sugar factory loomed behind the power plant. When I was a little girl I wanted to be an inventor, and when we passed the factory's smokestack I vowed to invent the best candies in the world. I had secretly wished that we would move to Sugar Factory Road, which was the most beautiful street name I had ever heard.

"Don't you have anything with you?" Baron said, glancing at me.

"Nope. Everything's at home."

"You can't live like that."

"I can for one night. Tomorrow I'll recruit one of the kids playing in the yard to go up and see if the apartment's empty."

"Aren't you supposed to be at work early?"

"Day off."

Baron shook his head and parked the car next to the Orthodox church. The golden domes glistened in the rain. He led me around the block to the portico of a pink building. He said that this portico marked the spot where the first four people were killed in the bombings of the Winter War, a fact he never mentioned when he was showing the place. The quartet had rushed to shelter from under the open skies, sighed with relief, and right then a bomb had fallen in the middle of the street, hurling shrapnel in every direction.

"Maybe their last thoughts were happy," I suggested. "'We're safe.'"

Unlike the stairwell in my building, this one didn't stink like cabbage soup. Baron fumbled with his key ring and told me to walk lightly; the people living here went to bed early. We climbed up to the top floor. Baron opened the door and told me to take off my wet shoes. He didn't want the place to look like a duck had waddled in from the bay.

The apartment was almost completely empty. The room we were standing in had a table and four chairs.

"Where am I supposed to crash? On the table?"

"It's the best I can do. They're coming to get the last of the furniture tomorrow. You have to be out of here by nine. I'm betraying the trust of the owner and my employer by letting you in here."

"You have a towel?"

"I'm not carrying one in my back pocket, no. There should be paper towels in the bathroom. Use them. And take the trash out with you. At least it's warm in here. A roof over your head."

Baron pulled a minibottle of vodka out of his breast pocket and offered me a swig.

"What have you done?"

"Nothing."

"Your eyes are as jittery as a rabbit's."

"I just need some rest. Can you please stop lecturing me, Dad."

Baron tilted his head and looked at me, chewing his lower lip. Then he shrugged and said, "I'll leave the bottle on the table. You need it more than I do. Remember: be out by nine."

"Yeah, yeah, yeah!"

Baron's aftershave continued to stink up the apartment after he left. I opened the kitchen window to air out the place. I moved the chair over to the window, looked out at a maple tree, where a few rust-red leaves still fluttered stubbornly on the branches. Baron had been right about what he said, even though I didn't want to admit it to his face. When I had lived with Rust, little things hadn't spooked me.

Rust's presence had been enough to calm me when my imagination started galloping. A graffiti artist shouldn't live alone. There's no way you can help getting paranoid.

The wind whirling up from the yard made me shiver. I curled up next to the radiator in the bedroom. I decided to stay in this warm little nest for a minute before I showered. The thought of water flowing down my skin seemed unpleasant, even if the water was hot. I shoved my frozen hands between my thighs and pressed my nose into a gap in the radiator. I didn't even have the energy to remove my fanny pack. Once again, I blamed myself for panicking; if I hadn't, Rust would still be alive. If I hadn't pushed the boat out, Rust would have hopped in and we would have rowed off into the horizon together—beyond the horizon, goddammit. The Rats would have been left scrambling around the rail yard, whipping their hairless tails.

We would have continued our life together. We would have painted trains. We would have slept next to each other, sharing one blanket, our legs intertwined. We would have traveled to Berlin next summer. We would have moved to Helsinki once I got into school. We would have lived happily ever after, painting and fucking.

But I pushed off. One uncontrolled stroke of the oars was all it had taken to create an impassable chasm between us. I had abandoned Rust. And Rust had died. I would be stuck here forever in the same town with Rust's murderer. Delivering newspapers. And living the same night over and over again like in that movie where the weatherman wakes up to the same day every morning. *Groundhog Day*.

And. AND. AND!

And is the most fateful word, in any language. *And* tells what happens when a poor wretch makes one single mistake. A cough at the wrong moment. A tiny lurch that sets off a sequence of consequences like a perpetual motion machine. Consequences linked by tens of *and*s.

Every *and* sinks you deeper into the swamp.

I had to get away from Kotka.

***

It was dark when I woke up. I heard a foghorn outside. I stood up. The only thing I could see beyond the window was a gray soup. I rubbed my eyes but it didn't go away. The heavy fog was veiling the maple tree and the rest of the courtyard. The kitchen window was still open. Fog was wafting in; it was like a living creature drifting through the apartment, touching everything with its cold fingers. A long tatter of mist reached the table.

The glowing red clock on the stove read a quarter to two. I sat down at the kitchen table and took a swig from the bottle Baron had left behind.

I smelled like sweat.

I went into the tiny bathroom, took off my clothes, and turned on the tap. I waited for the water to heat up. Silvery gloom percolated in through the little window.

I only spent a minute in the shower. I didn't want to wake up the neighbors. I was nothing but a shadow that moved while everyone else slept. I wasn't supposed to be here. I used my sweatpants to towel off. I'd make do in my panties for the rest of the night. The sweatpants would dry on the radiator by morning.

The bathroom window had fogged up from the steam. I drew a train track across the glass with my fingertip. Mom had told me that there was a train track next to our first home, back when Dad was still around. Long freight trains pulled by two locomotives would thunder by; as they passed, the spice jars would clink and clank on the shelves. In the springtime, the railroad ties smelled pungently of tar. One of the neighbors had quipped that I'd been dipped in a vat of tar the first time he saw me crawling among the fireweed and lupine in the yard. Dad had hung the neighbor from the coatrack and asked him to repeat himself.

The guy said, "Can't you take a joke?"

In the summer, people tarred their wooden boats on the shores of Kotkansaari. For Kotka natives, the smell of tar meant boat trips, seagulls, picnics on the islands. But for me, the smell of tar meant train tracks, a longing for rail yards and distant cities.

And Dad.

I was startled out of my thoughts by a click.

I softly stepped closer to the closed bathroom door and slowly locked it. I laid flat on the wet floor and put my ear up to the crack between the bottom of the door and the floor.

Someone was moving around the apartment.

It was more than one person. I heard sounds coming from two directions.

I pulled on my wet sweats, grabbed my fanny pack, and flattened back down on the floor. It was dark on the other side of the door.

One of the voices said, "Where's the scum?"

Suddenly someone twisted the door handle. The lock resisted.

"In here."

The door thrashed back and forth. I crouched there, frozen in place, until a piece of the doorjamb snapped off with a crack. I pushed against the door, trying to hold it closed. It slammed into me, throwing me backward across the toilet and into the shower. I grabbed the shower curtain, ripping it down from its hooks. A heavy animal was on top of me, pressing the shower curtain into my face. I couldn't breathe.

I tried to pound at the beast with my fist but my blows went wide. The oxygen rattled out of my lungs as I tried to push myself out from under the plastic curtain.

I grabbed the shower hose and used the showerhead as a club.

It didn't do any good. I was gasping but getting no air. My eyes were going dim.

Somehow I managed to open my fanny pack. I shook the can of spray paint, held it out, and sprayed. The plastic curtain was filling my mouth. The weight gave and I was able to climb up on my knees. Hot water was streaming down over both of us. The shower had turned on. The dark figure was rubbing his eyes. The lights were off, and we were veiled in steam.

I jerked open the small window, shoved my upper body through it. To the right, there was nothing but a sheer wall.

"Don't let the scum go!"

To the left there was a rainspout within reach and a ladder just beyond the fat metal pipe. I wriggled out of the window and was just barely able to reach the spout. Someone grabbed my legs. I kicked backward, shattering the window. The grip loosened and I propelled myself toward the spout. I knocked the wind out of myself and hung there like a falling maple leaf.

I managed to wrap my fingers around the ladder on the other side of the rainspout. A man's head thrust out of the bathroom window.

"Did he come down?" shouted someone down below.

Instead of climbing down, I started climbing up into the fog. The ladder continued to a metal roof, which glistened with tiny droplets of mist. I looked down. The man who was chasing me had made it through the window. He was already hanging from the spout and swinging himself onto the ladder.

"Get the fuck up here," he called down.

On the roof, the fog wrapped me in a gray blanket. I could only see an arm's length in front of me. I stumbled between two chimneys toward the ridge of the roof. I was barefoot, wearing nothing but soaking sweats and a wet T-shirt. I banged my knee against a ventilation duct and teetered on the sloped surface in the dense fog.

They're going to knock me down, I realized.

I couldn't see the edges of the roof.

Something touched my cheek. I screamed.

"There!" someone called out, far too close to me.

A jackdaw had settled on the chimney next to me to ruffle its feathers. Its wing had grazed my face. I circled around behind the metal duct, inched forward. My fingers hit on a gutter funnel. I was back at the edge of the roof.

It had to be more than a twenty-meter drop, but in the fog, the ground looked like a soft, inviting down mattress.

Maybe it would be better to jump before someone pushed me. Now I could still decide for myself.

There was a searing pain radiating through my foot. I ran my hand along the sole and found a wedge of glass sticking out of the ball of my foot. I pulled it out. My foot started to bleed; I took off my T-shirt and wrapped it around the sole to protect it.

I leaned against the ventilation duct in my wet sweats and sports bra. At least one man was up on the roof with me. His cautious steps echoed in the fog, boxing me in.

I started crawling along the edge of the roof. The metal slipped under my sweats, and I was terrified I would slide over the edge. I bumped into a ventilation duct and stopped behind it.

"She's over here."

The booming voice felt like it was coming from over my head, from the top of the duct. I twisted around; the jackdaw was eyeing me from above.

The fog was making sounds bounce around.

I no longer knew which side of the roof I was on. There was no light reflecting from the depths of the mist, so I figured I must still be on the courtyard side and not the street side. Fog was the perfect condition for painting. It gave you a hiding place. But here I was with only one good foot, waiting to get knocked off a roof.

"We can see you. You'd better come over here," a gruff male voice said.

It seemed to be coming from beyond the edge of the roof, from the emptiness.

Maybe they had those special goggles that you could use to see through the fog. Maybe they were prolonging the chase on purpose.

A sphere of light appeared in the darkness, like a lighthouse calling me to safe harbor.

"Goddammit, it's bouncing off the fog."

"Turn it off."

The sphere of light went out.

I pressed up closer to the metal duct when an upright figure glided past from above, a ghost. If I stayed here, it wouldn't be long before they caught me. My glass-gashed foot couldn't take running.

I felt the low lip that ran along the edge of the roof, the one the chimneysweeps jammed the soles of their boots into to stop their slide if they lost their balance. The lip felt like pretty slim reassurance, like I was using thread for a seat belt. I advanced along the edge at a crawl until I hit my head. A tall, dark wall rose above me. It had to be the next building. I didn't see a ladder. I lowered myself onto my stomach, leaned my head out over the edge of the roof and peered down. For a second I thought I could make out another metal roof a few yards below me. It looked to be an outbuilding or a wing of the main building.

"The fog's lifting," someone said behind me.

"Turn on your flashlight as soon as you can. Let's close this cage."

I took a deep breath, grabbed hold of the edge of the roof with both fists the way I had grabbed the edge of the table when I was learning to walk. I dropped down into the emptiness and dangled there. I stretched my toes, reaching for any sort of protrusion, but sheer stucco was all they found. My fingers slipped from the eaves.

I dropped. Or actually, I fell.

I tried to protect my cut foot but I still landed on it when I hit the metal roof. I cried out in pain and slammed over onto my side. Two flashlights turned on, one below and one above, penetrating the fog.

"She's on the lower roof!"

I limped away from the shouting, kept moving along the ridge of this second roof. The light was tracking me from the yard below like a bloodhound. I heard a thud behind me; someone had dropped to the lower roof.

"Where is she?" said someone from behind me.

"Fifty feet," I heard from below.

The metal roof came to an end. A ladder rose up the dark wall into the fog. I started to climb. It went on and on, as if I were scrambling up the smokestack at the fucking wood plant. I finally realized I was climbing, fingers trembling, to the roof of the City Theater's prop warehouse. I could hear the labored breathing of someone coming up the ladder after me.

Once I reached the top of the ladder I crawled along the edges of another roof, feeling my way around. The fog grew denser again and the pain radiated up from my foot and throughout my body. The stars dancing in my eyes weren't enough to light the way forward.

Suddenly, one of these guys bum-rushed me from the soup and with both hands shoved me into the emptiness. I fumbled wildly to get a grip on the edge of the roof, but I flew too far. I flailed in the air. My life didn't flash before my eyes. My thoughts were like the dense fog I was falling through.

My back slammed onto a flat roof to the rear of the prop storage. My ass felt like someone had run a spear through it. I cried out, rolled onto my side, and crawled forward. I caught a glimpse of someone ten feet above me standing at the edge of the warehouse. I had to get out of there.

Through the fog I could make out one more flat roof below me, a cluster of plastic chairs huddled on it. I tried to cut the distance by hanging off but my fingers wouldn't hold, and I fell again. I hit the seat of one of the plastic chairs, and both the chair and I toppled over. Two of the chair's legs broke. At first I thought the splitting crack was from my own limbs.

So much blood was rushing through my ears that I couldn't properly hear the cries of the men approaching from the upper roof. I hobbled over to the ladder I could see at the edge of the rooftop terrace, made it down to the street, and limped away through foggy Sibelius Park.

JERE

When I kicked down the bathroom door I felt jubilant, thinking it would all be over soon. It was the same triumphant sensation I'd get as a teenager playing ice hockey when I'd get the perfect shot on goal and knew before the puck left the blade of my stick that it was going to slam into the upper corner of the net.

I made out a figure flying backward; he tore down the shower curtain as he fell.

I jumped on top of him. At last, I had the destroyer of my home in my grasp, the killer of my car, the shamer of my family. I felt like mashing him through the drain and down into the sewer, which is where he had crawled from to harass normal people.

The Bacteria twitched below me; I crushed him against the floor. I realized that there would be no fingerprints if I strangled him through the shower curtain.

He flailed at me helplessly with the showerhead but it just glanced off my shoulders and face. Ville hits harder when he's upset.

That would have been all she wrote if my eyes hadn't suddenly been blinded by some burning, stinging substance. He was spraying me with fucking poison.

I jumped back and rubbed my eyes. Luckily the water from the shower was rinsing my face.

"Don't lose the scum," Raittila said from the doorway.

I clenched the leg of the Bacteria as he was climbing out the window. We were both soaking wet and I lost my grip. I pushed my head out the window. My blurred vision started to clear.

"It's a fucking girl," I blurted out. "A black one."

"It's your tormenter. Trust me," Raittila said behind me.

I could just barely squeeze out the tiny window. The fog made it hard to see. I called down to Hiililuoma to find out if the target was down below. He said no. I reached the ladder and twisted myself up to the roof in pursuit of the girl. I told Hiililuoma to follow me.

The ventilation ducts and the old chimneys looked like large blocks of stone looming in the mist. I climbed up to the middle of the roof; I had no desire to end up near the edge. I turned on my flashlight for a second. The light bounced back from the fog and blinded my still-aching eyes. It was like staring into the headlights of a semi.

"Give up," I shouted. Or tried to. It came out a whisper.

I wanted to get back to the ladder but I ended up on the street side of the roof. Beneath me, the spheres of the streetlamps glowed as pale as soap bubbles. It felt like I was at the edge of a swimming pool lit from below, and all I had to do was jump in and swim to the far side to get myself a gin and tonic from the bar. The kind of outside bar that was at the hotel where Mirjami and I honeymooned, open from morning until late at night. Service with a smile, a bartender in a sharp white shirt.

My teeth were chattering. My clothes were glued to my skin.

I had to put a stop to this shit. I wanted to live in peace. I wanted to get back to a beachside bar someday. Now all my money was going to repair work and deductibles, thanks to this Bacteria. We were going to have to take out a second mortgage.

A dark figure approached. I dropped down to one knee, gripping my collapsible baton, and steeled myself to whack her in the leg.

"Jere."

It was Hiiliuoma. He had climbed up the ladder. He started moving across the edge on the street side. I did the same on the courtyard side. A jackdaw cawed out in the gloom.

As I fumbled forward on the foggy roof, I started to doubt Raittila's "100 percent solid" tip. Instead of blocks of stone, the metal ventilation ducts now reminded me of the gapped walls of a fortification, which offered defenders shelter while allowing them a full view of invaders. My chest tightened at every one, making it hard to breathe; I was sure someone was going to attack me from behind.

It's just a girl, I kept telling myself. *A little black girl.*

"We can see you. The fog is lifting!" I shouted, victoriously. "The game is up!"

My voice ricocheted around in the dense fog, more ominous than silence. I heard heavy panting and a wail to my left.

"Did you get her?" I called to Hiiliuoma.

"She's on the lower roof."

What lower roof? Visibility was close to zero. I couldn't even make out my fingernails, even though I was flapping my hand right in front of my face. I kept crawling along the edge of the building. My shoes kept slipping as if the roof were greased.

"Just hang over the edge, it's a short drop to the next roof," Hiiliuoma said, appearing at my side.

"Shouldn't we have safety harnesses?"

"Where are we going to get safety harnesses?"

"I don't see a roof down there."

"Just go."

Hiililuoma half shoved me to the edge. Before I could hang down properly he prodded me and I fell.

What the hell? First he knocked the Bacteria off a wall, and now he's knocking me off a roof.

I slammed into the metal surface below.

The fog was just as heavy down there as up above. Frantic breathing ricocheted somewhere up ahead.

Goddamn Hiililuoma, I thought, as I chased the Bacteria along the roof. *He's trying to kill me. It's all the same to him. He doesn't care which one of us dies, me or the Bacteria. Both would be a nice addition to his CV.*

The wild panting was now echoing overhead. I found the ladder that the Bacteria had used to climb away. I started climbing after her. My fingers were so stiff that I couldn't curl them around the iron rungs. I had to keep stopping to blow into my palms and clap my hands together, using my elbows to lock myself to the ladder. I couldn't see the roof down below me anymore. Someone was aiming a flashlight up in my direction.

"Give up," I shouted.

No one answered.

I made it to the next roof. I waited at the ladder for Hiililuoma to show up; he didn't. I had no idea where Raittila was. Maybe they had both gone home to snuggle up with their women, leaving me here.

I started feeling my way across the roof. I couldn't see a thing. All I could hear was the chattering of my teeth and the pounding of my heart.

With each step I started getting more and more pissed off. Pissed off at Hiililuoma, who had gotten the promotion that should have been mine. Pissed off at Raittila, who had given the promotion to Hiililuoma and who served me cheap rotgut and Hiililuoma top-shelf Cognac. Pissed off at Raittila's wife, who looked at me like I was a roach on the bathroom floor. Pissed off at Hiililuoma's girlfriend, Johanna, who smiled at me a lot more invitingly and sexily than Mirjami had smiled in years. Pissed off at everyone who had been laughing and smirking at a round table as my home was invaded and my wife almost died of shock. I should be at Mirjami's side right now, not on some freezing roof. The person who pissed me off least was the black girl, even though she kept making me chase her along roofs. According to Raittila, she was to blame for everything and she kept slipping out of my grasp like piss in snow. She pissed me off least of all, but she still pissed me off. Of all of them, she was the only one I could get back at.

That's why I didn't hesitate when I made out a crouching figure through the tatters of fog. I just pushed, kicked, and smacked her over the edge of the roof. I heard her yelp and fall.

The thud came too soon.

METRO

The car slithered up out of the fog before I could get away. A voice called out, "Hey, whore, let me give you a ride. I'll take my clothes off, too." The man was hanging out the window, waving his shirt.

I wasn't actually naked. I was hobbling barefoot through the dead of a foggy November night in sweatpants and a sports bra. The red tail-lights vanished into the fog like the penetrating eyes of a cat. I heard a final honk followed by a burst of laughter.

The fog protected me, but it was also problematic. I couldn't see anyone approach until they were too close. I wouldn't be able to get away from a six-year-old on this leg.

I had broken off a branch from one of the trees in the park so I didn't have to lean on my gashed foot. I hobbled like a disabled vet. In Finland, racists always love to talk about the debt the country owes its vets when they're trying to justify why Finland doesn't need to take in any refugees. One time Dad had responded to them by explaining how in his hometown every third man was dead or lame because of war. He went on to tell them that there were a lot more war heroes and invalids there than in Finlahd. That was the time Dad had gotten his ass kicked worst of all; both eyes had been so swollen that it took a week before he could see straight.

That's when Dad decided to leave Finland. He gave up. I hated Dad for a long time because he gave in to the fearmongers and assholes but left me behind with them.

People in Finland find it really fucking hard to accept that things have been rough in other parts of the world. Sometimes it feels like most men between the ages of twenty and sixty are jerking off in their bathrooms to the Finnish flag, not a picture of a woman.

At Kiviniemi Bridge, an approaching van looked like a police vehicle so I ducked under the bridge's arches. I had no desire to be interrogated. There was a pile of wet cardboard under the bridge that smelled like vomit and glue. I hid under it when I heard the slosh of waves from the foggy strait. A dark boat was gliding under the bridge only a few meters away. It was helmed by a figure who looked like the ferryman of the dead.

I thought about staying there under the cardboard for the rest of the night, but I was too cold. If I fell asleep, I'd never wake up again.

The fog thickened in the inlet and the dull blare of a foghorn rang out from the direction of the harbor. Another one answered. And a third. I was trapped in a net of sirens.

I tossed the can of green spray paint into the water. I didn't want to get caught with it.

I climbed back onto the bridge and limped across to Hovinsaari. In the drifting gray gauze it was hard for me to find the right building. Jack and his mom lived on the fourth floor, but I couldn't see that high. Otherwise I would have recognized Jack's room from the red elf that hung there year-round. This guy Olsson from the building across the way had seen the elf the Christmas before last and thought it was a hanged man. He had called the police and demanded they come over. He met them in the entryway, jabbering about how he had just been waiting for some tragedy to take place in that building; it was full of the wrong sort of people, and unless it was broad daylight he didn't dare set foot outside without some means of self-defense.

Jack said that no television comedy could compare to the look on Olsson's face when the cops saw the red plastic elf in the window. "Technically it was hanged," said the police, "since the noose was wrapped around his neck and not his pointy cap. But we'd appreciate it if you didn't call in next time, Judge Olsson." Then they confiscated the bright red purse Olsson was carrying, with its brass-knuckle handle. Olsson protested that it was his grandmother's, from the war. Things had been just as restless on the city streets during wartime as they were nowadays, and decent people needed to be able to defend themselves, he'd argued.

Thinking about the story gave me the strength to climb the fire escape up to the fourth floor. This was starting to be too many ladders for one night. I didn't get how one bum leg could screw up your entire body. I was shivering, but my arms were on fire.

I found the familiar elf in the window, knocked on the glass. I had to tap out several series of raps before Jack's sleepy face appeared. He opened the window.

"I thought the upstairs neighbor was remodeling."

"At three in the morning?"

"Are you going to paint?" Jack asked. "You're really goddamn pale."

Jack grabbed me by the arms before I lost my grip on the ladder. Somehow he wrangled me in. I managed to hit my head on the edge of his desk, and the next thing I knew I was sprawled out on his grass-green shag rug. Jack shoved a newspaper under my feet, complaining I was getting stains everywhere. I didn't come to on my own. Jack had to pinch my cheeks and pull my hair.

"You can't stay here," he said.

I wasn't thinking straight. I had a hard time remembering how I had ended up on the grass. My head was filled with plaster instead of brains.

"I bandaged your foot," Jack whispered. "You busted open your knees too. I cleaned them, and the big gash on your palm."

I raised my right hand; it was wrapped in thick white gauze.

"Plus your whole body is covered in bruises," Jack added. "I didn't do anything about those."

"OK."

"Sorry, but you have to go," Jack said.

I managed a stutter: "W-why?"

"I can't let you sleep in my bed. My Mom will freak out if she finds out tomorrow morning I had a girl in my bed."

"I can be your girlfriend."

"Hey, take a look in the mirror. You'd need a slightly different skin tone for my mom."

"Come on, at least let me stay under your bed."

"No, I have a good place for you. You just have to put on some clothes first. These might be a little loose, but they're warm."

Jack helped me up from the rug and onto the bed. He had set out a shirt and a sweater and baggy pants for me. Then he gave me an over-coat, wool socks, and his own tennis shoes.

"My feet are a lot bigger than yours, but with the bandages, these shoes should work pretty well. I think. At least for your bandaged foot."

He forced me to drink a glass of water and a take an ibuprofen. Then we wandered through the dark two-bedroom apartment. I heard deep breathing coming from behind a door that was cracked open. Jack scavenged me a hat and mittens from a closet. The mitten didn't fit my bound hand. Jack led me up the stairs to the upper landing and opened the door to the attic.

"Fuck no," I said.

"It'll be good. I have a down sleeping bag for you. Rated minus ten. It's not going to be that cold tonight. I'll come up and see you in the morning as soon as my mom goes to work."

"Your mom works? I thought she just sat on the sofa, like my mom."

"She works at a furniture store. She sells sbfas."

"Does she test them at home?" I mumbled.

My mouth felt thick, like that time at the dentist's when they numbed it with a shot before they removed my wisdom teeth.

Jack helped me to the back corner of the attic, to our spot behind the cots. I collapsed on the spinach-green sofa, setting off a mushroom cloud of dust as if I had accidentally detonated a small nuclear explosion. Jack unzipped the sleeping bag he was carrying and stuffed me in. He told me to take off the coat but to leave on the hat.

He disappeared before I could even mumble thanks.

JERE

I was panting on the foggy street corner as Raittila stood next to me, talking into his phone. Chasing Bacteria didn't seem to have winded him at all.

I had climbed roofs and ladders and plunged through the fog for several blocks under the fancy streetlamps decorating Main Street and stopped now and again to catch the panicked clop of fleeing feet. A moment later I had been forced to admit that I had lost the trail. I went back. Raittila and Hiililuoma were waiting in the courtyard.

"We'll catch her," Raittila said as I bent over and tried to stop huffing. "But next time I'm going to ask you not to let the prey slip through your fingers after you're already on top of it."

"Let a girl slip through your fingers," Hiililuoma said disparagingly.

"You can't let the gender catch you off guard," Raittila said. "I thought you had learned that simple fact by now."

"She sprayed paint in my eyes, goddammit."

"Did you let her tits distract you?" Hiililuoma asked.

"Gender is the only thing we can't tell about smudgers in advance," Raittila said, as if he hadn't heard a word I'd said. "You have to be prepared for a fifty-fifty chance. Don't you remember anything from Vartia's visit? I guess not."

Raittila continued his call, turning his back on me. I cleared my throat, wiped the sweat from my face, and let my breathing normalize. Hiililuoma gave me the evil eye and clicked his tongue; it sounded like a judge's gavel. I glanced at my clock. It wasn't even two thirty yet.

Raittila was wrong. I remembered Vartia's visit perfectly well.

Last fall on training day, Raittila had introduced me and a dozen other security officers to a man in slacks and a blue blazer. He introduced himself as Vartia, *ia*, no *j*. Vartia opened his rolling briefcase and lifted out several thick folders that he had us pass around. They were full of photographs of tags scribbled on walls, bus stops, billboards, fences, and a hundred other places.

Under each photograph Vartia had carefully written an analysis of the tag in a tidy print that looked like a newspaper font. *They're called tags*, Vartia had begun. *For those of you who have a hard time remembering your high school English, that's spelled t-a-g.*

Vartia had divided every tag into an upper, middle, and lower zone. He explained that you could deduce a lot based solely on which of those three zones was highlighted in the smudge. Did most of the tags reach up to the pillared heights of the letters *l* and *k*? A script rising upward in this fashion spoke of the writer's tendency toward dreaming and building castles in the sky. A stress on the lower area of the script, on the other hand, indicated that the smudger was prisoner to his urges and corporal desires. In this case, the writer's decisions were guided less by rational thought and more by impulse.

Vartia projected a few sample tags onto the wall. He revealed how much you could deduce from nothing more than the shape of the letter. Rounded letters hid within them a romantic dominated by sentimentality in graffiti as well as in life. Straight letters told of superior powers of concentration; these smudgers were more determined and stubborn, and often the leaders of smudger cells. A script that curved to the right told of an extroverted personality, to the left, of an introverted one. The most dangerous smudgers were those whose tags varied arbitrarily between right and left slants; this characteristic spoke of the tagger's chronic instability.

"Of course, we start from the presumption that all smudgers are unstable in comparison to regular citizens, like us, who put bread on the table through regular work," Vartia added. "But there are different levels of instability. With a little practice, every one of you will be able to distinguish five different categories of tag slants. Number five is like a red alert for the army: it signifies the tagger is exceptionally dangerous and has a heightened propensity for violence."

For three hours, Vartia taught us how to analyze tags. We learned, for instance, what the size of the tag said about the person who made it. The creator of small tags probably suffered from an inferiority complex; the creator of a very large tag, on the other hand, was domineering and self-centered by nature. If the basic line of the tag was an upward slant, the smudger was ambitious, and it was important to catch him as quickly as possible. A tag sagging down spoke of its creator's potential depressive tendencies. He would be relatively easy to catch and to call to account for his deeds. The bad part was that depressive smudgers often ended up in the mental health system, and in that sense, a burden on society for the rest of their lives.

"But that's not your problem," Vartia noted. "Your job is to catch them and bring them to justice."

The exact age of the tagger was hard to deduce based on the tag. But it was possible to establish sufficiently accurate age parameters based on those smudgers who had been caught. The core group fell between the ages of fifteen and twenty-five.

"There's only one thing about the smudger we can't definitively deduce based on the tag," Vartia stressed. "Gender. Don't let gender fool you. Even though female smudgers are in the minority, they vandalize public and private spaces with as much gusto as males. Women are often more ruthless, fanatical smudgers, as a matter of fact. You shouldn't allow yourself to feel any particular pity for them."

According to Vartia, there were two clear reasons to analyze tags. The first was the creator's psychological profile: for many smudgers, handwriting was the only unique identifier. The tag was the smudger's birthmark, or an unusual tattoo that could be used to pick him out of the crowd despite the hoodie he had pulled down over his face.

The second reason for the systematic analysis of tags was maximizing an individual tagger's liability. Vartia had developed a computer program with which he was able to analyze the thousands of tags he had photographed. The software compared tags' curves, loops, slants, lettering, and intersection of lines like fingerprints, and was able to link different signatures to a single creator.

"If you catch one smudger, with this software we can link him to hundreds of other smudges."

Vartia had testified in numerous graffiti trials around Finland and used the circumstantial evidence he produced to hold those caught for one-off tags accountable for damages amounting to hundreds of thousands of euros.

"All you have to do is catch one smudger," Vartia said. "Either he pays for everyone else, or he reveals who the other members of the cell are so the colossal damages are spread among the whole cell. Often a smudger who gets caught will choose the latter option and give up his partners. In my experience, the loyalty of smudgers under pressure is, on average, mediocre, leaning toward weak."

Vartia was a math teacher by profession. After the training, we had all gone to the bar at Seurahuone for a drink. Vartia tossed back pints twice as fast as the rest of us and persistently tried to get women to join him on the dance floor.

Raittila saw me notice Vartia's pint-downing and hookup attempts and told me that broken marriages and substance abuse were typical among middle-aged mathematicians. Many of them experienced the glory of early genius as a golden sunset of sorts before they reached the age of twenty. That's when they catch a fleeting glimpse of a vision in which the tiniest speck flying in the wind and every snowflake falling from the sky are seamlessly integrated into this ingenious mechanism called the world. It happens when they are sound asleep. This insight into how the relationships between everything in the world, great and small, can be contained in a single formula comes in a flash that lasts no longer than an agonizing blink of an eye. By the time they wake up in the morning they've forgotten the formula. The only thing rolling through their brains is fading mist, and they can never access it again. After years of frustration they start nitpicking and drinking too much and arguing with their loved ones.

"Mathematicians who are disappointed in themselves are perfect witnesses for us," Raittila concluded. "They justify their conclusions so unequivocally that in the end it's all the same to the judge if the conclusions are right or wrong. The judiciary loves logic above all else."

"Do you have other handwriting analysts you use?" I asked.

"Of course, if the court wants a second opinion," Raittila said before ordering another pint for Vartia and patting him on the shoulder.

I was startled out of my thoughts when Hiililuoma pushed me in the back so hard it hurt. He gestured toward the car, where Raittila was already sitting in the passenger seat. Hiililuoma climbed in behind the wheel; I had to get in the back.

The fog wrapped around us like a gray tarp.

I could sense Hiililuoma's and Raittila's unspoken reprimands: *You let a girl beat you.*

I rubbed my eyes.

The car radio was playing faintly—many minutes of screeching, jangling glockenspiel and mechanical whirring, which the host eventually announced in his low, velvety voice was one of his all-time favorite pieces of modern music. "And here's another minor masterwork for the city and for the night," he crooned. The car filled with an out-of-tune, flutelike blowing and the clacking of castanets. I wasn't surprised that the station had scheduled him and his favorites to the slot when 99.99 percent of Finns were asleep.

"You mind changing the station?" I asked from the backseat.

"Yes. This will keep us awake," Raittila answered.

"What do we do now?"

"I have some nets in the water," Raittila answered. "Don't worry. This is almost over. But the last bit is completely up to you."

METRO

All I wanted to do was fall asleep. Instead I listened to the creaking of the metal roof, wondering why Baron had betrayed me.

I had caught the scent of his heavy musk wafting in under the bathroom door. Right before the door was bashed in. He'd known where I was staying in Karhuvuori and he'd led the Rats to my apartment. I had been right. Someone had been lurking in my apartment when I came home from my run. When I called him in the middle of the night, Baron reluctantly took me to the vacant apartment, though the whole time he wanted me to return to Terror Hill. To return to my apartment, into the grip of the Rats.

The supposed safe house had offered me only a moment's respite. Baron had let the Rats enter in the middle of the night so they could catch me. If I hadn't woken up at the time I normally did to deliver papers and stumbled into the shower, they would have caught me fast asleep. The way it went down I barely got away.

There in the sleeping bag, I moved my leg and grimaced as the pain shot up my thigh. I couldn't turn my head properly.

Now the Rats knew everything about me. They knew where I lived. They knew what I had done. I was sure Baron had told them I had painted Jere the Rat's car, and his house, twice. The first time, Baron had been in the car watching.

Not that it mattered. In Finland it didn't make a crap's worth of difference if you got caught in the act or not. Handwriting analysts bribed by the Rats participated in the hunt for graffiti artists. They would testify that a single graffiti artist's marks could be found in four hundred spots, even if the tags were totally different from each other. When you got caught for one work, you were forced to pay up retroactively for everything that the handwriting analysts said you had done. Regardless of whether or not you had bombed there.

Rust had said things were different in Germany. In Berlin, you only paid damages for the piece you got caught making. They didn't hang past paintings around your neck. The first graffiti writer to use a fire extinguisher was Just, from Berlin. He had been so stoked about his innovation that for the next two and a half weeks he sprayed his name on dozens of buildings in letters several meters high. On the eighteenth day, he was caught in the act. Just was only sentenced to pay damages for his most recent tag. He didn't have to pay for all the other ones, even though they all read JUST in letters three stories tall.

It's so funny that people claimed Germany was still a Nazi police state where citizens didn't have rights. Berlin was heaven for street artists. But I was stuck in Kotka.

If I went back to my place I'd get caught. I'd be slapped with six-figure damages that I'd never be able to pay off, even if I lived to the age of ninety-six, like my great-grandma. Well, first they'd beat me. Then the Rats probably would throw me down from somewhere really fucking high. Leave me on the train tracks. Drown me in steaming tar. Maybe I wouldn't have to worry about paying the damages, after all. I wouldn't be alive.

Dreaming about getting into university would be totally pointless. Or getting a job around here. In Finland, a black person convicted of doing graffiti is a less desirable colleague than a white-skinned rapist.

You could fill the city with huge advertising banners and billboards, but one single tag was too much. They called it a misuse of public space because street art was not under the control of corporations. More severe punishments were handed down for graffiti than for speeding through a crosswalk and hitting a kid.

I hated Jere Kalliola more than ever. He had ruined my life when he took Rust's. My eyes were watering. I convinced myself that it was because of a broken tailbone.

My thoughts wandered to Banksy, the world's most famous street artist. On a trip to Israel he painted an escape hatch on the West Bank barrier. A single one of his works was worth hundreds of thousands of euros. These days, if you had the balls to remove a Banksy from a wall you'd be the one who ended up in jail.

No one knew who Banksy was except for his friends. He had been able to rely on his friends throughout his career; they had been solid as a rock. His friends had never betrayed him, even though they had been promised stacks of cash, free flights, homes, bars of gold.

Who did I have? Baron. I wondered what he received for betraying me. A pine-tree air freshener and fuzzy dice for his company car is probably all it took.

One time in Bristol, Rats forced Banksy to run in a rail yard. He hid under a train for a long time in the middle of the night and while he was lying there, he studied the stenciled letters on the bottom of the car and decided that he was going to switch to stenciling so he could work more quickly on site. There's a mathematical graffiti formula: after five minutes, every extra minute at the site you're painting doubles your risk of getting caught. If you have a stencil, you can spend hours working out a piece at home instead of a few hurried minutes. Once you've finalized your vision you cut the work out of the paper and then just spray it on a wall outside. You can think about and prepare the pieces a hell of a lot more carefully.

One of Banksy's most famous stencils is of a little girl hugging a big bomb. It has spread around the world on T-shirts, postcards, and posters. A poster of *Bomb Hugger* hung in my place; it had been Rust's. Banksy painted the original in London, on a wall in the East End. Some money-grubbing shit scraped off the entire square meter of wall and sold it at Sotheby's, earning himself a house.

I'm the little girl hugging the bomb. Graffiti is my bomb, the bomb I detonate.

Rust had interpreted the image a little differently. He had claimed that the image symbolized that love can vanquish even the world's most heinous evil. Good always wins over evil, if good can just stand to be good even when it takes a boot to the head.

Rust was an example of what happens to good people in this Rat-run world.

If I stayed in place, I would die. Standing still is a death sentence. Rabbits learn that when they stop to stare at approaching headlights. Cars are greedy foxes that hunt at night.

I couldn't let myself fall asleep. I couldn't. I couldn't.

I shuddered and winced. Someone had tied me up; I couldn't move my hands. I couldn't see anything; they had put a hood over my head, like at Guantánamo.

I finally realized I was flailing around in the sleeping bag.

I turned and yelped. My ribs hurt so badly I couldn't even touch them. But at least the pain cleared my fog-clogged thoughts.

I had to get out of there.

I worked my way out of the sleeping bag. I opened the lid of the desk. We kept pencils and paper in there. I wrote two words.

I left the sleeping bag and hobbled across the attic. I wouldn't be able to make it far. My phone showed that it was a little past four; my battery was almost dead. My breath was steaming; I tried the doors of chicken-coop closets overflowing with stuff. They were locked except for the farthest one.

I slipped into the empty storage closet; the neighboring closet was packed with stuff: a sled and a pair of skis and stacks of cardboard boxes. There was a small gap where the ceiling sloped above the bulging mesh wall; it was big enough for me to squirm between the storage spaces.

I couldn't jump with my wounded leg. I pulled myself up the mesh wall and slid across sideways. A nail sticking down from the ceiling ripped open the back of my coat.

Coming down on the other side was easier than climbing up. The stacks of cardboard boxes were like stairs. I descended into the storage space. At the back, there were chairs heaped on top of each other and another piece of furniture that had caught my eye. A tall-sided crib the color of Swiss cheese. You couldn't see the crib from the door; the cardboard boxes and an old pram were in the way. Two pairs of ice skates hung from a nail knocked into a nearby crossbeam.

I had to raid a few of the cardboard boxes before I found some old clothes. I curled up in a heap at the bottom of the crib and covered myself with summery clothes and flowered curtains.

According to my phone, I had only slept for a minute before the Rats stormed the attic.

JERE

Raittila's phone came to life; the ringtone sounded like the blaring of an old-fashioned alarm clock, the kind that had woken me up during my childhood from two rooms away, where it had been rattling on my dad's nightstand.

Raittila exchanged a few words and then ordered Hiililuoma to drive to Hovinsaari.

"Is that where she is?" I asked.

"That's where she is."

Hiililuoma drove along the harbor. The fog was still hanging heavily and the harbor cranes looming through it looked like giraffes grazing on a nocturnal savanna.

"I should be with Mirjami," I said.

"They're not going to let you into the hospital this late," Raittila said. "Go at breakfast for coffee and sweet rolls. I'll come with you."

Hiililuoma cleared his throat. "I'm sorry about what happened to Mirjami."

"It's not your fault. Luckily she just hit her head."

We cruised along next to the bridge crossing the rail yard. One winter night I had been patrolling this area with Hiililuoma and a small white creature had suddenly appeared, darting in and out of the cracks so insanely fast it looked like it had seven siblings.

"You remember that ermine?" I asked.

"I thought I was seeing things," Hiililuoma answered.

For the first time in a long time, I felt a sense of brotherhood with him. It wasn't Hiililuoma's fault that he had been promoted. He probably had more nightmares than I did. Raittila started humming some tango that would have been more suitable for midsummer, and Hiililuoma slowly steered the car across Kivisalmi Bridge. We were driving across the cold world in a warm, motorized, three-man cocoon. I could only see about fifty feet down the road.

"You just have to trust that the road keeps going. Even if you can't see it," I said.

"Kalliola has hidden talents," Raittila said.

His tone wasn't mocking, it was encouraging, like my junior-high math teacher the time I got an A- on a test instead of the normal C-.

"What talents?" Hiililuoma asked.

"Philosophizing," Raittila said.

Hiililuoma grunted and nodded.

"You guys are so great," I said.

"All for one and one for all," Raittila replied. "It's the individualists of the world who end up shoveling the shit with a pitchfork."

He indicated a right turn to Hiililuoma as we passed a yellow art-nouveau building, gesturing for him to slow down. The drive would last a few more quiet moments. I had put on a dry shirt I found in the trunk; there weren't any extra pants. The legs and the ass of the pair I had on were wet from my wrestling match in the shower. I was sitting on a newspaper so the backseat wouldn't get wet. Raittila pressed his nose to the window and checked out the house numbers. He raised a hand, signaling for Hiililuoma to stop.

We waited silently in the car until a hooded ghost emerged from the fog and stepped out in front of the car.

Raittila told me to open the back door. A young guy climbed in next to me, rubbing his hands. I pulled the hood back from his head.

"This here is Ismo," Raittila said.

"Jack," Ismo said, staring at his feet.

"Ismo has a pretend name, Jack. Ismo thinks Ismo is a good man. But his bad half, Jack, likes to smudge around town."

"Not anymore."

"I've promised Ismo amnesty on our behalf if he helps us catch the person who smudged your house and car," Raittila said.

Ismo edged away when I turned to glare at him.

"I didn't mess with your property," he quickly reassured me. "I didn't have anything to do with it."

"Who did?" I asked.

"Metro."

"Who the fuck is Metro?"

"I don't know her real name."

"The black girl?"

"Yup."

"I was given that same name by another smudger who goes by Baron," Raittila interjected. "But reluctantly and only after I exerted relatively strenuous pressure."

"What's Metro's real name?"

"I don't know."

I slapped Ismo across the face.

"I really don't know," Ismo sniveled. "I only know her as Metro. Rust called her Metro, too."

"Who's Rust?"

"The smudger who fell from the roof of the Maritime Museum," Raittila said.

I thought for a minute. Did these smudger-scum think they were goddamn Brazilian soccer players or something, using pseudonyms? That was an offense to the Brazilians as a nation, soccer as a sport, and me as a human being.

"Where's Metro?" I asked, my lips right against Ismo's ear.

He raised a hand to his temple.

"Where?"

"In the attic," Ismo said. "I'll take you there. You don't have to shout."

Ismo led us into a building that vanished into the fog two floors up. Hiililuoma kept the door from clicking shut. Ismo was about to call the elevator, but Raittila's hand stopped him before he pressed the button.

"Let's go as quietly as possible, shall we?" he said.

Ismo climbed up first; I followed right on his heels, flashlight in hand so I'd be ready if he tried to pull anything. I didn't trust the kid; his eyes kept shifting from face to face. Up at the top landing we came to a gray metal door. I took the key from Ismo and softly cracked the door. Luckily the hinges didn't squeak. Ismo pointed right. I pushed him in front of me and followed him into the space, which was broken up by support beams. The narrow horizontal windows formed dim, clay-gray stripes. It was too dark for me to notice the hunk of metal on the floor, and I banged my leg on it. I had the urge to scream but I bit my lip. I lit the flashlight through my shirt for a second and checked what I had bumped into. A rusty two-sink drainboard. A little way ahead, the side of a fridge gleamed. Someone was using the attic as a landfill.

Ismo pointed into the corner behind a stack of cots. I had my telescoping baton in one hand, my flashlight in the other. I flicked it on. I took the final steps at a run. This time the Bacteria wasn't going to slip away.

The beam of the flashlight landed on a rumpled sleeping bag. A piece of paper had been left on the hood. It read: LATERZ. METRO

"For fuck's sake," I hissed.

I would have whacked Ismo with my baton and pepper-sprayed him if Raittila hadn't stepped in and pushed me onto a ratty old sofa.

"I didn't tell her. I didn't," Ismo said over and over.

Hiililuoma twisted his ear and gave him a solid punch to the gut. It had no effect on Ismo; he kept jabbering like a madman that he didn't know and didn't understand.

"Ismo doesn't know," Raittila said.

He was half lying on top of me, twisting my arm behind my back so hard my elbow ached.

"Let me go," I mumbled.

"I will if you promise to stay calm."

"Yeah, yeah, goddammit."

"Say it."

"I'll stay calm."

Raittila let me up and sat Ismo down on the lumpy sofa. The three of us stood there in front of him.

"Ismo, we're tired of this chase," Raittila said. "Now tell us where Metro is, or I'm going to head out of here and leave you to the boys."

"I don't know," Ismo insisted, his lip quivering.

"The girl won't make it far out there alone," Raittila said to me and Hiililuoma as Ismo shook his head. "We have one man waiting for her at Karhuvuori if she goes back there. Where else could she have gone?"

"Baron's place?" I suggested.

"We'd hear about it right away," Raittila said. "Baron has a direct line to me. Who else?"

"Smew," Ismo said faintly from the sofa.

"Who the hell is Smew?" I growled. "Some fucking bird?"

"It has to be Smew," Ismo said.

Raittila went over and quizzed Ismo on Smew's appearance and address. I didn't hear either one properly because I received a text message from Mirjami's mother:

WHERE ARE YOU? WE NEED YOU HERE. MIRJAMI LOST THE BABY.

METRO

I waited a second after the Rats had left, then I climbed out of the locked storage closet. The same nail scraped the back of my coat again. I had just made it over to the empty chicken coop when the door clicked again. I crouched down. Only one person entered.

It was Jack.

He headed to the furthest corner behind the heap of rusty cots; he left the heavy metal door cracked open. The lights in the stairwell went out.

I crept over to Jack. He was hunched over by the desk, using the light of his cell phone as he rolled up the sleeping bag I had left. I clubbed him on the back of the head with the jar of pickles he had brought up from the basement. The jar shattered, and my hand was drenched in the decades-old seasoned brine. The past smelled rotten.

I tugged the sleeping bag up around Jack's limp body and waited for him to wake up. For a second I was afraid I had hit him too hard; he was just lying there like a dead fish, with the dark splotch under his head spreading across the sofa.

Gradually Jack came to. He couldn't move his hands; I had cinched dozens of loops of rusty iron wire around the sleeping bag, wrapping him up like a baby. I had shut the attic door and brought over one of the ice skates from the storage closet where I had hidden; I pressed the blade against his windpipe.

"You goddamn traitor," I said.

Jack didn't reply. His eyes were still jittery. Blood had congealed at the top of his head, and shards of glass glistened in his puffy hair as if someone had sprayed it with glitter.

"I don't have anything to lose," I hissed. "I'll be happy to go to prison for killing the asshole traitor who gave me up."

"Take it easy."

"I thought Baron was the traitor, but it was you, after all."

"Baron betrayed you, too," Jack grumbled.

"And Smew?"

"Smew doesn't know anything."

"Yeah, right."

"He doesn't."

Jack tried to roll over. I knelt on his chest so he'd stay still. He stopped wriggling when the blade of the skate grazed the side of his neck.

"Hey, take it easy with that."

"Are you the one who told them Rust and I would be painting down at the tracks?" I asked.

"Does it really matter who did it?"

"It was you." I spit in his face. "You never came to see me after Rust died. Baron did. You didn't have the guts. You were too ashamed, you Rat whore."

"I never wanted Rust to die," Jack blurted out. "Believe me."

"Why did you tell the Rats?"

Jack glared at me with hostile eyes before he said, "I just tape walls. I don't want to go to jail for stuff you did."

"Stuff I did?"

"You've gotten way out of hand."

"I'm the one who caused this mess?"

"Everything was totally fucking fine before you showed up," Jack said in a more irritated voice. "Rust went crazy over you. He started taking too many risks. He never painted trains until you showed up. He was just trying to impress you. Before that, he used to go around to abandoned buildings with us. Painted in places the Rats didn't patrol."

"I loved Rust," I wailed.

"I've known Rust since first grade," Jack snapped. "I knew him a hell of a lot better than you did. He spent time with us before he met you. You ruined him. You broke up our gang."

"I didn't ruin anyone."

"Yeah, of course not. You just radiate that black light of yours and imagine it brings sunshine to people's lives. But all you really do is drag everyone around you deeper and deeper into the shit. Like Baron."

"What did you say?"

I pressed my knee into Jack's chest, fighting the urge to punch the skate into his jugular. That would serve him right.

"Baron is totally screwed because of the damages he's supposed to pay in Sweden from the days he used to paint there," Jack gasped. "He owes tens of thousands to some loan sharks in Stockholm. He's working here under a fake name. If anyone finds out his real identity he'll lose his job. The people he owes money to will be on his ass, too. See, Sun Queen, more than anything he wants to keep his job and stay out of trouble. Forget his former life. He wants exactly what you hate. He wants to live in a house in the suburbs, he wants to have a little yard and a trampoline and two kids and a leather sofa and a sauna that he heats up every evening, and he wants to be able to put a satellite dish up on the roof and watch three soccer matches back-to-back on weekends from that leather sofa and kick the ball around with his son in the yard. He doesn't want to be some shitty little rebel who runs around all night being hunted by the authorities. You dragged Rust into your personal revolution, and after that you dragged Baron in. You should have seen the relief on Baron's face when he gave the Rats the keys to the place you were staying. Once you're out of the picture we can all go back to living in peace."

Jack stopped talking, his Adam's apple pumped furiously against the blade of the skate. Just a tiny thrust was all it would take to rid myself of this traitor.

"They promised me a job," he croaked.

"As a Rat?"

"They're not Rats, they're security officers."

"You've got to be fucking kidding me. You're already working for them. You make extra for overtime tonight?"

"Hey, I'm prepared to do just about anything to get out of this shit hole I've lived in my whole life. It's not going to happen painting trains and bombing walls. Once you're poor, you're always poor. It's a longer journey from here to a house in Mussalo than it is from Porvoo to Peking, goddammit."

"Is that how Smew thinks, too?"

"Smew left half his brains at the bottom of that lake. He's happy photographing the world crumbling around him and living off his mom for the rest of his fucking life, waiting in breadlines for cans of tuna fish. He doesn't want to own anything. No one who hasn't drowned in a muddy pond at least once in his lifetime thinks the way he does."

"I do."

"You're a special case. It's patently obvious. Congratulations. I'd clap if I could."

I couldn't stand the malicious glint in Jack's eyes so I whacked him with the skate. To my credit it wasn't with the blade to his throat, but the boot to his temple. He didn't lose his life, but he did lose consciousness.

I loosened the coils of iron wire from around Jack's limp body and pulled his cell phone out of his pocket. In his other pocket I found the key to his 125cc. I packed Jack back up into his down bag and pulled the iron wire around him as tightly as I could. Maybe they'd find his mummified body twenty years from now in the corner of the attic. I went down to the courtyard without encountering any signs of life except the aroma of coffee wafting out from one mail slot. The fog had lifted, but the sun hadn't come up yet. It just coming up on five. This night from hell had lasted longer than the whole entire month leading up to it.

I started up Jack's moped and cruised back to Kotkansaari along the back roads past the sugar factory. I had no desire to be a candy inventor anymore. The sea surged to my right; in the lights of Hirssaari opposite, the estuary looked like molten copper that would swallow anyone who dared dip in their toes.

I rode past the place where the Russian truck drivers would lay over; four of them were camping there tonight. In the winter, the truck drivers fished on the ice of the nearby bay; they would keep fishing on the year's last, crisp, bread-thin ice at the Mussalo Bridge long after the locals had switched to boats. Once I talked to one who spoke a little English. He didn't think fishing on melting ice was especially risky. Near his home in Russia, in an inlet of the Gulf of Finland, men would be fishing for almost a month still; sometimes they ended up drifting for days on big ice floes. They just had to remember to bring along an extra bottle of vodka as a first aid kit and they'd be fine. As the raft shrank, the group would huddle closer; they kept each other plenty warm. Then a helicopter would appear on the horizon at the last minute to pluck them to safety. Usually. The last time, a few had been forced to swim home. The Russian had wrapped up his story with a hoarse laugh.

I couldn't take sitting on the seat; I just stood on the pedals. It was tough on the pitted dirt road; every time I hit a bump, it felt like someone was slamming me in the ass with a sledgehammer. When I reached the end of Via Dolorosa I shoved the bike into a stand of willows sprouting out of the wasteland. Pallets, a couple of honey buckets, and a pyramid of dead batteries had been left next to the bushes. The bakers were hard at work at the Vaasa Mills bakery; the smell of fresh sweet rolls condensed around me more heavily than last night's fog. I hadn't eaten anything in almost twenty-four hours.

Limping up from the shore I approached the familiar warehouse. It was dark, and there weren't any cars parked outside the neighboring corrugated-metal building. The hoarders of stolen goods were snoring away under their warm quilts, dreaming of new investment opportunities and schemes for accumulating wealth. Unlike me.

The nearby Hankkija silo seemed like the only friend in my life whose foundations hadn't given way.

I slipped into the warehouse from the unlocked side window and found what I was looking for.

With my fucked-up leg and aching arms it took me a long time to reach the catwalk fifteen feet up. Once my fingers stopped trembling I searched Jack's phone for Olavi Raittila's phone number and sent him a text message. I closed my eyes. The ibuprofen was starting to wear off, and the throbbing pain in the sole of my foot was getting worse and worse. I counted the throbs; I almost made it to two hundred before the reply from Raittila beeped on Jack's phone: *OK.*

I smashed Jack's SIM card and then the entire phone with a huge rusty bolt. Then I rolled onto my stomach and started counting the throbs again, starting from zero. If I made it to a thousand before they got here, they were slower than I imagined.

JERE

According to the information we had wrung out of Ismo, Smew lived in Metsola. The main thing I remembered from his litany was that Smew lived with his mom, just like Ismo. All of these goddamn smudger-scum were fatherless. That's one thing I was going to make sure never happened to Ville.

Before we left the attic, Raittila made Ismo swear that he would not say anything about what had just happened. We hadn't been to see him, and neither had Metro. If he said anything about that night's events, Raittila would nail the kid for smudging and heap millions of euros in damages on his bony shoulders.

The mood during the ride to Metsola was totally different from the mood when we had arrived in Hovinsaari. It felt like there was an extra passenger in the car: Mirjami.

Hiililuoma drove slowly past the wooden houses; the yards here were a lot bigger than in Mussalo and were dotted with berry bushes and fruit trees. Garden swings continued to defy the snow.

I was all for ringing the doorbell once we got to Smew's place, but Raittila told me to cool down. It wasn't even five in the morning yet.

"The best alternative would be to wait until later," Raittila suggested.

"I'm not waiting anymore," I said.

"I understand that. So we'll go with the second-best alternative."

I had shown the text message from Mirjami's mother to Raittila and Hiililuoma back in the attic as soon as I got it. They hadn't had a lot to add. Raittila had muttered, *Oh shit.* Then he had cleared his throat and apologized *with all his heart.*

Through the gauze of mist, we staked out the small wooden house where Smew lived with his mother. Three leafless apple trees dominated the sloping yard. Surrounded by fog and the skeletons of trees, the house looked more like a witch's cottage than the sky-blue idyll the stammering Ismo had described in the attic.

Raittila tapped at his phone and told the person who answered to call Smew now, *I repeat NOW*, and tell him it was an emergency and to come out to the black car waiting in front of the house immediately, *I repeat IMMEDIATELY*. They'd be driving on from there. It was about Metro, she had ended up in serious trouble, *I repeat SERIOUS trouble*, and only Smew could help.

"Who did you call?" I asked after Raittila hung up.

"Baron. He can act as Smew's deke."

"Deke?"

"Decoy. The wooden duck that lures his pals over into the range of the hunters' shotguns."

"I don't know much about duck hunting," I said.

"You'll learn today."

We had to wait about ten minutes. Then the door to the wooden house opened and a young man in a baggy coat slipped out. He straightened up on the stairs when he heard a dog bark. The kid was actually a lot taller than he seemed at first. He kept walking at an odd slouch; his back was as hunched as a professional beggar's.

I had climbed out of the car right after Raittila's phone call and was now following his progress. The kid glanced in the direction of the Toyota when Hiililuoma flicked the lights on and off. Raittila reached back to open the back door as Smew approached the car.

I bolted out from under the gnarled branches of the apple tree. Smew managed to turn halfway around before I whacked him. Hiililuoma climbed out to open up the trunk. I held on to the limply twitching kid while Hiililuoma drew duct tape across his mouth; Hiililuoma used the same roll to tape his hands behind his back, and then his legs.

We had pulled on ski masks so the kid wouldn't be able to ID us. We lifted him into the trunk and I slammed it shut. I glanced back at the wooden house. No lights had come on inside. Mom was fast asleep, like Sleeping Beauty.

I climbed in on the passenger side, and Raittila, who had scooted over into the driver's seat, started up the Toyota. Hiililuoma didn't climb in; he was going to hang out by the house until he got a message from either me or Raittila. It was possible that Metro was either a) in the house at the moment or b) on her way there. Until we got the facts out of Smew we had to make sure we covered every possible scenario.

We had decided to take Smew to Jylppy, where among the car lots there was a cluster of industrial halls and warehouses that we patrolled. They were ideal spots for interrogation. Plus, the industrial area was close to Smew's house. If Metro appeared there we'd have no trouble getting back quickly.

We had already passed the water tower when Raittila's phone beeped.

"Hiililuoma?" I asked. "Did the girl show up?"

"No," Raittila said thoughtfully. "It's from that kid from Hovinsaari. Ismo. The message says where Metro will be at six."

Raittila handed the phone to me and turned around at the next intersection. Instead of Jylppy, we headed to Kotkansaari. We passed the soccer pitch, home field of the local pride and joy, the Kotka Workers Football Club—a team originally scraped together from the longshoremen's one-room flats. Over the generations, the players had grown skilled in techniques other than the ruthless slide tackle that had been the longshoremen's forte. But during games, the visiting team was still directed to the girls' dressing room, as decades of tradition dictated.

We drove past the outdoor swimming pool and skirted Tupakkavuori Hill. Raittila turned right, heading downhill on a rain-gouged dirt road that I didn't remember ever having been on. A brick smokestack rose to the left; according to the rusty sign, it belonged to a smokehouse. We continued up to two warehouses with sloped roofs.

"It's around here somewhere. There should be a green letter *A* on the door," Raittila said.

I circled the warehouses on foot. Rusty beams jutted up between them at overlapping intervals; to me they looked like antitank barriers from the war. Two cylinders rose in the background like the towers of a castle. Near them I found a long building marked with the *A*. The metal door was closed with a fat crossbar and a heavy padlock. I went back to tell Raittila; he brought the car around.

"We still have over half an hour," Raittila said, glancing at his watch. "Let's take the kid out. Then I'll park the car off a little farther."

I opened the trunk and yanked Smew out onto the gravel. He whimpered; I pulled the tape off his mouth and the whimper intensified into whining.

"If you don't shut your mouth this instant, I'm going to fill it with this fist," I said slowly.

I didn't have to repeat myself.

I cut the duct tape from around his legs with my knife, though I left his hands taped.

"You know this place?" I asked.

Smew nodded.

"Is this your hbme base?"

Another nod.

"Goddamn terrorists. How do we get in there?"

"The window," Smew mumbled.

I let him lead the way. I kept a firm grip on his shoulder to keep him from running away. After a few steps I realized that this was a pointless measure. Smew's legs had fallen asleep in the trunk; he was lucky he could even walk. He stopped at a small rectangular window that was six feet off the ground.

"How the fuck do you get up there?" I asked.

"We're all able to."

"Why doesn't one of you just go in and open the door?"

"It's not our lock."

"Of course not. So you break in every time. That's a lot more natural for you than using a key."

When Raittila got back, I turned Smew over to him and climbed in through the window. The Bacteria had brought over a portable grill someone had left behind in the wasteland and used it boost themselves up and into the warehouse. The window had been left unlatched from the inside, and I was able to push open the pane.

The only way I could fit was by aiming my arms through first in a diving position. I couldn't see how long a drop it was to the floor; probably the same six-foot drop as on the outside. I could make out a few broken windows along the upper edge of the wall, but the dawn hadn't penetrated the darkness yet. Inside or outside.

I prepared to fall hands first and roll to the floor ukemi-style but my hands struck raw lumber almost immediately. I felt around. Wooden pallets had been stacked under the window so entering didn't demand a leap into the depths.

As soon as I made it down, I turned on my flashlight, sweeping the beam across the interior of the warehouse. It was empty. There were more loose pallets strewn across the floor, as well as some torn cardboard boxes. A bonfire had been lit in the middle of the floor at some point; smashed beer cans were among the ashes.

"Just a second," I called out the end window.

At the far end of the warehouse I spotted an alcove where there was a lump that looked like a hunched-over person. I headed toward it. Something pale fluttered in the glare of my flashlight for a second, then disappeared. The hairs on the back of my neck immediately stood up. I kept moving, ready to pounce and defend myself.

The first thing I noticed was the interior wall. It wasn't standing; it was toppled over. The window frame was lying against the floor of the warehouse.

I aimed the flashlight into the depths of the alcove. An empty room flickered in the beam of light, as did a couple of other plywood walls that had tumbled to the floor. The big lump turned out to be a bathtub.

I shined the flashlight around the alcove. No one. A coatrack was screwed to the one wall that was still standing; there was nothing hanging from it. The only thing left of the bed was a split mattress showing off its springs.

The white creature I had already encountered once was moving at the fringes of the beam of light. I dodged and prepared to strike. The flashlight landed on a picture of a woman with big boobs. Like almost everything else in here it was falling off the wall. The draft coming in through the broken windows set the paper fluttering, making the woman toss her hips like a belly dancer.

I stepped closer to the tub. There was still a faucet at one end with separate taps for hot and cold. Out of curiosity I twisted both of them. To my surprise, water started flowing into the tub, but just cold water.

I went back to explain to Raittila how to enter. I helped haul in Smew; Raittila pushed himself in right after.

I taped Smew's mouth again and shoved him into the tub. He shook his head wildly. I made him swear to be still and stay quiet.

Raittila went over to wait under the window at the end. I stayed next to the tub.

The clock advanced painfully slowly. My wet clothes were making me cold; I did squats to stay warm.

No one had shown up at the warehouse by six. From the far end of the warehouse, Raittila signaled ten more minutes.

Smew whimpered something; I slapped him on the head. He ought to be happy, getting to spend quality time in the tub.

The only time I had used a tub was on our honeymoon. During our week on Santorini Mirjami and I had stayed in a two-room suite with a spacious bathroom, and from the broad balcony we could admire the turquoise sea and the caldera down below—the deep, underwater crater that a volcanic explosion from thousands of years ago had left behind. Every night we filled the tub and sat in it drinking the local white wine; it tasted of ash and was so cold it tingled. Sometimes we fed each other cherries; we'd spit the pits out the window.

Back then we didn't have our own house. Or Ville. On those evenings in the tub, we'd plan our future. We decided that we'd try for two children, a girl and a boy, and I secretly hoped that the first one would be a boy. We also decided that we'd come back to this hotel regularly, and the next visit would be at the latest three years from our honeymoon; we'd come to the same suite, splash around in the same tub, and we'd eat dark, juicy cherries and toast and savor each other and our happiness. There wasn't a couple in the world happier than we were.

We still hadn't gone back to Santorini, and it was seven years since our honeymoon. We did have our own house. And a son. The girl had been on the way. According to the ultrasounds, it had been a girl.

I bit my lip. I thought about Mirjami, pale in the hospital with the dead baby inside her. I thought about my vandalized home. Before Metro came along, our plans had been going exactly the way we had envisioned in the tub in Santorini. One filthy Bacteria hadn't just made a mess of our walls, she had messed up our entire lives.

***

At a quarter to seven it was clear to me that Metro wasn't going to show. I was freezing in spite of my calisthenics, and my fingers ached when I bent them. Raittila suggested we wait half an hour longer.

I was done waiting.

I was sure that Smew could lead us to Metro. Interrogating him had been our original plan. I brought my face up to Smew, who was staring out of the tub with glazed eyes, and asked him if he understood everything I said. Smew nodded.

"There are only two things that I want to know. I could give a crap about what you've done. A flying fucking crap. Now we're not talking about you, we're talking about Metro. If you answer my two questions, you'll walk out of here a free man, and you can forget that we even exist. You can go to sleep, you can sleep all day long, you can skip the whole day. Two questions, two answers. Then we're done. Do you understand what I just said?"

Smew moved his head. I interpreted it as another nod.

"First question: What is Metro's real name? Second question: Where is Metro?"

I pulled back the tape from Smew's mouth.

"I don't know Metro's real name. No one does."

"That's a hell of a bad answer," I said.

I jammed the plug in the tub and turned the water on. Smew flailed and tried to get out. I yanked his legs over the sides so his head slid down to the bottom.

"No water," he begged.

"You smell like you could use a bath."

I turned on the tap. The water rushed into the tub. Smew whimpered and tried to get up, his hands were taped behind his back and he could only push himself with his shoulders.

I turned off the water for a second.

"First question: What's Metro's real name?"

"I don't know, goddammit. I don't know. I don't, goddammit."

"I don't believe you."

I turned the torrent of water back on. When the water got up to Smew's earlobes he started thrashing around like he was having an epileptic seizure. I pressed both of his shoulders down with my hands.

"Second question: Where's Metro?"

"I don't know. I slept at home. There's no way I could know. I haven't seen her in days."

"Where's Metro?"

"Let me out of here."

Water splashed into Smew's mouth, and that's when he completely freaked out. I pushed his head underwater so he'd calm down. He tried to kick me, but all his wriggling did was sink him deeper into the tub. I locked him sideways at the bottom with his legs bent up against his chest. He wasn't able to move. I turned off the water. He gasped for breath.

"What's Metro's real name?"

"Viivi! I don't know. Siru! Taru! I heard it once. Give me a second and I'll remember it."

"You're full of shit. You're going to tell me Metro's real name now, or you're going to drown. If you tell me the wrong name you're going to drown."

"Let me out of here," Smew cried. "I can't think."

"Where's Metro?"

"Let me go."

"Tell me first. Where's Metro? What's Metro's real name?"

I turned the water on full blast. Raittila had appeared behind me; I asked if Metro had shown up yet. He shook his head. Smew was almost totally under the surface; his left shoulder was the only visible part of him, sticking out of the water like a solitary gray rock. I yanked Smew's head out so we could see him.

"Where's Metro? What's Metro's real name?"

"Dad, don't drown me. Don't drown me, Dad," he begged, retching.

I was so fucking fed up with people who couldn't give simple answers to simple questions. I pressed the kid's head under the surface.

I heard a faint rattling overhead as the wind whirled across the metal roof. I watched the bursts of bubbles spill from Smew's mouth and waited for them to die out. He didn't know what drowning was yet; maybe he'd give me a proper answer if he drowned once in his life.

A few more bubbles. One more. Now they stopped.

Then an incredible pain struck me from behind. It felt like I was being torn in two.

METRO

I was watching from the catwalk as the Rat wriggled through the little window and into the warehouse. The light from his flashlight meandered along the walls. I was lying silently on top of a blanket. The dark blanket would prevent the Rat from seeing me, even if he happened to turn the flashlight upward for a second. The light explored the walls, painted its yellowish, squiggling graffiti, and then turned back to the floor.

The Rat announced in a loud voice, "Just a second."

I heard him cross the warehouse.

So there was one more outside. At least one more.

The Rat headed for the windowless end of the space. He turned on the tap and muttered to himself. I peered over the edge of the blanket. He was bending over the tub.

Before long, the Rat walked back across the warehouse, and the next one crawled in. The Rat gave the newcomer a hand. And then a third figure dove in through the window. After dusting off his clothes he made his way over to the long wall, to the locked door, and flicked the switch. The lights didn't come on; I had removed the fuse. The beams of the flashlights danced around and then came together.

I could see that one of the people was Smew. He was holding his hands at this weird low angle the whole time. They shoved him into the tub. One of the Rats went back over to the window; the other one stayed with Smew.

The Rats were wearing ski masks so I couldn't ID them. The flashlights went out. It was quiet; the only thing I could hear was the occasional clank from the tub.

Smew's arrival was a complete surprise to me. I didn't know what to make of it. My head was buzzing like a beehive. Had Smew betrayed me, too? But he couldn't have been the one to lead the Rats here because I had lured them with Jack's phone.

A faint cough carried up from below. The Rat at the tub was huffing; I could see from above how he spun his arms and did squats over and over.

I counted to a hundred. I counted again.

I had to pee.

I stayed there with my cheek against the blanket, looking at the gloom-darkened wall opposite. I imagined the 360-degree mural I had dreamed of painting with Rust: the city of Kotka through a seagull's eyes. We would have created a panorama of the city as seen from high above the rooftops and smokestacks, over the market square. On the left, on the long wall, you'd catch the tip of the gliding gull's wing, the other one on the far wall.

This piece was the only one that Rust had planned several versions of on paper; normally he didn't want to leave any plans of his works for the Rats to find. The sea and the sky would have encircled the island of downtown. At the end of the warehouse, above the tub, we would have painted the old water tower, which looked like a lighthouse; from the top of it you could see the hills of Suursaari Island, which now belonged to Russia.

If you continued on into the gleaming horizon, you'd be able to go all the way to, say, Buenos Aires. Across the very water that splashed up along the shores of Kotkansaari, the water we had rowed across that night with cans of spray paint in our bags.

We had planned on painting the panorama next spring, as soon as the weather warmed up.

I could hear rapid steps below. The Rats conferred briefly, then went back to their stations. The Rat lurking at the tub did more and more squats, jumped in place, shook his arms. He really was cold. I was relatively warm up above in the clothes Jack had given me; I stretched my limbs so they wouldn't go completely numb.

"I'm so goddamn wet," the Rat huffed down below.

It took me a second to figure out how he had gotten so wet. It was foggy outside, but it hadn't rained. It wasn't until a few minutes later that my congealed brain realized that it had to be the same guy who had attacked me in the shower. He was still wearing the same gear as when he strangled and beat me.

The Rats were debating; they turned on their flashlights. The wet Rat was tired of waiting. He was talking to Smew in a tone that was growing increasingly furious, explaining how he only wanted to know two things: my real name and where I was.

Smew was unable to answer either question. He couldn't have even if he wanted to. I knew he didn't know.

The Rat turned on the water and started filling up the tub. Smew struggled to get up but he couldn't use his hands. The Rat pressed Smew down to the bottom of the tub, turned off the tap, and asked him the same questions again. Smew begged the Rat not to let any more water into the tub.

The other Rat stood a little farther back, watching. He didn't interfere when his ski-masked colleague dunked Smew under the surface.

I gnawed on the blanket. Someone had jammed matches into my eyelids; I was forced to watch, even though I wanted to close my eyes.

The Rat brought Smew's head to the surface. The Rat asked his questions again.

Smew sputtered and begged his dad not to drown him. He had regressed into the little boy in the rowboat whose pops had tossed him overboard. He was sinking back through the water-lily stalks to the muddy bottom.

I couldn't fucking take it anymore.

I waited for the Rat to push Smew back into the tub and hold his head underwater. Then I rolled out the extinguisher, which was next to me on the blanket. The same one I had filled with pressurized air and paint, the same one Smew and I had carried here and left in the tub where Smew was being drowned right now. The same one I had hauled up to the catwalk when I got to the warehouse using the hooks, tracks, and cables hanging from the ceiling.

I pushed the extinguisher off the blanket and over the edge of the catwalk. It had been a cold, hard bedmate. I turned onto my side and curled up into a ball, shielded my head between my hands, put my palms over my ears, and opened my mouth.

The shock wave threw me into the wall face-first. A grate hit me in the back. My nose was bleeding. I was able to crawl up onto my knees. My legs still worked. A dent and a tear had appeared on the gridiron next to me; something had flown against it, and hard. I looked down at the floor of the warehouse and hobbled down the ladder as quickly as I could.

The extinguisher had exploded a lot more powerfully than I had imagined. The paint inside it had dyed most of the nearby walls a glowing orange. Orange ripples and rays were spreading across the floor, as if a supernova had popped.

I limped over to the tub. Smew was still below the surface. I grabbed him by the collar and jerked his head up into the air. As soon as I let go he slid back down to the bottom. I managed to wrench his upper body over the edge of the tub; he hung jackknifed there with his legs in the tub, his upper body over the floor.

Over the floor that was now an orange mingled with darker splotches.

When it hit the floor, the extinguisher shredded into pieces. The base was flipped over and jagged metal spikes radiated out from it like a crown. Bits of metal had flown meters from the spot where the extinguisher had slammed into the floor.

The iron tub had protected the submerged Smew; nothing had protected the Rats.

The shock wave had blown the ski mask off the head of one of them. But the thing that had proved fatal was the jagged piece of metal that had ripped open his throat. The Rat was lying on his side, one leg bent underneath him, a surprised expression on his face, like a child who has just seen his first shooting star.

The second Rat was lying on his back next to the tub. His face was still hidden by the ski mask. I made my way through the pool of blood and paint and pulled the cap from his head.

Jere Kalliola was still alive. But he wouldn't be for long. The side had blown off the extinguisher and severed both of his legs at the thigh. One foot lay a couple yards away in a grimy pool. The other one had flown beyond the area illuminated by the flashlight.

"Jere," I said.

He gasped as helplessly as a little fish I caught one time as a kid. Dad had tugged my hair for just standing there and letting the little red-eyed creature suffer.

"Why?" Jere managed to say.

"You knocked Rust down from the roof."

"I didn't knock Rust down. It was Hiililuoma," he said laboriously, one syllable at a time.

"The report said you were on the roof," I hissed. "Hiililuoma was below."

"The report was a lie."

Jere's words made me feel hollow inside.

If the man who was lying mangled on the floor was telling the truth, I had been exacting revenge on the wrong person all along.

I watched the life go out of him as Smew hacked and vomited up the water from his lungs.

Jere was still struggling to choke something out. I had to squat down next to him to catch what he was saying amid the gasps.

"What's your real name?" he asked.

"Maria," I said.

"Maria, you killed my child," Jere breathed softly into my ear, like reeds rustling in the breeze.

I went rigid. Jere blinked rapidly; at first I thought he was trying to telegraph something to me, but he was crying. I took him by the hand and held it until the blinking stopped.

I helped Smew out of the tub and freed the hands that were bound behind his back. I yanked the plug out of the tub. I led Smew along the wall so he wouldn't dirty himself with the paint and blood pooling in the middle of the floor.

"I drowned, Mommy," he murmured.

"Don't you go fucking crazy on me now, too," I said.

I half forced Smew out the window. I heard him clatter against the grill; he had managed to knock it over. I went back up to the catwalk and got the blanket I had been lying on and took it with me. It was stained with orange splotches; it reminded me of a leopard skin.

Then it was just the two flashlights burning in the dark warehouse. The batteries of one were dying; it gave off a dim, trembling beam of light. From where I was standing it looked like Jere still had legs and he was just resting for a moment. At sunrise, in the middle of a glowing orange sea.

I slipped out the window. The sun hadn't risen yet.

MARIA

I shook the can and added some orange paint to the dark-skinned woman's shirt. I was creating a piece on the bedroom wall of a top-floor apartment in a sixteen-story building.

In the image, a man and a woman were embracing and kissing each other. Behind them, all the way to the blistering side walls, spread the Kotkansaari I had painted, its harbor cranes, the gray rocks, and the archipelago around it.

I was the woman, and Rust was the man.

Outside the window, I could make out real harbor cranes. They jutted up, rust-footed, on the shores of the Pripyat River.

A crack in the ceiling was allowing in a steady curtain of water. A birch sprouted from the floor at the foot of the queen-size bed; its roots raised the plastic floor into snakelike knots. The birch was bursting with buds.

I pulled off my mask and stepped over to the window. Lenin Square opened up before me, now scrubland; to one side stood the Energetik Culture Palace. Its extinguished neon letters no longer looked so energetic, but wrinkled as raisins. Across the square rose the sumptuous

Polissya Hotel with balconies now populated by songbirds instead of tourists. They nested in the trees rooted to the concrete balconies. The last hotel guests had waved from the balconies in 1986.

Behind the hotel there was an amusement park, with the frozen Ferris wheel looming above it all. Smew and I had wandered through the amusement park that same morning before dawn. Early morning and late evening were the best times to explore Pripyat because those were the only moments when the reactor tourists who dropped by the ghost town for a few hours weren't around.

Smew had taken a series of shots of bumper cars that had been waiting for drivers on mossy tracks for over a quarter of a century. The ropes at a nearby tug-of-war stand had disintegrated and tangled into spiderwebs, and grand prizes had stared down at us from the walls of the raffle shack: big, furry teddy bears with bow ties around their necks. Surprisingly many only had one button eye left. Near their fur, the gauge raced up to almost three thousand; I suggested to Smew that maybe the purpose of the gadget was to measure the craving for affection that had concentrated in the fur, not the amount of radiation.

"Maybe. Maybe not," Smew said.

While he was shooting the bumper cars Smew told me that the amusement park had never officially opened. The official opening day was supposed to have been May 1, 1986, but Chernobyl's Reactor 4 had been destroyed less than a week earlier. Unofficially, the amusement park had been open for thirty-six hours, from the time of the reactor's collapse to the evacuation of Pripyat. The residents had not been informed about the accident, and they had spent a day and a half in joyful bliss, reveling and laughing on the carousel, swings, and bumper cars as the radiation showered down on them and the cotton candy they were holding, as heavily as rain in a thunderstorm.

I sat in one of the Ferris wheel's sunflower-yellow cars; Smew showed me the previous day's catch from his camera. Photos of a floor strewn with dusty gas masks. The maternity clinic at the hospital, where the ward was full of abandoned cribs. Their boxlike metal frames and tall legs made them look like the skeletons of wildebeests.

But for Smew, the most important shots were the ones from families' homes. He and Vorkuta had systematically entered apartments and recorded the life that had come to a standstill almost thirty years earlier. One was of a cigarette pack left behind on a table; the newspaper dated April 1986 next to it was opened to the sports pages. Another was of a board game that had been left unfinished. In a third, a drawing hung over a child's bed, in which the owner of the bed was flying into space on a rocket and waving at his parents standing back down on Earth.

They were all smiling.

Smew had continued on to the amusement park to photograph. I had headed back to the apartment building. The forest had taken over Pripyat's streets, and over the years the lanes had turned into an overgrown jungle. Berlin's most famous street is the mile-long *Unter den Linden*, Under the Lindens. There were plenty of streets here that could have been renamed: In the Jungle, In the Bushes, Under the Birches, In the Thickets.

On the way back, I had dropped by the Energetik Culture Palace; the gym had a wall covered by wooden bars, and a lone rope still hung from the ceiling. I held the radiation gauge near the rope; a climber could expect to get an extra dose of gamma from the hemp. Two-thirds cesium, one-third strontium.

A blackbird was perched on the pommel horse in the corner. I expected it to blast its flute into the decaying room. When it didn't, I started singing on its behalf: "The songbird bridled the horse, the songbird bridled the horse. The horse it galloped off, the horse it galloped off."

I clapped my hands, the blackbird didn't move. I stepped closer. It was a blackened gull, charred whole. The tips of a couple feathers from one of its wings tenaciously held on to their whiteness.

The bars on the wall didn't give off any more radiation than the surroundings. I yanked them to see how sturdy they were, then I climbed up to the top and hung there upside down.

When you gaze at a postnuclear landscape upside down, it doesn't look half bad.

I just don't have the energy to hang upside down all the time.

I stepped away from the window, put the mask back on, and continued painting the embracing couple.

Water dribbled down to the foot of the bed at an accelerating pace. Pretty soon it would be fair to call it a waterfall.

Smew had told me that morning at the Ferris wheel that Jack was in prison. He had already been there for a while, but the information had just reached us now. We had spent the first part of the winter in Estonia and then slowly made our way down south through the Baltic countries toward Ukraine.

At first Smew had suspected that Jack was being prosecuted for his old graffiti, but he had apparently also been sentenced for the deaths of Jere and the other Rat, Olavi Raittila.

The same morning I had saved Smew from the bathtub I had left Jack's moped outside the warehouse. I had put the bloody, paint-stained running shoes I had borrowed from him under the seat. The police had found them hidden there, and Jack had been accused of two homicides.

Maybe I could say something on his behalf. Maybe not.

Ever since Rust's death, innocent people had been suffering. The actual murderer was still on the loose: Hiililuoma.

Smew was bunking with Vorkuta in the same apartment and I was in the next apartment over. Vorkuta's two Russian friends had claimed a corner suite two floors down.

Yes, staying in Pripyat was strictly forbidden. The skull and cross-bones was the most common tag.

We had founded our very own bed-and-breakfast. For five.

Vorkuta was planning on picking false morels for dinner. The dish sounded suspect; I thought false morels were deadly even when they hadn't absorbed excess radioactivity.

"I'll parboil them an extra time," Smew said after he had listened to Vorkuta's explanations.

I intended on keeping the radiation gauge at hand and measuring every forkful.

My piece was almost finished. I hadn't been able to paint it in the warehouse in Kotkansaari. There was no one to stop me here.

Underneath the kissing man and woman, I added their names.

MARIA
LOVES
MARKUS

ABOUT THE AUTHOR

Photo © 2014 Havu Järvelä

Jari Järvelä has written novels, short stories, and essays, as well as plays for the stage and radio. He currently resides in Kotka, Finland, living between the ocean and a river. Naples and Marseille are his favorite cities because nothing works in them but everything works out, giving their citizens reasons to believe in miracles. His hobbies include karate, wines, and history. He is also passionate about punk music and fifteenth-century paintings, both of which indulge frenzied creation.

ABOUT THE TRANSLATOR

Photo © 2015 Lisa Loop

Kristian London has translated numerous Finnish-language plays and novels, including Petri Tamminen's *Crime Novel* and Harri Nykänen's *Nights of Awe*, a WLT notable translation of 2012. A native of the Pacific Northwest, he currently divides his time between Seattle and Helsinki.